THE TEA PLANTER'S
SON

THE TEA PLANTER'S
SON

AN ANGLO-INDIAN LIFE

JIMMY PYKE

PARTRIDGE
A Penguin Random House Company

To order additional copies of this book, contact
Partridge India
000 800 10062 62
orders.india@partridgepublishing.com

www.partridgepublishing.com/india

CONTENTS

For my daughter, Teresa

When my daughter was a teenager, she said to me,
"Dad, you read so many novels, surely you can write one."
Teresa, this is it.

ACKNOWLEDGMENTS

Thank you to my family and friends who read some chapters of the book and encouraged me to carry on, just at the time I was thinking of giving up.

I also thank my editor, Lewis Ward (London) for his help and advice.

Love, hope, fear, faith
—these make humanity;
these are its sign and note and
character.

Robert Browning

GLOSSARY

Anglo-Indian

Originally meant a person of British ancestry living in India. But subsequently a person of mixed British Indian blood (half-caste).

11-plus—examination in last year of primary schools to gain admission to various types of secondary school

A & E department—Accident and Emergency department of a hospital

aama—mother

ackee—considered a fruit but it is cooked and used as a vegetable. It forms one half of Jamaica's national dish of ackee and salt fish

ayah—maid, often companion for the woman of the house and child minder

babu—father

banana split—ice cream-based desert served on a long dish called a boat

baronet—British hereditary title of honour, and the man has the title Sir

bazaar—market

bearer—butler

bhai—younger brother

bhainee—younger sister

bhaju—grandfather, also used as affectionate and respectful greeting to an elderly man biris—thin, often flavoured, cigarette made of tobacco wrapped in a tendu leaf

black tie—semi-formal wear; dinner jacket and matching trousers, white dress shirt, bow tie and black shoes

boo to a goose—emphasising someone is very timid

bottle blonde—dyed or bleached blonde hair

bowju—grandmother, also used as an affectionate and respectful greeting to an elderly woman

burra baba—affectionate and respectful term referring to minor

burra sahib—senior Englishman or other European e.g. proprietor, manager

Carey Street—euphemism for being bankrupt or in debt

caro mia—my dear (Italian)

chaprassi—senior overseer

Cheshire Cat—cat in Alice in Wonderland known for its mischievous grin

chaukidar—village policeman

Chin—one of the ethnic groups in Burma of Tibeto-Burmese origin (Burmese)

chorie—daughter

chota hazri—light breakfast

chullah—cooking stove

churpee—cheese consumed by Nepali and Tibetans in Nepal; the hard variety is like chewing gum

COPD—Chronic obstructive pulmonary disease

dacoits—criminals who engage in organized robbery and murder

dhal—lentil

dhupii—Japanese cedar tree

didi—older sister

DIY—do-it-yourself

doko—baskets made from bamboo

Durga Puja—annual Hindu festival that celebrates worship of the goddess, Durga (meaning "the invincible")

ERPC test—evacuation of retained products of conception test

Eton Mess—mixture of strawberries, pieces of meringue and cream dessert

football pools—betting pool based on predicting the outcome of top-level association football matches taking place in the coming week

Foyles—well-known bookshop in Charing Cross, London

French letters—condom

godown—warehouse

guinea—one pound and one shilling

Gurkha—Nepali soldier in British and Indian regiments

Haiti—Caribbean country occupying part of an island with Dominican Republic

havildar—police sergeant

Ingaleik—English (Burmese word)

jack of all trade—person competent with many skills

jetha—oldest son

kancha—youngest or young son

Kancha—youngest or young daughter

khola—mountain stream

kebab—dish of pieces of meat, fish, or vegetables roasted or grilled on a skewer or spit

kofta—meat ball dish

labourer line—group of huts for occupation by workers

luncheon voucher—voucher for a specified amount issued by employers to low paid employees redeemable at restaurants and cafes for food

maharajah—a high ranking Hindu king or prince in India

makai—maize

mama—uncle

Marie Curie nurse—nurse from a charity who provide
 hands-on care during the terminal stages of cancer in the
 patient's home
Marks & Spencer—major British retail chain of shops
Maymyo—May's town (Burmese word)
memsahib—respectful title used by an Indian in addressing
 an Englishwoman or other European, and sometimes a
 woman employer
momo—Nepali style of dumpling
Mughlai—Rich food cooked with aromatic spices, nuts and
 dried fruits; result of the Mughal rule in India
murwah—a kind of millet from which liquor is brewed
namaste—most common form of acknowledgment in the
 Indian sub-continent—meaning, "I bow to the divine in
 you"
nawab—a Muslim prince or powerful landowner in India
Neej Kaman—nearby garden
Nepali—people from Nepal
New Commonwealth—decolonised countries, mainly
 non-white and developing
nimbu pani—lime soda
Paki—British offensive slang, used as a disparaging term for a
 person of Pakistani or South Asian birth or descent
pani-wallah—water-carrier and cook's assistant
peon—postman
poppadum—thin crisp Indian bread
quinta—wines, including port, that originate from a single
 estate in Portugal (Portuguese word)
Rai—surname of an ethno-linguistic group in Nepal
ramrow—well
ramree—pretty
RMS—Royal Mail ship
saag—greens

sahib—a respectful title used by an Indian in addressing an Englishman or other European

Sicilian—someone from Sicily the largest island in the Mediterranean Sea

scotch bonnet—a very hot variety of chilli pepper

shilling—five pence

Sisters of Charity of Nazareth—with special concern for health care

sola topee—lightweight cloth-covered helmet made of cork or pith

solicitor—English lawyer

supari—beetle nut

sweeper—very low caste Hindu

syce—groom

thana—police station

thakin—Master (Burmese word)

tiffin—lunch

thunderbox—a portable boxlike lavatory seat placed over a bucket

tonga—horse drawn carriage

vanda mataram—poem and later song, "I love thee, Mother." The first two verses are now the official song of India *contra* the national anthem

white tie—formal evening wear; dress coat and matching trousers, white stiff fronted cotton shirt with detachable collar, white shirt, low cut waistcoat, white bow tie and black court shoe

yam—vegetable. Tuber of a tropical vine

CHAPTER 1

THE ENGLISH TEA PLANTER

1914 to 1937

Lewis Stephens was born in England on July 10, 1914 in the seaside town of Hove in the county of Sussex.

His father, Joseph Stephens, was His Britannic Majesty's Vice Consul in Haiti at the time, and his mother, Phyllis James, was the daughter of a doctor in Wales. They met on a sea voyage from America, where Joseph had been working in the Boston Consulate.

Theirs was not a quick romance; she had a long line of suitors and it took two years of correspondence and meetings before she agreed to be his wife.

Phyllis had returned to England because of the political unrest in Haiti; six presidents had been assassinated or overthrown in the previous three years.

President Michel Oreste had deserted his country; and on that day, January 27, 1914, Joseph found himself suddenly in the line of fire from soldiers clearing a large open space and was fortunately not hit.

As soon as the Revolution was terminated by the election of President Oreste Zamor, Joseph had arranged for his pregnant wife to return to England.

Lewis was brought up by nannies and he changed schools more often than he could remember. Due to his father's postings, he studied in schools in places as diverse as Port-au-Prince Haiti, Laurenco Marques in Portuguese East Africa, Mexico, Basle and Hamburg.

Lewis saw little of his parents, and later he would remember his father as a workaholic, and his mother as a beautiful lady all dressed up and smelling of perfume, who would come fleetingly to the nursery to wish him good night before going to a diplomatic party.

Lewis was expected to join the diplomatic corps like his father so after Cambridge University, he sat for the entrance examinations.

When his parents came from abroad on leave to the family home in Sussex, Lewis then 23 years old took the opportunity to speak to them about his future.

Life in the Stephens family was very formal. At dinner, it was the normal procedure at home for the men to wear white tie when there were guests and for Phyllis or any women guests to wear ankle length sleeveless dress with a wrap and evening shoes; but as there were no guests that night, father and son were in black tie. Lewis took the opportunity to address his father.

"Father, may I have a word please?"

"Of course" said his father.

"I have been thinking of my future. I think I have passed the entrance exams, but I would prefer to take some time off and travel. I had in mind going to Asia and working there for a year or so, and then deciding about my career."

"Really, Lewis," his mother said. "You do continue to surprise us. Why do you want to waste time travelling to Asia of all places?"

"Mother, not everyone wants to be a diplomat like Father. I am not sure that I do. I may want to, but I need time to think about it."

Lewis' mother turned to her husband, "Darling, what do you have to say about this?"

"Son it is your life, but you are making a mistake. You should think of your career first."

To which Lewis, like many a young person, said nothing.

Without his parents' blessing, Lewis went to London to see an uncle, who was a successful City trader. He was greeted warmly, and after what Lewis had to say, the uncle offered some advice.

"Lewis if I was thinking of going to Asia, I would think of India. Just the other day I was speaking to my solicitor who has been asked to find an assistant manager for a tea estate in the Himalayas—now that would be an adventure, and you might make some money as well."

Lewis had never thought of becoming a tea planter, but instinctively thought he would consider it and asked his uncle how he might go about it. So his uncle introduced him to his solicitor friend.

Lewis went to see this solicitor in his office at Lincoln's Inn in Central London. He was not to know then, but many years later his son would be working there.

Before keeping the appointment, Lewis had carried out some basic research. He learnt that in the 1850 experiments to grow tea in the Darjeeling region had been successful leading to rapid development of the tea industry. Lewis was surprised to learn that there were now some 98.8 square miles under tea in the region and the population in tea estates was about 150,000.

"How is your uncle?" the solicitor asked Lewis. "We were at Cambridge together. He is a fine man, and he has done well for himself. You know Lewis, we lawyers can have an interesting life, but never wealthy." After a pause the solicitor continued, "My client is an Englishman who owns a tea estate in India—it is in the Himalayas where the weather is suitable. The region is known as Darjeeling. He has formed extensions to his existing tea estate and it is now too big for him to manage. So I have been asked to recruit an assistant manager as it is traditional there for a Briton to be appointed to such a post."

Lewis said, "Sir, what type of work would the assistant manager do? I have no idea."

The solicitor was unable to provide any detailed information.

"You would learn as you go along; and you would have to be a jack of all trades," said the solicitor.

"If you select me, when would I have to leave England?"

"Right away," said the solicitor, before giving the details of the employment contract.

The successful candidate would be employed for a maximum of five years with six months leave at the end of the term. The employer would pay the return sea fares. However if the candidate ended his contract before the third year, he would have to repay the cost of the outward journey. The salary would be paid in Indian Rupees with any bonus paid in Pound Sterling in England. Living accommodation, with servants, would be provided at the tea estate.

"Can you please explain the bonus system?" asked Lewis.

"I really don't know anything about it," replied the solicitor. "You will have to find out when you get there." Lewis was puzzled by this response but concluded that the answer was truthful rather than evasive, and after all was the solicitor not a friend of his uncle?

After a week, the solicitor telephoned.

"Lewis I have made my decision. I can offer you the post of assistant manager at Neej Kaman Tea Estate; and if you are interested I will send you the employment contract."

"Thank you, Sir," said Lewis. "I am minded to accept, but first I will study the contract and take some advice before coming back to you."

Lewis spoke with his father, who remained sceptical.

"Are you sure you want to go to India? Your future would be more secure working for the diplomatic corps, and you would do a lot of travelling and live abroad, which is what you want, is it not?" said his father.

"Father, I do not want all that responsibility or to have to work as hard as you do—not at this moment. I would like to travel on my own and take my time deciding what to do with the rest of my life, and who knows I may even earn a fortune."

"It is obvious you have made up your mind, so I cannot stop you. You will have to leave your mother to me. And let me know what I can do for you."

Lewis thanked his father, signed the employment contract and sent it back to the solicitor. He felt both relieved and worried.

Lewis would later claim that he was probably the only candidate for the post considering the low salary that was on offer.

This is how Lewis became a tea planter.

CHAPTER 2

Journey to the Himalayas

1937

Much to the annoyance of his mother, especially as she had noticed that the only child of a wealthy baronet had a crush on her son, Lewis left England just after Christmas 1937 at the age of 23 to seek his fortune in India.

"If you decide to come back," his father said as they parted, "don't let your pride stop you from asking for my help."

Lewis boarded the motor vessel Circassia in Liverpool on her voyage to Bombay, a journey of some 4,599 miles. Other than during World War II, this was the route Circassia served for her entire commercial career; 23 years later, Lewis' son would board the same ship in Bombay bound for Liverpool.

The ship carried 300 passengers and 187 crewmembers. By the time it reached Gibraltar, Lewis had struck up a friendship with a pretty girl from Aberdeen who was travelling to join her engineer fiancé in India, and as she was ready for an on-board romance this made the journey very enjoyable.

On arriving in Bombay, Lewis wished his new friend well and on parting, he promised to keep in touch with her, and she gave her fiancée's business address for such communication. The two of them continued communicating for many years, giving news of family life and events that took place in each other's lives.

After spending a week in Bombay, Lewis caught the train to Calcutta, which meant travelling right across India from the west to the east. After spending another week sightseeing in Calcutta, he travelled on another train going north to the railway town of Siliguri in the foothills of the Himalayas.

At Siliguri Station, Lewis caught a narrow gauge train, known as the Toy Train, going to Darjeeling. UNESCO would one day designate the Toy Train as a World Heritage Site.

The travel agent in Calcutta had told Lewis to get off the train at the bazaar named Sonada, where transport to Neej Kaman Tea Estate would be waiting.

CHAPTER 3

SONADA

1938

If this hamlet in the Himalayas was in America or Australia, it would be called a one horse town. In India it was described as a local bazaar, and the population numbered about 250.

Sonada is found in Darjeeling District in the northern part of Bengal 6,552 feet above sea level and at 26° 57, north latitude and 88°, 14, east longitude.

It comprised in 1938 of a small railway station (incorporating a godown, which decades later was gutted by fire due to an electrical short-circuit caused by a rogue monkey); the sub-post and telegraph office; thana with one havildar and four chaukidars; a primary school run by the Church of Scotland who had been the most important influence in the spread of education in the area; a small Roman Catholic chapel established in 1937 by the Salesians of Don Bosco, a religious institute founded in Italy; a few shops; huts occupied mainly by families of Nepalese descent but also by a Chinese family who owned a piggery, a grass cutter who was a Burmese widow with a young son, an Afghan moneylender, an Indian doctor; and surprisingly, six English style bungalows with whitewashed walls, red corrugated iron roofs and chimneys but no electricity.

No one understood why the English and Scottish sahibs built these bungalows in an area which was cold and damp with cloud and fog rising from the valley and hanging for days, when ten miles away there was the principal town of Darjeeling milder and with a backdrop of hills of eternal snow.

The residents of the bungalows waited eagerly each weekday for the peon to deliver the post and the newspapers, which were at least two day old. If these residents were lucky, the peon would also deliver magazines from Britain (always referred by the residents as home), which would be several months old. So the expatriates living in Sonada would be reading and discussing out of date news, gossips and fashion.

There were no tourists or casual visitors in Sonada; however the Nepal Macaque monkeys, the Himalayan flying squirrel, pheasant and the Indian wild boar were regularly seen; and the older residents spoke of Himalayan black bears, mountain goats, Bengal barking deer and even clouded leopards that they had seen in the years gone by.

There were two roads going through Sonada. The main road leading to Darjeeling had shops along the hillside selling groceries, basic household provisions and equipment for the nearby tea estates; and there was a butcher selling pork, goats, and, on special days, fowls. The residents had to travel to Darjeeling to buy anything else.

The second road led from the tea estates below, including Neej Kaman Tea Estate, to Sonada and its railway station. The hairpin road was as steep as could be.

Following the British and the Bible, the railway had come to Darjeeling District in 1881. The railway line was laid on about the same alignment as the main road and criss-crossed it. At some points it was so close to the huts that passengers could lean out of the compartment windows and touch some part of a building.

Landslides were common around Sonada resulting in traffic being held up and sometimes making the roads and railway inaccessible. The landslides occurred during or immediately after the Monsoons and would leave scars, which were features of the area.

In Sonada, the highlight of the day was when the Toy Train came through. The trains coming up from the foothill on the way to Darjeeling stopped for the few passengers and for unloading the post and goods including rice and other grains, coal and other merchandise for the tea estates, but primarily to replenish the water required for the steam engines.

The early morning train was called the milk train as it carried the milk, which had been collected along the route to be sold in Darjeeling; and in the early afternoon, the second train arrived in Sonada and as it carried the mail, not surprisingly it was known as the mail train. The third train came down from Darjeeling in the late afternoon carrying the passengers, mail, potatoes, cardamoms, oranges and timber as well as the tea chests which were loaded in the goods carriages destined for the auction houses of Calcutta and London.

Just past Sonada, on the way to Darjeeling, there was a khola where the women met to gossip, wash clothes and try to dry them on the banks; and it was also where the funeral pyres were lit.

CHAPTER 4

NEEJ KAMAN TEA ESTATE

1938

The Calcutta travel agent had told Lewis that transport would be waiting for him in Sonada.

To Lewis' surprise, the final stage of the long journey from England was a downhill ride from Sonada to Neej Kaman Tea Estate by pony.

Lewis was handed a letter from the owner of the tea estate who was apologising that his Austin 7, which had a low gear box suited for the hills of Darjeeling, was unavailable due to petrol rationing.

As he rode down to Neej Kaman, the scenery overwhelmed Lewis. The tea bushes and flora were in bloom. The hills were covered in beautiful scarlet rhododendrons and white and pink flowers of magnolias and michaelias and there were forests of tree ferns, birches, acers, pines as well as clusters of large, evergreen trees towering over the land, which Lewis later found out were called dhupii.

Neej Kaman Tea Estate consisted of 1,545 acres, about 790 acres of which were cultivated for tea.

The owner was a Mr George Sinclair. His father had initially obtained a lease of land, which he had named Neej Kaman, for 30 years for cultivation of tea; and later he had negotiated with the Government to purchase the freehold title on favourable terms.

11

The first task undertaken by Sinclair's father was to clear the jungle; then the hills had to be terraced to prevent rain-erosion.

He had raised the tea in Neej Kaman from seed. After germination, the seedlings were reared for up to three years in a nursery before the China-hybrid was planted out. It took about another seven years for the tea bushes to reach maturity.

During this period Sinclair's father had built a small factory, whose motive power was derived from a turbine driven by water to avoid the cost of fuel. Having little capital, he had managed to install only the most basic machinery in the factory.

The labourers employed at Neej Kaman were mostly of Nepali descent, and therefore the language used was Nepali.

The original labourers had been Nepali immigrants. Such immigration was no longer permitted by the time Lewis had arrived. But there was no shortage of labourers as the present generation descended from the original wave of immigrants were keen to work in the tea garden because of the benefits. Labourers were paid partly in cash and partly by the provision of free housing, and there were basic medical treatment, subsidized rice and cereal ration, as well as primary education for their children.

George Sinclair, known as the burra sahib, was born in Neej Kaman in 1889. When his father died, he took over the tea estate at the age of 20.

The burra sahib had learnt about tea management through trial and error; and as he could ill afford to employ an engineer full time to maintain the factory machinery, he had from long experience learnt how to repair ordinary breakages.

The burra sahib was a bachelor in the eyes of the members of the Planters Club and their guests, although he had a Nepali mistress living next to his own bungalow for some time. He also had 12 Nepali servants tendering to his needs and those of his 10 dogs.

Lewis arrived at the burra sahib's bungalow, which was comfortable with shelves in every room containing books shipped from England, which he would read before going to bed.

"Welcome, Mr Stephens," said the burra sahib. "I am happy to welcome you and I hope you will like it here."

"Thank you Sir," said Lewis. "I look forward to working for you."

Lewis' first impression of the burra sahib was that he looked worried and in poor health. Lewis later found out this was due to the burra sahib being a workaholic and having money-related worries, particularly as a result of a hailstorm that had destroyed the previous year's crop and a breakdown of machinery in the pruning season the year before.

After the usual exchange of information, news about the home country and a good tiffin, the burra sahib took Lewis to the assistant manager's bungalow. This had been built quickly and inexpensively. It had the benefit of electric lights, a living room, kitchen, a bedroom with a bathroom, which contained a basin and bathtub. However there was no running water and no toilet facilities other than a thunderbox, which was cleared by the sweeper twice a day.

The burra sahib was full of praise for this dwelling.

"The bungalow is water-tight," he said.

"That's good, Sir," said Lewis but he remembered the luxurious diplomatic residences that he had lived in as he was growing up.

Lewis was then introduced to his servants being the bearer, the cook and the sweeper, all of whom had been taught their tasks by memsahibs who had previously resided in the bungalow. They were ready to please the young assistant manager, and they hoped that their poor wages would be supplemented by bonuses on his birthdays and Christmases, as was the case with his predecessors.

CHAPTER 5

A DAY'S WORK FOR THE ASSISTANT MANAGER

1938

The days for the assistant manager were long and arduous.

At seven o'clock in the morning, Lewis had to be present at a meeting with the labourers so that the burra sahib could allot the field work for the day—be it manuring, plucking, pruning, forking, lopping, weeding, building works, constructing revetment walls and contour drains or repairing the roads and bridle-paths.

He would then accompany the burra sahib by pony along the zig-zag roads and bridle paths learning the basic facts of tea planting and picking up Nepali words, which he practised on his own each night. As Lewis was interested in languages having studied Modern Languages at University, he picked up the Nepali spoken language quite easily.

He learnt to inspect the tea bushes, deal with blights which could destroy the leaves, decide when, where and how much to replant; when and where to prune or pluck the tender young shoots or buds and not the older leaves which would be too coarse in flavour.

Following lunch at the burra sahib's bungalow with a glass of cold beer or homemade lime juice, Lewis then had to go to the factory to be taught the process of making tea (withering, rolling, fermentation, firing and drying, sorting, tasting and packing) by the factory overseer, whilst the burra sahib went to the office to deal with the paperwork.

As the months passed, Lewis had to inspect the machineries to see that they were thoroughly clean and oiled; check that the factory workers were keeping the temperature of the machines at the required level and ensure that there were adequate supplies, particularly of packing tea chests.

After making sure that the factory was cleaned at the end of the day which would be around six o'clock, a tired Lewis would return to his bungalow for a bath and dinner by which time it was 9.30 p.m. and time to go to bed.

All this work had to be done for a salary that, whilst not enough to save, was sufficient to live on and socialise at the Planters Club one weekend a month.

As the only people he could speak to in Neej Kaman were the servants and labourers (in broken Nepali) and the burra sahib, Lewis looked forward to the weekends at the Planters Club for recreation, social chat and female company.

CHAPTER 6

SEX AT THE PLANTERS CLUB

1938-39

The Planters Club had been established in 1868 by tea planters in the centre of Darjeeling town. The founders had chosen a site with a view of one of the most awe-inspiring vistas in the world—the Himalayan mountain range with Mount Kanchenjunga, the third highest mountain, as the centrepiece.

It was the meeting place for the planters and their guests, churchmen and the more important expatriates that lived in the District.

The Club had a lending library, a billiards room and a long bar. There was both residential accommodation and stables, as the normal way of journeying to the Club from the nearby tea estates was on horseback.

On his weekends off, Lewis wearing his sola topee, safari suit and breeches would ride up to Sonada and catch the Toy Train to Darjeeling town on Saturday morning, stay the weekend at the Planter's Club and return the same way on the Monday.

On arriving at the Club, Lewis looked forward to a hot bath, haircut and shave. After changing to more formal clothes, he would participate in the conversation, which included local and overseas news, gossip, the state of the tea estates, prices, grumbles about employers and labourers all supplemented by never-ending beers, pink gins and whiskies. It was claimed that more bottles of Scotch whisky were exported to the Planters Club than to any other club in India.

The get-together at the Planters Club was a local affair, and any outsider would find the conversations humdrum.

Thankfully there was also female company as the Club was the place where the bored wives, who felt isolated by great distances, would come to exchange gossip and talk about flower and vegetable gardens, changes in fashion, cooking and problems with servants. They also came to party and dance, and flirt with the tea planters.

One of the infrequent guests was the Reverend Louis Hunter of the Church of Scotland. He had laboured for years to convert the locals and to minister to the spiritual needs of the expatriates. He had been reasonably successful with conversions and as a result he received funds to open a new station some 40 miles from Darjeeling town; but he found on his visits to the Club that the expatriates were more interested in having a good time.

The wife of this devout and noble Scottish missionary was Kate Hunter, at 38 some 15 years younger than her husband. She was a handsome and fruitful looking woman according to the women, and voluptuous in the eyes of the male members of the Club.

Kate had been supporting God's work for eight years in the Himalayas; and unsurprisingly she was tired, bored and looking for some excitement. She therefore tried to be a frequent guest at the Club. As soon as she laid her eye on the assistant manager of

Neej Kaman Tea Estate one summer day in 1938, she decided that he would be her next conquest.

Kate took up with Lewis, and their affair continued until the winter of 1939.

The Durga Puja weekend in 1939 was on October 21. Guests at the Planters Club, other than Kate, were in the holiday spirit. She had managed to slip away for the weekend to the Club with the intention of telling Lewis her latest news and to discuss their future.

"Are you listening, Lewis?" said Kate.

"Of course. Kate, what is it?"

"Louis has been recalled to Glasgow, and we're returning home after Christmas."

"Oh crikey" said Lewis as he sipped his whisky and soda.

"Is that all you have to say?" said an irate Kate.

There was nothing more said about the coming departure whilst they danced to Someday Sweetheart and the music of Sid Millward and his Band on the gramophone and when they slipped into the paramour's room at the Club; but Kate now realised, if she had not done so already, that there was no future with Lewis.

That winter Kate and her husband, without any fuss, returned to Scotland where many years later she became the bishop's wife.

Lewis was sorry that Kate had left, but he had no intention of being in a permanent relationship with her. So his life continued.

CHAPTER 7

WORK GOES ON

1940

After two years of working for him, Lewis decided to ask the burra sahib for a pay rise and to enquire about his bonus. He went to the burra sahib's bungalow.

"Sahib, the burra sahib is out," said the senior bearer. "I will inform him of your visit."

Being curious Lewis decided to go past the home of his employer's Nepali mistress.

The house was built of wood and mud and had a thatched roof. Steps led to a verandah then came the walls of the building. Alongside the house Lewis saw a smaller building, which looked like the kitchen and then a cowshed and a cardamom kiln to dry the rhizomes.

As he approached the house, Lewis saw a woman in her late 40's, quite pretty but plump and no more than 5 feet in height, sitting on a stool in the verandah. She was wearing a cotton sari and shawl. She was laughing and talking in Nepali to someone inside. Lewis recognised the voice that replied—it was the burra sahib speaking; and when he came out, Lewis was amused to see him in a Nepali outfit with sandals and smoking a pipe. Lewis decided not to disturb him.

The next time Lewis met the burra sahib, the latter was wearing the tea planter outfit, namely his sola topee, cravat, boots and a worn safari suit; and of course he was smoking his pipe.

"Mr Sinclair, would it be possible to have a word with you?" said Lewis.

"Go on, what's on your mind?"

"Sir, I have been working for you now for two years, and I was wondering if it would be possible for you to give me a pay rise, and also let me know when my two year bonuses will be paid?"

The burra sahib seemed to be considering this request, and Lewis was hopeful.

"I think it is time you called me George" began the employer, "and may I address you as Lewis?"

"Of course," said Lewis.

The burra sahib shook his head.

"Lewis, I wish I could, but tea prices have been down the last few years, and as you know production has not increased. We're in a business with little profit. Maybe next year?"

Lewis was fuming, but only said, "I hope so."

That Christmas, in appreciation of his hard work and loyalty, the burra sahib gave Lewis a present, a bottle of non-vintage port.

"He could have at least given me a single quinta vintage," thought Lewis.

There were times when Lewis considered moving on, but he had to complete his fixed term contract. So he carried on, but he was determined to find a better posting when his contract ended.

Unexpectedly around the Easter period, Lewis received a letter from the solicitor from London who had interviewed him. The letter said that the Lewis' uncle, who had suggested he become a tea planter, had died. This was news to Lewis; and he was even more surprised to find that the deceased had left him a legacy of fifteen hundred guineas.

This money enabled Lewis to make the assistant manager's bungalow more comfortable purchasing a new bed, bedside table, a wardrobe and a Bush radio model SUG73 with four shortwave bands costing £17 plus carriage. Lewis would later put some of the remaining money towards the price of a bungalow in Sonada.

It was March 1940 and time for picking the tea leaves known as the first flush. Lewis rode to the east sector of the Neej Kaman to see if the tea bushes were ready. He noticed a group of girls waiting for instructions. There was one pretty girl who looked serene and sure of herself in contrast to the others. Lewis would later say that he was taken aback by her look and composure.

Lewis learnt that the girl was a daughter of the chaprassi of Neej Kaman and that her name was Mylie. When the next day he saw her again, he winked at her and she blushed and looked down.

Whenever he came to the sector where the girl was working, Lewis would look for her; and tease her in broken Nepali saying such things as "Mylie, are you ramrow?" instead of "Mylie, you are ramree." Mylie did not appear to be best pleased, and would look embarrassed and turn away.

CHAPTER 8
THE ILLITERATE TEA PICKER
1940

Mylie was the second eldest daughter of the Nepali chaprassi of Neej Kaman Tea Estate. She did not know the exact date, but had been told that she was born in the summer of 1923.

During her lifetime, Mylie had three given names. When she was born she was given the name of Lakshmi (Hindu Goddess of wealth, prosperity, fortune, and embodiment of beauty); and on conversion to the Catholic faith, the Christian name of Teresa (the name of the Catholic Chapel in Sonada). However all her life she was known as Mylie.

It was the custom amongst the Nepali to be addressed according to the sequence of birth. So the eldest daughter was known as Jettie, then Mylie, Sylie followed by Kylie and so on until the youngest was called Kanchie. There were lots of Jettie, Mylie, Sylie, Kylie and Kanchie in Neej Kaman and Sonada, but somehow or other there was never a problem of mistaken identity.

Mylie's mother had died in childbirth; and her father re-married and eventually there were seven children from his two marriages living under one roof.

At Neej Kaman, children were only educated to primary school level. The main reason why they did not progress to secondary level was because it would have taken up to two hours, each way, to walk to and from the senior school in Sonada.

The ultimate aim of the boys who could write and do additions and subtractions was to work in the office or the factory, while the rest of the male students would become labourers in the tea estate or the surrounding villages; but the girls could only look forward to household chores, and to being employed as tea pickers during the plucking seasons which lasted from March to November.

Following the death of her mother, her father spoke to Mylie.

"There is no need for you to go to school," he said. "You are needed here in the kitchen." She was eight years old at the time.

At the age of thirteen, Mylie became the oldest woman in the household after her eldest sister got married. This lasted until her father remarried the following year.

At the age of fifteen, life changed again.

"I have arranged for you to join the girls from the labour line," said her father "to work as a tea picker during the plucking seasons. I need more money coming into the house."

The end result was that Mylie grew up illiterate, and remained so for the rest of her life.

Mylie discovered that work was divided unequally between men and women. Whilst her father worked better for a short period under the influence of opium, he would then feel tired and drowsy. Meanwhile her brothers would play around after what they claimed was a hard day at school.

"How can it be a hard day when you go to school for half a day, and I am working from five in the morning till late at night?" asked Mylie, and no male could give an answer.

All of Mylie's meagre wages as a tea picker went to her father, except for a few Rupees she saved over many months and which she spent on her first pair of wooden sandals as she was by now embarrassed walking barefoot and a tattoo on her right arm of Lakshmi. The latter decision she regretted in later life.

Therefore her father thought Mylie was a very lucky girl and he could see the results for himself too when she, at the age of 17, told him annoyingly that the young sahib had been flirting with her in broken Nepali.

CHAPTER 9

THE FATHER-IN-LAW

1940

Mylie's father was 52 years old, which was old in the Himalayas. He held the senior post of chaprassi of Neej Kaman, and was therefore respectfully called Bhaju by everyone.

Bhaju had inherited the post of chaprassi from his father as traditionally employment in the tea estates was on family basis. His father was a hill tribesman who had been recruited as a labourer at Neej Kaman from a village across the border in Nepal. After working hard, showing a bit of intelligence and the ability to carry out the sahib's instructions, he had been promoted to chaprassi then the highest post in a tea garden for a Nepali.

Bhaju's family home was situated in a labourer line.

The main building had a large front room, which was used as a bedroom at night, as well as three smaller bedrooms and a kitchen. The kitchen had a chullah made of mud with no chimney to ensure that the smoke was channelled out.

The family had to use an outside dry (non-flush) latrine with manual scavenging, that is to say, human faeces were manually collected into buckets using brooms and spades and carried to an area where the waste was discarded.

There were additional low cost buildings for chicken, cows, goats and pigs.

The buildings were made of bamboo and a mixture of mud and cow dung with corrugated iron sheets for the roofs.

There was electricity for lighting the sahibs' bungalows and for lighting and driving the machineries in the factory, but none in the labourer lines, although it was said that the Darjeeling district had installed the first hydro-electrical undertaking in India in 1897. So the family relied on candles and kerosene wick lamps for lighting, and charcoal or firewood for cooking and heating during the cold winters.

The huts had no running water, but households had access to water that came from a khola to a communal tank in the labourer line via bamboo pipes. There was non-stop grumbling about lack of constant water due to the bamboo pipes leaking or some neighbours diverting water to irrigate their vegetable plots.

The only telephones were at the owner's bungalow and the factory. If a message had to be sent urgently or for business, someone had to go by pony or on foot to the sub-post and telegraph office in the neighbouring town of Sonada to send a telegram.

The chaprassi had the benefit of a small plot of land where, with the help of his family, he grew cauliflower, potato, makai, murwah and saag to sell to the shops in Sonada. He also grew poppy, from which opium was derived, for his personal use.

Bhaju had not only inherited his father's employment but also his habits of supari chewing and opium, both difficult-to-kick.

He had to work long hours to sustain his large family; and chewing supari, which is known to be a mild stimulant, and smoking opium helped him to relax and get some relief from pain and anxiety—pain from the hard labour cultivating vegetables in addition to his daily work as a chaprassi; anxiety resulting from his inability to redeem the outstanding loans due to the Afghan moneylender from Sonada, such loans having been taken out for his first wife's funeral and then for his eldest daughter's dowry. But the results were not always pleasant for the family, particularly when he became lethargic, had mood changes, complained of headaches, or suffered from nightmares.

CHAPTER 10

THE ARRANGEMENT

1940

Nothing further than flirting with Mylie would have happened had Lewis not gone to the Planter's Club and met Alfred Ferguson, the assistant manager of a neighbouring tea estate.

Ferguson came from a well-to-do landowner family in England; and the local gossip was that he had been sent to India following his expulsion from University for having an affair with the disabled tutor's wife.

When he had visited Ferguson's bungalow, Lewis noticed that a Nepali woman called Kanchie was living with him. Thinking of Mylie, Lewis asked how they came to live together. Ferguson explained the procedure of getting the father's permission for the arrangement—the handing of gifts to the parents along with assurances that the girl would be cared for and financially looked after.

Lewis mentioned that he had been smitten with Mylie; and after hearing about her, Ferguson made a suggestion.

"Would you like me to send Kanchie to see Mylie's father on your behalf and agree an arrangement?"

"There is no harm," replied Lewis. "Yes Alfred, please go ahead. But warn Kanchie that the father is a sly dog."

So Kanchie, accompanied by her father, went to see Mylie's father. She had been asked by Ferguson to make such offer as seemed reasonable to her for a successful arrangement. Kanchie knew Mylie's family including the fact that Mylie's father had a loan from the Afghan moneylender from Sonada, so she thought she had an advantage.

"Namaste, Mama" said Kanchie, respectfully referring to him as uncle, as she bowed and kissed his feet. She and her own father were taken into the front room and after sitting down, pleasantries were exchanged and glasses of hot tea were given to the guests.

"You have come for a reason, so please begin," said Bhaju.

"Mama I do not know if you know that the young sahib has shown an interest in our bhainee, Mylie."

Bhaju nodded.

"I have been asked," Kanchie went on, "to bring these gifts for you from the sahib as a token of his respect for you, and to ask for your permission for Mylie to join his household."

She then handed over three silk saris and blouse material for Mylie's stepmother and six bottles of foreign brandy for Bhaju.

"The sahib knows that you are from the Rai clan, and that alcohol is important for the worship ceremonies," said Kanchie. Bhaju looked pleased.

"I am happy to know that the sahib has learnt about our customs, but what does he offer for Mylie's future?"

Kanchie was prepared for this question. She untied the knot in her sari and gave him a white envelope.

Bhaju opened the envelope, and looked at Kanchie.

"Can the sahib give a bit more for Mylie's future?"

Kanchie was again prepared.

"Mama, this is more than Alfred sahib gave my father," said Kanchie. At this her father nodded.

Bhaju seemed satisfied. He was about to say something, when Kanchie interrupted.

"The sahib will arrange for the ration shop to increase the food ration for the family at his cost."

"I am happy that the sahib is such a kind man," said Bhaju. "Can he also help with medical treatments for us?"

"Sahib, this will not be a problem," replied Kanchie.

All this time Mylie was in the kitchen. Leaving her father to continue talking with Mylie's father, Kanchie went to see her and realised that Mylie had been listening to the conversation.

"So Bhainee, you know what is going on," Kanchie said. "Do you want to go and live with the sahib in his bungalow?

"But who is going to help stepmother with the household work?" asked Mylie.

"This is not a problem. She will make other arrangements."

So it was agreed that Kanchie would collect Mylie in seven days' time; and in the intervening period, Kanchie would go with her to buy clothes, at the young sahib's expense, to take with her to his bungalow.

After the evening meal, Mylie helped her stepmother to clear and clean the kitchen.

"Mylie, you are my daughter," began the stepmother. "You have done everything for your family out of love, and now it is time for you to leave us and give your love to the sahib. This will be good for you and one day if you have the sahib's children it will be good for them also. You will no longer be poor. I ask you to accept the arrangement. I will miss you, and remember to come to see us."

"Aama I am scared," said Mylie. "What happens if one day the sahib does not want me?"

"My daughter, you should not worry about these things. If anything goes wrong, you will come back home. Now go and speak to your father."

So Mylie left the kitchen to find her father lying in his bed smoking his opium as she had seen every night. She just sat down and said nothing.

"Mylie I give my blessing," he said softly. "Just remember to save some money for yourself just in case. You can save a little at a time and keep it for an emergency."

Mylie never forgot this wise advice from her father.

Over the next seven days Kanchie came in Ferguson sahib's jeep to take Mylie to the big town of Darjeeling. This was the first time Mylie had been in a motor vehicle, and she felt embarrassed as it drove past her tea picker friends. Whenever they saw her, they would stop plucking tea and wave to her. Mylie thought they looked happy for her.

On their excursions to Darjeeling Mylie, who was wearing her best cotton sari and her only wooden sandals, acquired her first silk saris and leather shoes. The tailor came to the sari shop and measured her up for her blouses; and Kanchie bargained and bought some Kashmiri shawls for her.

"So, bhainee what do you think of your purchases?" asked Kanchie.

"I do not want the sahib to spend too much money on me," replied Mylie.

Kanchie laughed.

"The sahib can afford it."

Kanchie then took Mylie to a restaurant, again for the first time. However Mylie could not enjoy the curry and rice, as she could not eat with her fingers. She tried to eat with a stainless steel spoon like Kanchie was doing, but she thought it did not taste as good that way.

It was all a strange experiences for Mylie, and more so when Kanchie took her to the Chinese lady hairdresser who started to wash her hair.

"Memsahib, please don't," said Mylie. "I can wash my hair".

The hairdresser laughed. "You are sweet. Please don't worry. I am paid to wash your hair."

She then cut Mylie's hair, dried it with a towel and combed it stylishly. When Mylie saw herself in the mirror, she was quite shocked.

"Mylie bhainee, I can see why Lewis sahib wants you," said Kanchie.

Mylie blushed.

Kanchie then took her to the upper part of Darjeeling, which catered for the expatriates and richer locals.

Kanchie pointed to the Planters Club from the road below, named Commercial Row (which was later re-named Nehru Road).

"This is where the sahibs and memsahibs meet. We're not allowed in."

"Why?" asked Mylie.

"We're not good enough," replied Kanchie.

They then went to the photographic shop named Das Studio in Commercial Row, and Kanchie asked the shop assistant to take a portrait photograph of Mylie.

The benevolent proprietor, Mr Das told his assistant that he would take the photograph. He took Mylie to his studio and gave her a smile.

"Chorie, do not look so scared. I am going to take a lovely photo of you. The camera will love you."

Years later, the black and white photograph was displayed by her son in the living room of his house.

"Your mother was beautiful," they would say. "She looks just like a young Aung San Suu Kyi."

Every evening when she got home, Mylie would have to display all her purchases to her family who would look in wonder. Her sisters would watch Mylie try the clothes and learn to walk in her new shoes as they ate the biscuits, cakes and sweets that their older sister had bought for them. As for Bhaju, he would be grinning like the cat that got the cream.

Then the day came for Mylie to leave home and join Lewis sahib. Everyone was in tears. They were sorry that Mylie was leaving, but anticipating an improvement in their lives with the sahib being part of their family.

"Bhainee, it is time to go," said Kanchie.

After paying respect to her father and stepmother, Mylie left the labourer line, with her recent purchases, promising to visit the family as often as possible. As for the neighbours who were looking at what was going on, Mylie thought they looked unhappy and concluded that they must be jealous.

So in the summer of 1940 at the age of 17, Mylie, accompanied by Kanchie, drove down to the young sahib's bungalow, which was two miles away, situated just above the factory and surrounded by a garden plot and a mandarin orange orchard.

CHAPTER 11

LIVING TOGETHER

1940

As Mylie got out of the jeep, Lewis came up to her.

"Mylie, I am happy to see you have come. Don't be worried. Come and meet our servants who will help you."

Mylie was then introduced to the bearer, a distant relative who was smiling all the time, the cook who was looking at her curiously and the sweeper who could not have bowed lower. Standing behind them was another person, her sister Kylie. Mylie was pleased to see her.

"Kylie will stay with us so you will not feel alone," said Lewis.

Mylie bowed. "Sahib—thank you. You are a kind man." Lewis laughed.

"You must not call me sahib. Lewis is my name and you should use this name. I am going to work, but I will come back for tiffin when I will see you again. Please go with the bearer."

Mylie said goodbye to Kanchie, thanked her for all her help and followed the bearer.

The bearer took Mylie to her bedroom, where she noticed there were two single beds, one for her and one for Kylie.

"Memsahib," the bearer said (which astonished Mylie). "I will put your clothes away in the cupboard.

The sweeper will get your bath ready, and then tiffin will be served when the sahib comes back."

All this was too much for Mylie, who sat on her bed and did not know what to do next.

"Sister" said Kylie. "I came yesterday and they showed me around and I was told the work that the servants do. I can show you around, and please remember there is nothing for you to do. Cooking, cleaning everything will be done by the servants."

"If I have nothing to do, how will time pass?" Mylie thought.

So Kylie and the bearer took Mylie around the bungalow and the garden. The cook explained the dishes he was cooking—English food for the sahib, chicken curry, rice and dhal with accompanying homemade pickle for her.

"What about the food for Kylie and you all?" asked Mylie. The cook smiled.

"Memsahib, please do not worry. We will have food for us as well."

The first meal that Mylie and Lewis ate together was tiffin. Lewis had a chicken salad, and watched Mylie trying to eat her food with a spoon.

"Mylie, if you want to eat with your fingers, you can. I will show how to eat with a knife, fork and spoon like I do once you have settled down."

Mylie was grateful.

"I will be a good student," she said. They both laughed.

She stayed in her bedroom with Kylie until Lewis came back in the evening.

"Sahib has come," said the bearer. "Memsahib, please come with me. Would you like a drink?"

"Tea?" replied Mylie, and met Lewis in the living room.

"Are you alright Mylie? This is now your home, and you can do what you want."

Mylie was not used to having two cooked meals in a day. So when dinner was being served, she asked to be excused and went back to her bedroom.

In the next few weeks, Mylie would find that Lewis had already left for work when she woke up. She would meet Lewis when he came home for his tiffin break and then after his factory work. At tiffin times and evenings, they walked around the garden plot and the orchard. Lewis explained things as the days passed. He would tease her and they both laughed a lot. Mylie began to feel more relaxed in his company, but she still felt a little awkward with the servants.

Mylie had no experience of employing servants, but she had the knack of dealing with them without causing ill will. She would help them, much against their protestation, to make sure that the bungalow was properly cleaned and maintained. But she did not interfere with the cook, other than to ask him to make the curries hotter.

She asked for help from the bearer, who liked her as soon as he realised his senior position in the household was not being challenged. He arranged for the drapery shop owner and tailor from Sonada to come and see her. And Mylie consulted him when choosing new curtains, bed linen and a Chinese carpet for the living room.

With the help of Kylie and the sweeper, she also worked in the garden plot, so that by the following summer there were delightful flower and vegetable gardens where before there had been patches of weeds.

About a month after Mylie had come to live at his bungalow, Lewis said that she may wish to move into his bedroom and Kylie could go home to see the family. Mylie consented, and this was the start of Mylie and Lewis living together.

CHAPTER 12

SURPRISES AND
A CONVERSION

1940-41

About a fortnight after Mylie moved bedrooms, Kylie brought an urgent message from their father that he would like to see Mylie. Expecting the worst, Mylie asked Lewis for permission to go immediately. Lewis laughed.

"You do not have to ask for permission. Visit your family as often as you want, but give the bearer notice so he can arrange for transport for you."

"I could not find a better husband," Mylie thought, for as far as she was concerned, she was Lewis' wife.

Mylie hurriedly arrived at her family home and saw her father, who looked healthy enough. So she thought the Afghan moneylender must be causing him grief, and she wondered how she could help. However this was not the reason for the invitation.

"Your stepmother has something to ask you," said her father.

So off Mylie went to see her; and her stepmother spoke to her somewhat shyly.

"Your father had heard a rumour many years ago that the sahibs have tails. He wants to know how long is the sahib's tail?"

Mylie did not know whether to laugh or cry.

"I do not know if Nepali men have tails, but the sahib does not have one." She never found out if her father was disappointed.

It was quite embarrassing when Mylie returned home to answer Lewis' question as to what was wrong with her father.

"No, he just wanted advice about the animals," she said.

A regular visitor to the assistant manager's bungalow was Father Giovanni Nigrelli, an enthusiastic Sicilian Salesian priest. He was the parish priest for Sonada and the neighbouring tea estates.

Father Nigrelli would walk to all corners of his parish, which meant that he visited Neej Kaman once every two months to see his few parishioners there, to give communion to those who could not walk for some two hours up to the small chapel in Sonada to attend Mass at six thirty in the morning; to try and convert a soul or two, and to have a nice English meal with one of the sahibs. If pressed by his host, he could also be persuaded to have a dram or two.

It was Lewis' turn to entertain Father Nigrelli.

"Father," Lewis began, "I am not sure if you know that I was baptised in the Church of England, but I am not a practising Christian."

"I did not know. Am I to try and convert you? Ha ha," said the priest.

"Not likely, Father. But the reason I raise this matter is because I have been thinking that it would be a good idea for Mylie to learn a religion. And as there is no Anglican Church here, why not learn about Catholicism?"

Father scooped a spoonful of rice pudding and custard.

"I will be happy to talk about our Church to Mylie, or maybe even better send our Nepali Catechist to teach her."

And this is how Mylie became a Catholic.

Life carried on in the assistant manager's bungalow in Neej Kaman.

Lewis continued working hard even though there was no increase in salary and the word bonus no longer existed in a dictionary as far as the burra sahib was concerned. Meanwhile Mylie spent her time keeping their bungalow spotless and, much to Lewis' surprise, maintaining the vegetable garden so well they became self sufficient.

Mylie was also adept at using a treadle sewing machine and could knit a woollen sweater, a pair of gloves or a scarf for Lewis in no time at all (Mylie's little secret was that Kylie was helping her).

Mylie had always wanted to see a peacock, so Lewis purchased one that roamed around the garden of the bungalow.

Lewis was surprised to find how enjoyable it was for the silence to be broken by the shrill raucous shrieks of the blue peacock; and to walk around the garden plot selecting the vegetable to be taken to the kitchen, or to pick the mandarin oranges to give to the cook, who was an expert marmalade maker.

Lewis would spend time after dinner teaching Mylie lots of things, but when he tried to teach her to speak English words, she just could not get it as her mind wandered to the household chores that she would need to supervise next day. However she was good at playing Ludo, snakes and ladders and other board games.

Lewis thought that this was the first time he had a home. The only cloud in the horizon was that the world was at war; and, signal permitting, he would listen intently every morning and night to the BBC World Service News, and wonder what he could do to support his countrymen other than to grow tea.

CHAPTER 13

HERE COMES THE BRIDE

1942

Father Nigrelli was very happy that Mylie had been converted. It raised the profile of the Church as far as Neej Kaman was concerned. As Mylie had transport, she brought other Catholics with her from Neej Kaman for Sunday Masses, and he could not help but notice that there was an increase in the weekly collections.

As for Mylie, she was pleased that Lewis thought she was clever enough to be taught.

She found the story of Jesus Christ as explained by the Catechist most interesting, and the idea of someone suffering for others was as noble as any Hindu gods that she had been told about.

She found a purpose in life, that is to say, to live a good life and go to Heaven. She had to be disciplined; not eat meat on Fridays; go to Mass at six thirty every Sunday morning and on Days of Obligations; say her daily prayers; confess her wrongdoings, promise not to do them again and expect God to forgive her; and help her family and neighbours, which she was doing anyway.

But she could not get used to her Christian name of Teresa. She preferred to be called Mylie.

And she did not know why the Mass was said in some foreign language which she was told was called

Latin. No one, other than Father Nigrelli, knew this language so what was this all about?

Whilst Mylie was thinking about her religion, Lewis was thinking about his relationship with Mylie, his future plans and the war, which had not touched him yet.

One day in early April 1942 the two of them were sitting in the garden, one enjoying a pink gin, and the other salty nimbu pani.

"Mylie," Lewis said. "I have asked Father Nigrelli to stay with us this weekend. I would like to get some advice from him. Please ask the cook to prepare his favourites for Sunday tiffin—a roast chicken meal and meringue with strawberries and cream. He will like that. The poor man needs a break. Father said he would say the Sunday Mass at the factory, so please tell the other Catholics."

Mylie had no idea what advice was being sought, but she went off to ask the bearer to prepare a bedroom for the important guest and to inform the cook as to the menu.

That Saturday morning, the driver went to fetch Father Nigrelli from Sonada. Father had a siesta after tiffin and the evening was spent discussing with Lewis the war, the tea industry, news of other residents and the state of the Catholic Church in the region, with half a bottle of blended Scotch whisky by his side.

The next morning Father said Mass after which he and Lewis went for a long walk before Sunday tiffin. When they came back, Father spoke to Mylie.

"The sahib and I have been talking about you; and we both think it is best, as you are a Catholic, that you should not live in sin and you must get married. Is there anything you would like to say?"

Mylie had nothing to say except that she did not want to live in sin.

Alfred Ferguson, the best man, and Kanchie, the bridesmaid, accompanied the couple to the Chapel. They were also the witnesses.

The wedding took place at St Teresa Roman Catholic Church, Sonada with Father Nigrelli proudly officiating on March 17, 1942.

The bride's father had to give his consent as Mylie was only 19, but neither he nor his family attended the wedding for the official reason that he was unwell. The true reasons were that he did not want to participate in a foreign religious ceremony; he did not know what he and his family had to do; and he did not want to spend money buying more new clothes for his family. After all, had he not kitted them during the Puja holidays last October? But he was pleased that his daughter was getting married, especially when he received a wedding gift from Lewis contained in a white envelope.

No one from the Planters Club, other than Ferguson, attended the wedding. The Club members and their guests could not believe Lewis was marrying an illiterate native, when he could quite easily just live with her like many of them did, and one in fact had two mistresses, one in the north sector of his tea estate and the other in the south.

"Has he gone mad?" was the common cry.

After the service, the wedding party went from the Chapel to Ferguson's bungalow, where a wedding breakfast had been prepared. There was so much food that afterwards the servants and their families became the unofficial guests and ate all the leftovers without having to give wedding presents in exchange.

It was also rumoured that the bearer, cook, and sweeper at the assistant manager's bungalow in Neej Kaman celebrated the wedding with the bridegroom's foreign whisky; and next morning, an exasperated Mylie went to see her husband.

"I do not know what is going on," she complained. "All of them have headaches. Where are the aspirins?"

There was no honeymoon, and in any case Mylie would not have known of this custom. But Lewis did give her six gold bracelets, which were the first pieces of jewellery she had ever owned. When the Tea Planter's son left for London for his studies many moons later, Mylie gave these to him as security for hard times.

It was July and Mylie noticed that she had not been bleeding during the previous three months. She thought nothing of it until she began to feel tired, nauseous and sick. She also noticed her breasts had become larger and felt tender.

The doctor from Sonada was called, and after examining Mylie and asking a few pertinent questions, he went to the living room and spoke to the sahib.

"I have carried out all investigations and can report that the Memsahib is expecting a child."

When Lewis next met Ferguson at the Planters Club, he told him about the pregnancy.

"Oh God," said Alfred. "Do you want me to arrange an abortion? There is a doctor in town, who is discreet."

"No," Lewis replied. "There is no need for that."

"When is the baby due?"

"I believe in the beginning of the New Year."

"How do you feel about all this?" asked Alfred.

"Less worried than I expected. But I can just hear my mother saying 'Well, there goes his career' and my father agreeing," said Lewis.

"Let me know if I can help in anyway," said Ferguson. But no help was requested.

CHAPTER 14

WORLD WAR II

1942

Once he had settled down in Neej Kaman, Lewis like other younger tea planters in the Darjeeling District joined the North Bengal Mounted Rifles. This was a voluntary force and while most of the corps was mounted, some men used motor vehicles in place of horses. The corps operated as the local defence, which really meant there was not much to do, as there was no enemy at the door. However there were some members serving in combat alongside the regular forces.

On March 8, 1942 the Japanese took control of Rangoon, the capital of Burma. They closed the 700-mile Burma Road, the route used to transport war supplies that was unloaded in Rangoon and sent to China for Generalissimo Chiang Kai-shek, who was being supported by the West. Therefore there was an urgent need to find a new supply route to China.

It was decided that a new road would be built from the small town of Ledo in Assam, India to Kunming in China with parts of the Burma Road being used. It would be constructed by the Americans, sixty per cent of whom would be African-Americans, with the help of the British and Chinese authorities.

By the time the road had been completed, about 35,000 Indian workers had been deployed, of whom some 8000 labourers were provided by the tea estates under the auspices of the Indian Tea Association, for general road construction.

In December 1942 Lewis and some other tea planters were ordered not to serve in combat, but to accompany the Nepali labourers from the tea estates to Ledo to work on the new road. The authorities came to the conclusion that the Nepali labourers would be more likely to obey superiors they knew when they were being paid so little to work in hostile territory.

Before he could leave, Lewis had to find accommodation for Mylie, as the assistant manager's bungalow at Neej Kaman would be required by his replacement.

Knowing that Mylie had no knowledge about the war other than that three of her brothers had joined the Gurkha Rifles as foot soldiers, Lewis sat her down and tried to explain why the war was taking place, why he had to leave and why she had to move out of the bungalow.

As two of her brothers were fighting in North Africa with the 4th Indian Division, which had a Gurkha element, Mylie had a question.

"Are you going to fight like my brothers?"

"No," Lewis replied, "I am going to supervise our Nepali labourers who will build a new road to China."

"Why does another road have to be built? There must be so many roads already," said Mylie.

Lewis patiently explained the reason why a new road was required.

"How long will you go for?" asked Mylie.

Lewis could only say that he did not know.

"There is a war and I am needed. Now Mylie, the burra sahib wants you to leave our bungalow, as the new sahib will require it. I have to find a new home for you."

Mylie was quite happy to go back to her father's home, but Lewis would have none of it, especially as the baby was due the following month.

CHAPTER 15
Brightside Cottage, Sonada

1942

Once more Ferguson came to Lewis' rescue. He had heard in town that the owner of a bungalow in Sonada was returning home to England and he was looking for a buyer.

Lewis and Mylie went to see Brightside Cottage. It was a well-maintained bungalow, except for one broken windowpane. It consisted of living and dining rooms, kitchen, a small study, and three bedrooms with ensuite bathrooms, each of which had a basin, bath, running cold water but no toilet cistern. Just as in Neej Kaman, the residents had the use of thunderboxes.

There was no electricity, and lighting was dependent on gas and kerosene lamps, but each room had a functioning fireplace. And the pride and joy of the owner was located in the dining room—a kerosene-powered refrigerator.

The bungalow was surrounded by a rose garden, and it came with a two-acre vegetable plot. There was also a labourer line consisting of four huts.

Lewis agreed a price for the bungalow and the contents which included a piano which neither Lewis nor Mylie could play.

"Mr Lewis," said the owner, "I am happy to sell to you but it must be on one condition. There is a Burmese widow who has worked for my family from Assam to here. She has a young son. They live in the labourer line and I need your assurance that they can continue living rent-free in their home. She is loyal and hardworking so if you need someone she would be the right person." Lewis readily agreed, as there were other units in the line for his servants; also the grass cutter could be useful to Mylie.

Brightside Cottage was situated above the main road to Darjeeling and the railway track, on the far side of Sonada alongside the khola.

The owner had laid a lead pipe from the khola to the cottage, but it was prudent not to use this water for drinking purposes because of pollution, and during the autumn and winter months Mylie would find that the supply was depleted.

Fortunately there was a spring above the bungalow from which water was collected in a storage tank before being supplied by lead pipe to the kitchen of Brightside Cottage.

"Mylie, make sure the water is boiled before you drink it," advised Lewis.

"Yes, I will," said Mylie, but she and the servants would happily drink the water as it came out of the kitchen tap because, as they said, "It is sweeter than boiled water."

Lewis and Mylie moved into Brightside Cottage with her sister, Kylie and the cook from Neej Kaman. Lewis decided to employ the bearer and the sweeper who were already working at the bungalow and living in the labourer line.

By now Kylie was 17 and had become streetwise. So she asked her older sister if she could be designated as the baby's ayah.

"Why?" asked Mylie.

"Then I can get monthly wages, and not only pocket money," Kylie replied. Mylie laughed.

"If that is what you want, I will speak to the sahib and arrange it."

Three years later Kylie left Brightside Cottage causing a scandal in Sonada, which was talked about for years to come. What happened was that Kylie ran away with the married cook from a lower Nepali clan working at Hillside, much to the annoyance of his employers. A traveller recounted some years later that he had seen them in a village 80 miles away running a roadside café with Kylie so popular with the truck drivers that her husband was always in a jealous mood.

Whenever she thought of her younger sister, Mylie would smile.

"Kylie must have saved all her wages as I continued giving her pocket money."

In the beginning of December 1942, Quartermaster Lewis Stephens of the North Bengal Mounted Rifles along with one hundred and fifty labourers, at the request of the Indian Tea Association, left his pregnant wife and travelled to the town of Ledo to start military service. Mylie, the neighbours, the servants, families, friends and all and sundry waived their red handkerchiefs, the local traditional custom to say goodbye, as the Toy Train left Sonada Railway Station that day.

But before he left, Lewis got an assurance from the local Indian doctor that if there were any complications with the pregnancy, Mylie would be taken immediately to the Planters Hospital in Darjeeling.

In the absence of her husband, Mylie began her new life in Sonada.

CHAPTER 16
Neighbours in Sonada
1942

Hillside was a one-and-a half storey-bungalow built on a plot of five acres for a Mrs Foster and her son, Tim. It was next to Brightside Cottage.

The Fosters came from a Purnea family. The town of Purnea, situated in the State of Bihar was sometimes referred to as the Poor man's Darjeeling—Poor man's because there were some expatriates who could not afford to holiday in Darjeeling, and Poor man's Darjeeling because Purnea's favourable climate was said to be comparable to that of Darjeeling.

Following his mother's death and his retirement from tea, Tim spent half his time in Purnea and the other half at Hillside.

Although obese, Tim's reputation was as a ballroom dancer. According to those who knew of these things, he was an excellent dancer and very light on his feet—floating over the floor of the ballroom like a balloon.

Whilst living at Hillside, Tim put a bullet through his head. There was no suicide note, but the local gossip was that he had killed himself because his young Nepali driver had made a sexual allegation against him and the police were investigating.

Following Tim's death, Hillside was sold to a Mr and Mrs Thompson who built a tennis court and established a croquet lawn. He had been a captain in the Royal Engineers Regiment when he came to India, and he had moved on to be a senior railway official until he took early retirement. They lived in style thanks to the generous gratuity he had received from the railway company.

Below Hillside and just above the railway track there was a bungalow with a porch owned by retiree Major James Massey and grandly named Sonada House.

The Major used to be the recruitment officer of the Gurkhas, and had been living in Sonada House since his recent retirement. He was a tall Englishman with a white handlebar moustache who always wore a Harris Tweed jacket and brown trilby. He was the pillar of the community, and at 52 the most eligible bachelor in Sonada if not in Darjeeling District, invariably invited to all parties in the area. He was a regular cock amongst the hens and the heartthrob of all the old biddies. He was called Major Mercy behind his back because he was always ready to come to the aid of someone in need, as Mylie would later find out.

Mrs Nicholls occupied the next bungalow named Azalea Cottage. She was a widow who had a reputation and was often the subject of gossip at Mrs Thompson's whist drives. However, Mrs Nicholls seemed to shrug this off, and kept her Nepali toy-boy quite openly under her roof.

The fifth bungalow was Roseneath the home of the McIntyre family. The bungalow was named after Mr McIntyre's village lying in the eastern shore of the Roseneath peninsular near Glasgow, Scotland.

The husband was a Scottish tea planter, who had been an engineer in the Merchant Navy until he had arrived in India. He had impulsively resigned his post when the ship docked in Calcutta, and had found his way to Darjeeling after seeing a newspaper advertisement for an engineer for the tea estates. From repairing machineries in the factories, he had become a tea planter. He had a Nepali wife and one son named John.

It was the standout building in Sonada as it had a weathervane with the traditional cockerel design and letters indicating the compass points on the roof. Mr McIntyre had brought it from Scotland, and as the locals had never seen such an object before, it was for them a sight to behold.

Whilst the other British bungalows were situated away from the railway station, the sixth, which had no name, was located directly opposite. Mr Hunt lived there with his Nepali mistress; and it was whispered that he had a wife, resembling Queen Victoria, living in the North of England, whom he would visit every few years. He was a charming man and an authority on philately. If you thought you had found a rare stamp, you showed it to Mr Hunt for his opinion. People used to say that he had also written a book on Himalayan orchids published in England whilst he was a tea planter, but no one had seen it.

The Chinese couple lived with their mothers-in-law and their three young daughters in the upper part of Sonada. They were second-generation residents. Both their fathers had come from China at a time when experienced tea workers were required at the start of the tea industry in Darjeeling.

The couple earned their living by selling pig manure to the local farmers, meat to the local butcher, and sausages and bacon to the sahibs, hotels and restaurants in nearby Darjeeling.

Thankfully for the other residents, the piggery was located in an isolated area so that the foul smell did not cause a nuisance. They bred black coloured Chwanche pigs until the early 1960s, after which they imported more exotic breeds from Nepal like Yorkshire, Hampshire and Pakhribas blacks.

The Afghan moneylender had come to India as a member of the retinue that accompanied Afghan Princesses when they came to live in exile in Kalimpong, another town in the Darjeeling District. Having left their service, he had come to Sonada and started a moneylending business, popular with the poorer residents of Sonada and the neighbouring tea estates who needed money to deal with emergencies, to find dowry for their daughters or to cover the cost of weddings and funerals.

The moneylender did not see anything was wrong with his business because he was just assisting those who needed the money. However, as he charged extortionate rates of interest, was a ruthless operator showing no mercy and harassed borrowers for weekly payments, and because one shopkeeper had committed suicide after being unable to make the payments, and another defaulting borrower had been beaten up, the moneylender was the most feared and hated person in Sonada.

CHAPTER 17
OUR ANGLO-INDIAN
1943

The boy was born in Brightside Cottage.

The Nepali midwife with no medical training but with lots of experience of delivering babies in Sonada and the surrounding area was considered by the locals, including Mylie, to be more knowledgeable on the subject of childbirth than the Indian doctor practising in the hamlet. Nevertheless she was hesitant.

"Memsahib," she said to Mylie, "I do not want any trouble with the sahib if something goes wrong. Please let the doctor deliver your baby."

The doctor meanwhile tried to reassure Mylie.

"Memsahib, why are you worrying? The sahib has already spoken to me, and asked me to take care of everything."

"But how will you be paid?"

"Please don't worry about it. The sahib will pay me. Now Memsahib, please go and rest," said the doctor.

Alfred Stephens was born on January 24, 1943.

The doctor delivered the boy, and rushed to Sonada Post Office to send a telegram to Lewis care of the Indian Tea Association in Assam, which read:

"Sir (stop) Difficult delivery (stop) Son and Memsahib healthy (stop) Dr (stop)." He had forgotten to state Alfred's date of birth.

Six months later the boy was baptised into the Roman Catholic faith by Father Nigrelli, the Salesian parish priest, and his birth was recorded in the Baptism Register as in those days there was no Birth Registry in Sonada.

The boy was given the Christian name of Alfred. He later wondered why he had not been named Francis as he was born on the feast day of St Francis de Sales, the patron of the Salesians of Don Bosco. He learnt that this was because his father wanted him named after his best friend, Alfred Ferguson.

"I hope he was not a sinner, as I would rather have been named after a saint," Alfred would jokingly say.

Lewis missed both events because of military service.

No one knew the reaction of Lewis when he received news of his first—born child.

But when Mylie sent her bearer to Neej Kaman to give the good news to her father, the first question the grandfather asked was whether the boy was white like the sahib. Mylie was very angry with her father for asking this question. Therefore the bearer did not tell Mylie his reply ("No Bhaju. Your grandson is dark skinned.")

Alfred was designated as an Anglo-Indian, the term approved by the British for half-castes.

CHAPTER 18

THE ANGLO-INDIANS

In 1600 Queen Elizabeth I granted a Charter to the East India Company to start trading operations with India. As the years went by, the Company established its trading posts, trading factories and military strongholds manned by employees from back home, whose women did not join them.

It was not surprising, then, that these sahibs began relationships with local girls, and some married them. In 1687, copying the policy of the Portuguese in their colonies such as Goa, the Company encouraged such marriages, believing they were in its best interest. They even offered to pay a pagoda (five Rupees) to the mother of any child born out of a mixed marriage when the child was christened. These children were known as Eurasians or half-castes.

The Eurasian males considered themselves to be Company men, and to belong to a higher class than the native Indians. Fathers sent their sons to England to study or educated them in the best schools in India on the basis that the Company would employ them. The golden period for Eurasians lasted until 1785.

However between 1786 and 1796, the Company passed orders that stopped Eurasian men from being sent to England to be educated, and thereby preventing them from being employed in the civil and military forces of the Company. They were also disqualified from service in the army except in a few designated low grades such as drummer.

The result was that there developed a social and cultural gap between the British and Eurasians, who felt that they were being treated unfairly and looked elsewhere for work. Some of them managed to find employment with the local rajahs and nawabs; others joined groups of irregular infantry and cavalry or took up employment as clerks with mercantile houses.

Then it was ordered in 1832 that English was to be taught in all Indian schools. The consequence was that it was not long before Indians started applying for posts, which, because of their knowledge of the English language, the Eurasians had considered were theirs.

When in 1833 the Charter of the East India Company was renewed, it provided that no native or natural born subject of His Majesty should, by reason of his religion, place of birth, descent or colour, be prohibited from holding any place, office, or employment under the Company. The Eurasians looked forward to better opportunities, but as the higher posts in the Company were recruited in England, in practice only the lower ones were available to them.

Fortunately for the Eurasians, the telegraph system in India was inaugurated in 1851, and the first railway service started in 1853. These developments resulted in Eurasians being recruited because of their education and greater knowledge of English.

Alfred would have been designated a Eurasian, but in 1911 the Government decided to replace Eurasian with the new term of Anglo-Indian, after a concerted effort by Eurasians to change this terminology to politically and culturally distance themselves from the native Indians and to acknowledge their heritage as Britishers.

In the Government of India Act 1935, an Anglo-Indians were the only minority community to be defined. Section 366(2) stated that an Anglo-Indian was a person whose father or any of whose other male progenitors in the male line is or was of European descent but who is a domiciled within India and is or was born within India of parents habitually resident in the country and not established there for temporary purposes only.

The next major change in the lives of Anglo-Indians took place following India's Independence Day in 1947.

The key points of the definition in section 366(2) of the 1935 Act were retained in 1950 when Anglo-Indians were listed as an official minority group in India's Constitution.

The prejudices that Anglo-Indians faced started in the domestic situation.

The sahib, like Lewis, was the king of the castle. His household followed his English lifestyle, and he would socialise only with other sahibs and very important Indians in venues such as army messes or clubs, enjoying hunting and partying, playing polo or attending horse race meetings.

The native wife, like Mylie, or mistress would not accompany the sahib on these social activities, unless she came from an important Indian family. Her role was to attend to the needs of the sahib and their children, and run the household. At home she would be found more often than not in the kitchen, supervising the servants and surrounded by her own family and friends.

Their children, like Alfred, the first generation of Anglo-Indians, would be educated in schools catered for their class, unless the sahib could afford to send them to Britain (and the Government allowed them to).

When mixing with others, these Anglo-Indians were more likely to talk about their fathers than their mothers, and copy the airs and graces of a sahib.

In the Anglo-Indian community itself, there was a division between those with fair and dark skin. Many of the former with blue eyes and light brown hair tried to pass as British to escape prejudice or to feel superior, as Alfred would find out when he went to boarding school.

CHAPTER 19
THE LEDO ROAD
1942-44

Lewis and his labourers travelled by train all the way to the shabby town of Ledo in the north eastern tip of the province of Assam in the Brahmaputra River Valley.

Whilst he was settling down and learning about the mammoth task ahead, Lewis received the telegram giving him the news of the birth of his first-born son. Lewis did think that the doctor could have provided more information about mother and son, but at least the telegram had reached him.

"It's a boy," said Lewis, and made this news the excuse to join the American soldiers and nurses who were partying in one of the tents.

The days passed with Lewis supervising the labourers who worked on the first 38 miles of the new road starting from the railhead at Ledo. This new road came to be known as the Ledo Road and later the Stilwell Road in honour of an American General. When completed, it was 1079 mile in length and was considered to be about the greatest engineering project undertaken in time of war.

The new road hacked through dense rain forest started as a steep and narrow trail to Pangsau Pass nicknamed Hell Pass because of its difficulty. The Pass was about 4,500 feet above sea level.

The tea labourers' contract stated that they would be stationed at high altitudes throughout their service because they were used to it. So Lewis felt cold throughout his military service and he longed for warmer weather or at least warmer military clothes. When he had his first leave to Sonada, he would make sure to return with more scarves, sweaters and gloves knitted by Mylie (with the help of Kylie) and a hot water bottle.

The men suffered great hardship as the work progressed, particularly during the Monsoons, which started in July and ended in September. The rainfall was heavy and destroyed the work that had been done; trees were brought down; clothing and tents went mouldy and rotten.

Lewis took his first leave in the beginning of November 1943 and returned to Sonada. He went home by train with those labourers whose contracts had ended. Lewis was pleased to reach Brightside Cottage and to see his wife, his son named Alfred and the bungalow with a garden displaying roses, geraniums, chrysanthemums and gladioli. In addition, as the garden was in an exposed location and therefore subject to strong winds, Mylie had planted small clusters of dhupii trees, which would grow to at least fifty feet high, to reduce the wind speed and provide shelter to the plants.

Mylie was disturbed to see that her husband was all skin and bone, and poor Lewis was forced to have chicken soup day in and day out.

"Chicken soup is good," said Mylie. "It will fatten you up." When Lewis protested, Mylie held firm.

"Why do you think we give chicken soup to pregnant women? Because it is good."

As for his relationship with his son, Lewis played with Alfred and found him amusing, but he concluded that he was not father material and thought that he would not want a second child.

After a month's leave, Lewis returned to the Ledo Road in better condition that when he had come to Sonada.

As soon as Lewis left, Mylie got together a group of her women friends, both in Sonada and Neej Kaman, to start a knitting club. This idea soon caught the imagination of others and the women spent any spare time clicking their needles for the menfolk in the Ledo Road. The men were very happy to receive woollen sweaters, scarves, socks and gloves from back home.

The work continued on the Ledo Road. But during his second Monsoons working on the Road, Lewis became ill. It started with a pain in his side, and then he found it difficult to breathe; he had high fever and felt very weak and was unable to move.

The American Army doctor diagnosed that Lewis had a serious form of malaria, which did not surprise the doctor, as the Ledo Road area was highly receptive to malaria transmission due to the excessive and prolonged rainfall.

As there was no hospital nearby, all Lewis could do was to take the tablets that were prescribed and hope that he would recover sooner rather than later. The doctor regularly tested him; and finally he advised his superiors that as soon as Lewis felt he could travel, he should return home for better treatment. This is how a very weak Lewis returned to Sonada in September 1944 and became a tea planter again.

Lewis was looking even worse on his second homecoming. So besides being force-fed with chicken soup, Mylie called the witchdoctor from Neej Kaman, who demanded two black-feathered cocks for sacrifice.

Mylie sent the servants and anyone else available to search and buy two Harringhata Blacks, which unfortunately for the searchers are very alert, highly mobile and capable of escaping predator attack.

Following the ceremony, the witchdoctor returned home with the two dead chicken and a white envelope.

Lewis recovered and while Mylie was convinced that the witchdoctor was responsible for her husband's recovery to good health, Lewis knew it was the quinine prescribed by the American doctor and at the Planters Hospital, adjacent to the Club.

CHAPTER 20
NEW HORIZONS
1944-1946

Lewis did not return to the assistant manager's bungalow in Neej Kaman. However he did go to see George Sinclair, the burra sahib.

"Lewis, we have all heard about how well you handled the labourers in the Ledo Road and I have seen the way you settled down in my Estate, so will you return? In a few years I will retire and you can be the manager."

However Lewis had already made up his mind.

"George, I am grateful. But I would like to seek greener pastures—you understand?"

The two men parted in good terms.

It did not surprise Lewis that a leading tea company invited him to Calcutta for an interview.

"Mr Stephens, our managers in Darjeeling speak highly of you, both your work as assistant manager at Neej Kaman and when you were in the Ledo Road. Therefore I would like to offer you the post of manager at Hopetown Tea Estate. The post is vacant and if terms can be agreed, you can start as soon as you return to Darjeeling," said the managing director. "Personnel will explain the terms and if you do not mind, arrange for a medical?"

As Hopetown Tea Estate was bigger than Neej Kaman (1,977 acres of which 1,100 acres were in cultivation) and as his new employer was not a sole proprietor but a major company, Lewis accepted the offer immediately and returned to Brightside Cottage to tell Mylie the good news.

"I am now the burra sahib of Hopetown."

The benefits of being promoted to the post of manager of a tea estate were not only an increase in salary and bonuses (although perhaps not the latter when working for Mr Sinclair at Neej Kaman), but also taking possession of a bigger bungalow, having more servants, delegating the drudgery work to the assistant manager and having more leisure time. But the negative sides were that the manager was responsible for the labour, he had to enter into tough negotiations with the merchants regarding the supply of ration for the labourers, deal with the office work and the accounts, and worst of all face his superiors at head office when the quality of the tea was not up to standard or the anticipated profit from the estate did not materialise.

The couple discussed the move to the manager's bungalow at Hopetown.

"Why don't you move to the bungalow and I can come and spend some time there and the rest of the time in Brightside?" said Mylie.

"Why is that?"

"There is no point in leaving Brightside empty, and Alfred has his friends here. At Hopetown he will have no one to play with."

Lewis thought about it.

"Alright, I will move to Hopetown and the two of you can come over as and when."

This is how it ended up with Mylie and Alfred spending one week at Hopetown and the following week in Brightside.

Every third weekend, Lewis enjoyed the facilities offered at the Planters Club; but as they were not welcomed at the Club, Mylie and Alfred would remain either in Hopetown or Brightside Cottage.

CHAPTER 21

THE BURMESE GRASS CUTTER AND HER SON

The Burmese grass cutter, whose name no one knew in Sonada, but whom everyone called Bowju had been living with her son Kancha in the labourer line alongside Brightside Cottage when Lewis bought the property.

Their hut was built with mud and cow dung with corrugated iron sheets for the roof. It had two rooms, the front being the kitchen with a mud fireplace with no chimney and a small window, while at the back the bedroom had a wooden bed where Bowju slept whilst Kancha slept on the floor. The lighting was by kerosene wick lamps.

They would bathe and wash themselves and everything else in the khola nearby. But for cooking and drinking water, one of them had to walk to the spring located on higher ground and bring back water in an earthen pitcher at least twice a day. It is not surprising then that mother and son regularly suffered from diarrhoea and gastroenteritis.

When Alfred was allowed to visit them in the evenings, he would squat on the kitchen floor with Bowju and watch her cooking tasty dishes, which cost next to nothing. On occasions, there was meat which Alfred's Mother had given her; and sometimes wild fowl, rabbit or pheasant which lived in the forests and were killed by her young son.

Bowju would go to the jungle in the early morning to cut the grass with her sickle or take the dead wood for firewood and transport it in her doko to sell to the bungalow owners. In season, she would harvest the cardamom growing in the shadowy part of the forest and sell it to the local shops.

She would forage for stinging nettles, bamboo shoots, the tips of bracken ferns, flowers, mushrooms, wild tomatoes and watercress from the springs all of which she would make into casseroles, curries and soups. These dishes were eaten either with rice or chapattis made from whole wheat purchased from the Government ration shops.

His mother, his ayah (who had replaced Kylie) and the cook forbade Alfred from eating Bowju's dishes.

"You will get worms in your stomach" was the common warning, and he would have nightmares every time he tasted one of Bowju's delicacies.

Alfred would also not refuse the hand-made tea with salt offered to him by Bowju, who was adept at illegally plucking tealeaves from the nearby tea estates and making the tea at home.

Alfred was curious.

"Tell me," he would say to Kancha, "how did your mother come to Sonada?"

"Burra baba, it is a long story," Kancha would say shaking his head like an adult. Maybe thought Alfred, Kancha did not know either.

However, as Alfred was growing up, he and Bowju became very fond of each other, and slowly over time she told her story to him.

Bowju was born in Rangoon in Burma. Her given name was Kyi (meaning clear), which the inhabitants of

Sonada did not know. Her parents were from Bombay, and her father was a docker. They had come to Burma as economic immigrants.

She was 16 years old when she was sent to work as a domestic for an Ingaleik family in Maymyo. This town was on the hills and, according to Bowju, the weather was like in Darjeeling but not as cold as in Sonada. The nearest big town, Mandalay, was 25 miles away.

The following year her parents arranged for Bowju to marry an older Indian boy. His parents had given him a Burmese name, Maung Myat.

Maung's parents were from Goa in India and had immigrated to Rangoon before he was born. The father worked as a docker alongside Bowju's father.

Maung worked as a junior butler at a mansion named Candacraig, which had been built as holiday accommodation in Maymyo for the employees of the Bombay Burmah Trading Company. Following their marriage, Bowju went to live with him in the Candacraig servants' quarters while continuing to work for her own employers.

"My husband was always complaining how cold it was in Maymyo," Bowju would say to Alfred. "It would have been too cold for him here in Sonada." And they would laugh as the cold wind blew through her hut.

In the summer of 1939, Bowju and Maung had a healthy boy much to their delight.

"Do you know burra baba, I went to work the day after Kancha was born," said Bowju to Alfred with a smile.

In Christmas 1941, the Ingaleik thakin were talking about the Japanese, the bombing in Rangoon and the need to leave Burma. Bowju did not know why the

Japanese were bombing Rangoon, but it had something to do with fighting against the Ingaleik.

After Christmas, the Ingaleik thakin and their families started leaving Maymyo in a hurry to return to their countries or to go to India. So both Bowju and her husband became unemployed, and it was not too long before Maung came to a decision.

"I have spoken to our neighbours," he said, "They're leaving for India, and we should go also before the Japanese come and punish us for working for the Ingaleik."

"Do we have to go?" Bowju asked.

"I think so," Maung replied.

"If this is what you want, then I will get ready," said Bowju.

So towards the end of April 1942, the couple and their son joined several thousand Indians from Maymyo and the neighbouring areas on the long march to India. They left their worldly goods behind taking just a few clothes and some food. The young couple did not know where they were going and what was involved, but decided simply to follow their neighbours.

The rumour amongst those leaving was that the Indian Government had arranged safe passage, and there would be no hardship along the way. Sadly this was not the case.

Their journey took them through ill-defined tracks and thick forests. The Monsoons had arrived early that year, so they had to cope with continuous rainfall, and travelling became more and more difficult.

The migrants were deprived of sleep, as wherever they settled down for the night they were warned to beware of Burmese and Chin dacoits, leeches and dangerous animals.

They had little to eat and Bowju had to learn from the others how to recognize edible plants in the forest and cook them. This came in handy later when she lived in Sonada.

They moved from one makeshift refugee camp to another where they were fortunate to be provided with basic medicine, rice, dhal, salt and tea. But they did not stay too long because the camps were so filthy.

On reaching the foothills the travellers were told that they had to get permits before they could climb over the mountains to India. Maung managed to get the permits by explaining that his parents were Indians and that they had arranged accommodation in Bombay, which was far from the truth.

They continued with their journey through the mountainous tracks, which were treacherous due to the continual rain. Maung and Bowju suffered from lack of sleep, exhaustion and malnutrition.

"Burra baba," Bowju said to Alfred, "by this time a lot of people became ill and we saw some dying. I prayed to God to look after us." But this was not to be.

Maung started getting diarrhoea, and then he could not stop vomiting and complained of pain. He got weaker and weaker, but he insisted on carrying on.

"We must not stop," he said, "because if we do we will be left behind. We have come such a long way and we're nearly in India."

Maung died at the age of 28 before reaching the final refugee camp in India. Bowju did not know then what illness he died of, but she was later told that it must have been cholera.

"Burra baba, I had nothing to live for, but I had to carry on for Kancha's sake. " Both she and Alfred would shed a tear.

It had taken just under three months for Bowju and Kancha by now in a skeletal condition to reach the final refugee camp in India, which was in Imphal, a busy town in the princely state of Manipur.

In the Imphal refugee camp, Bowju and her son were given proper food, clean water, clothes and camp beds in one of the sheds. They were also inoculated against cholera. Bowju remembered how nice it was to eat fresh vegetables, wash and change her clothes.

They were at the camp for several weeks, before they were moved by bus to another town, the name of which she could not remember. There Bowju was interviewed and when they learnt she had been a domestic for an English family in Burma, she was told that arrangements would be made for her to be an ayah for a sahib family in Assam and that the sahib was a tea planter.

Bowju did not know where Assam was, but she accepted the post, as it would give her and Kancha a home.

The sahib's family was very good to them so Bowju readily agreed to accompany them when he was posted to a tea estate in Darjeeling.

When the sahib resigned from his post, he bought Brightside Cottage and that is how Bowju and Kancha came to live in its labourer line.

"I hate war," said Alfred after listening to Bowju's story.

Years later Alfred would tell the story of the Burmese grass cutter at dinner parties in London, and everyone would ask what happened to her.

"In early 1968, I received a letter, written on my mother's behalf as she was illiterate, giving me news that exposure to chullah smoke emanating from the firewood used while cooking meals resulted in her suffering from a combination of bronchitis and emphysema. The condition was non-reversible and she died of lung damage. She was 49 years when she passed away. I was heartbroken."

"She would have died of COPD," said a doctor friend.

"What is that?"

"Chronic obstructive pulmonary disease is common in the hills where cold temperatures force a heavier exposure to biomass fuels in poorly ventilated dwellings. Women, who do most of the cooking for rural households, are the most affected."

"What about her son?"

"The following year, I went home for the first time since I had left in 1962. I discovered that Bowju's son, Kancha, was no longer living there. He had joined as a cook in an Indian Gurkha Regiment based in Delhi.

"Twenty-three years later, I received, out of the blue, a letter from Kancha. In broken English it said that he had gone to Sonada on leave and had been given my address.

"He had retired from the Army and was working as a night watchman at a hospital in Madras; and that he was now a widower with no children."

Alfred sent money regularly to Kancha until he died in 1997 at the age of 58 years. Alfred never found out the cause of his childhood friend's death, and only came to know of it when his standing order was cancelled.

CHAPTER 22
RELIGIOUS PREJUDICE
1946-1947

Alfred witnessed two incidents that had lifelong effects on him. The incidents showed him how divisive religion can be; but on the positive side, the incidents helped to form his character and point him to his career.

In 1946 the Muslim League was the ministry in power in the province of Bengal, of which Darjeeling District formed part.

The League chose August 16 as Direct Action Day to put pressure on the British to create a new nation, Pakistan, for Muslims during the transfer of power. The Congress Party, whose members were mostly Hindus, opposed the idea of a new nation being carved out of British India.

There was a riot, which continued for three days, in the provincial city, Calcutta. Several thousand Muslims and Hindus were killed; and it was reported that over 100,000 residents had been made homeless.

The authorities were anxious that the violence did not spread outside Calcutta, but it had a life of its own; and soon the harassment of Muslims reached Hopetown Tea Estate.

There were Muslim bakers living in several of the tea estates in the Darjeeling District, including at Hopetown. They would bake in their huts and walk miles barefoot carrying the goodies in large tin boxes on their turbaned heads, moving from one tea estate to another and from one labourer line to another selling their Indian sweets, bread, buns, biscuits and cakes.

These bakers had left their families in faraway villages in the region that is now named Bangladesh to earn a crust in the Himalayas; if they had a good year, they could go to their villages for a holiday with their small savings.

Alfred would observe them buying cheap toys, trinkets and cotton saris and shawls for their families from the local shops, and he would imagine how they would be welcomed when they got home.

It was a working day, and both Lewis and his assistant manager had gone to the bank in Darjeeling and no doubt to socialise at the Planter's Club, when three frightened Muslim bakers, living in Hopetown, came running to the manager's bungalow and asked to speak to the memsahib.

"Memsahib," they said, "the Hindus came to our hut, threw a pig's head and then started throwing stones, calling us names and threatening to set us on fire. We ran away to ask for your help."

"Bearer bhai," said the memsahib, "take them to the kitchen and look after them. Tell everyone not to say that they're here."

The bakers were most relieved and could not thank the kind Memsahib enough.

By this time the chasing mob consisting of about 60 men had come up to the front garden of the bungalow, and having got their breaths back, started shouting slogans such as Vanda Mataram.

Mylie called the pani-wallah, who was the fittest of her servants, and told him to run and bring the Hindu doctor to help her.

The doctor came with another man, who was introduced to Mylie. After a short discussion this man went to the mob, spoke to them and the men quickly dispersed.

Alfred was very taken by this result.

"Who is that man?" he asked the bearer. "What does he do?"

"Baba," replied the bearer, "he is the doctor's brother who has come from Calcutta. I think he is a lawyer." Alfred decided right there and then that he too would be a lawyer and help the persecuted.

In 1969, after a gap of seven years, Alfred came from London on a holiday to Sonada. He took the opportunity of visiting Hopetown Tea Estate and looked up the doctor and his brother. Alfred recognised the latter, and reminded him about the Muslim incident and how witnessing this incident had influenced him to become a lawyer.

"Mr Basu, what did you say to the mob that made them go home? I could not believe how you did it."

"Ah yes. I remember it well. I told them that the burra sahib was thinking of increasing their wages soon, and they should go home before he came back."

"My God, what a brilliant idea you had."

"No, sahib. It was not my idea—your mother told me what to say. After all I was only a clerk in a lawyer's office."

Alfred smiled as he remembered dear Mrs Thompson used to say, "Alfred, remember in life—all that glitters is not gold."

The Durga Puja, the biggest religious festival in Bengal and celebrated with great excitement, started on October 21, 1947.

As it has been the tradition for families to get together, Mylie went with Alfred and Kylie to see their family in Neej Kaman. The family were happy to see them, especially when they saw that Mylie was laden with gifts and money.

Due to Mylie's non-stop generosity the family were more affluent than their neighbours, who were getting even more jealous. Mylie was amused to learn that one of them had taken his 16 year old daughter all dressed up to the assistant manager's bungalow, but the new occupant had thrown them out.

Mylie was sitting on a stool in her family's kitchen surrounded by the womenfolk gossiping away, and Alfred was playing not far from her. There was much laughter, and all was well with the world until her father came back from work.

When he saw Alfred in the kitchen, Mylie's father screamed.

"Get that boy out. He is unclean."

"What are you talking about?" said a shocked Mylie.

"Your son cannot enter our Hindu kitchen as he is a half-caste. In fact you should also not be in the kitchen as you have become a Christian."

"If my son is not welcome, then I don't want to be in this house," replied Mylie. "Kylie go and call the driver."

So Mylie left with Alfred and Kylie; and although she continued to send money to her father to make his life easier, she never returned to her father's home until news reached her years later that he was seriously ill and her father wanted to see her.

As for Alfred, he was deeply disturbed. He did not understand his grandfather's behaviour, and never forgot this hurtful incident.

When Alfred was 15 years old, Mylie had a visitor from Neej Kaman.

"Our father is very ill," said the visitor, Mylie's oldest brother. "He has lost a lot of weight. We do not know what is wrong with him. He sent me to tell you that he wants to see you."

Mylie and Kylie went to see him and they were shocked at his appearance—he was looking old and thin.

The foolish man had been relying only on the witchdoctor, so Mylie called for the doctor from Sonada to come immediately. He in turn called for the doctor from Planters Hospital to make an urgent home visit. The diagnosis of the two doctors was that Mylie's father had oral cancer, which was closely related to his habit of supari chewing.

Mylie postponed Kylie and her return to Brightside Cottage; they stayed with their father for the next few weeks.

Over the following year Mylie visited her father every other weekend; and Alfred accompanied her when he was home from school. Alfred could see things were not looking good—not only did his grandfather have oral cancer, but he was also an opium addict.

One day Alfred was asked what he thought of his grandfather.

"Bhaju," said Alfred, "Mummy says that you are an idiot. If you had eaten the vegetables that you grew and sold the opium, you would have been healthier and we would all have been rich."

"Don't make me laugh," replied his grandfather. "I am sorry for losing my temper and throwing Alfred out of the kitchen," he then went on to say to Mylie.

"It happened a long time ago and there is nothing to be sorry for," replied Mylie, "You just rest."

Alfred's grandfather died five weeks after this conversation.

Before the funeral took place, there were people calling at Bhaju's home to pay respect. Mylie and her siblings were moved that so many came. But it was ruined when the Afghan moneylender from Sonada arrived wearing his turban loosely around his head and carrying a stave for self-protection.

He wanted to see the eldest brother, who passed him onto Mylie.

"Memsahib, are you settling the debt owed by your father?"

"What debt? My father has been paying you weekly for years. I cannot believe he still owes you," said Mylie, and her brothers concurred.

"He still owes. I want to know it will be paid, Memsahib, before I go," said the arrogant man.

"I will guarantee it. Now leave as we have guests," said a very angry Mylie. Alfred had never seen her angrier.

The moneylender left just as her brothers, supported by their cousins, were getting ready to assault him for insulting their father's memory.

When Mylie got back to Brightside Cottage, she called for the moneylender to find out how much was outstanding. He checked his ledger book and mentioned a figure, which was so ridiculous that Mylie laughed at him. She asked for a breakdown, but no written statement was handed over. After much haggling, they agreed a figure, and Mylie paid him off making sure that he gave a receipt with his thumbprint on it.

Alfred watched what was going on and saw, which his mother did not, the moneylender purse his mouth in a self-satisfied smirk as he left.

When he became a lawyer, Alfred vowed he would fight for the underprivileged.

CHAPTER 23

THOSE WERE THE DAYS

1947-48

Like Mr Sinclair, Mr Hunt (of the bungalow with no name) had a library in his Sonada home. Unlike Mr Sinclair, he would allow Alfred to see his picture books, and this how Alfred, who did not know how to read or write until the age of 6, learnt about the rest of the world whilst living in a hamlet in the Himalayas.

As he was growing up, one of Alfred's favourite pastimes was to go to the forest surrounding Sonada with Kancha to watch for birds, as the region was rich in bird life.

"Is there anything more beautiful?" Alfred thought as he watched a blue Indian three-toed kingfisher, a yellow naped or a golden backed woodpecker fly past; and the two boys would remain silent so they could listen to a cuckoo or the sweet-sounding call of a Kokla green pigeon.

Kancha's lack of formal education did not prevent him from being able to differentiate between a laughing thrush, babbler, Ashy wood pigeon or a flycatcher as well as identify all the birdcalls.

Kancha also knew which birds were tasty. After killing a bird with his catapult, all Kancha needed were two large stones, dry wood, salt and a box of matches to prepare a feast. This would be accompanied by fresh cool spring water to drink; and as far as Alfred was concerned, no bottled water would ever match its taste.

As his mother had taught him, Kancha would brush his teeth with charcoal ash after eating the feast so that stains were removed and breath made fresh; and Alfred would copy him.

"Kancha, how did you learn about birds?" Alfred would ask.

"My mother helped me and then I just got to know," the boy would reply.

Although Kancha was older, he was always respectful and would call Alfred—burra baba. But he could not help but giggle whenever Alfred tried to kill a bird with a catapult and always missed.

To add to his talents, Kancha knew how to make a kite and fly it, unlike Alfred for whom a kite had to be bought. In the kite season, which was in windy February time, they and the other local children would go to a meadow above Brightside Cottage and spend hours competing with each other, and Alfred trying to impress the Chinese girls. Again Alfred was useless in getting his kite to fly, so Kancha had to set it up and Alfred then would take over.

"It's useful to be a burra baba," thought Alfred.

In his later years, Alfred would smile and think how Bowju and Kancha made a mockery of the English saying: "Jack of all trades and master of none."

On many a day, Alfred would be late for a meal, afternoon siesta or evening bath time; or he would return with scratches on his arms or legs.

"If you are late again" or "If you cut yourself again," his mother would say, "I am going to stop you playing with Kancha," but she never did.

At the neighbouring bungalow, Hillside, there were shooting parties, games of croquet or tennis, whist drives, music (as Mrs Thompson had been a semi-professional pianist), dancing and lots of laughter.

Alfred was happy when Mr Thompson asked him if he would like to go shooting.

"Yes Sir," he said.

His mother gave Alfred permission, and he was able to accompany Mr Thompson who had a reputation for not suffering fools gladly. Mr Thompson was tall and looked down at Alfred.

"I am his Gurkha foot soldier," thought Alfred.

They went hunting accompanied by Mr Thompson's bearer who would carry a twelve-bore shotgun for his employer. He would shoot deer, pheasants and other game birds around Sonada and the neighbouring tea estates. That is, until one day Mr Thompson shot a deer.

"Come on Alfred. Let's get the deer," he said.

As they approached, Alfred could not help but notice that the animal was still alive and it seemed to be looking at him with sorrowful eyes. Alfred decided there and then that he would never go hunting again.

But this did not stop Alfred visiting Hillside as Mr Thompson's wife had taken a great liking to the boy.

Whenever he visited Mrs Thompson, he became the lucky beneficiary of her cook's roasts, stews, cucumber and watercress sandwiches as well as the best tipsy pudding.

Alfred admired Mrs Thompson, who always smelt lovely (Guerlain Champs Elysees perfume), had lipstick on, her eyebrows and nails were manicured unlike Alfred's mother and his aunties; wore clothes usually in bottle green or donkey brown colours that showed her hourglass figure, little hats and shoes with high thick heels.

"Yes, she is so ___." Alfred could not think of a word that suited, until many years later he realised that the word was "elegant".

Mrs Thompson made him listen to music on her HMV wind-up gramophone so he learnt tunes such as—Irene, good night Irene; Oh my darling, Clementine; Veni, vedi vici, and those from the film, The Great Waltz.

When he did not want to listen to music, Alfred would hide the gramophone needles much to Mrs Thompson's irritation.

"Bearer, where are those bloody gramophone needles?" Alfred noticed that the sahibs and memsahibs frequently said—bloody, so he went around using the word.

"Bloody, Kancha where are you?" or "Bloody, Mummy is calling me."

Alfred also had to endure Mrs Thompson's monologue in fluent Nepali on meningitis, mumps, chicken pox, her ulcers and dietary needs and the side effects of various medicines.

"Alfred," she would say, "Do you remember the symptoms for chicken pox?"

"Yes, Aunty."

"What are they?"

"Spots on face and body, fever, muscle pain."

"Well done, Alfred."

But the boy would be thinking.

"I wish I was playing with Kancha"; or as he got older, "I wish I was playing doctor and nurses with my Chinese friends."

When Alfred was 12 years old and in boarding school, Mr Thompson had a massive heart attack and died.

Until he went to England, Alfred would make a point of visiting Mrs Thompson every day he was on school holidays. He would listen as she reminisced, and talked about the good old days.

Alfred discovered Mrs Thompson had been married before.

"My first husband was a Viscount—that means, Alfred, a peer of the realm. One day you can find out what that means. In those days I was called Lady. Within six months of our marriage, I found the Viscount was a boring man. I left him; and later I met Uncle and came to India as divorced women are not popular in English society."

Alfred also found out that she was lonely.

"You know Alfred," she would say, "since Uncle died, no one has bothered to keep in contact with me. Mark my words—this is what happens when you are a widow."

"No Aunty," Alfred would reply, "I will not be a widow."

"You silly boy," and Mrs Thompson would laugh.

Alfred noticed that as the years went by Mrs Thompson was unable to live on her widow's pension, which was not inflation proof.

She had to reduce her entertainment and then her staff, followed by the sale of her car, piano and furniture in sequence until she was living in genteel poverty in one room in Hillside with an elderly ayah and a small shaggy black and white dog named Sunny.

Alfred, by then living in London, was given the news one day in 1965 that when Sunny had to be put down, Mrs Thompson, by then old white-haired and eccentric, sent her only servant to buy a half bottle of local brandy from the liquor shop and a stout piece of rope from the bazaar. When the ayah came to Hillside the next morning, she found Mrs Thompson hanging from the staircase.

Later whenever someone said that money does not bring happiness, Alfred would think of Mrs Thompson.

"Who says money is not important. Not having money is a tragedy," Alfred would comment. And he would say a little prayer for the most elegant lady in his life, and wish she had lived a little longer so he could have helped her financially.

CHAPTER 24

THE PARTING

1948

Lewis could look back and be proud of what he had achieved in Hopetown Tea Estate since he had taken up the post of manager.

The labour productivity had increased and the yield was better than head office in Calcutta expected. Lewis attributed this to his idea of influencing the workers to feel that they belonged to Hopetown, no more so than by them supporting the Hopetown's football team to compete in the Darjeeling Football League. It came as a considerable shock to all that in the first year of competition, the Hopetown football team reached the semi-final only to lose to Darjeeling Police, who were the champion team.

As for the quality of tea, the employer's brokers noted that Lewis had instructed the tea pickers that only the finest two leafs and a bud, which are the extreme ends of the small succulent shoots of the plant, should be picked to give Hopetown's tea a special flavour, which was described as muscatel.

Alfred's birthday in 1948 was on a Saturday, and as he and his mother were residing in Brightside Cottage, Lewis was going to the birthday party via the Planters Club.

Amongst the post he collected at the Club was a letter from his employers. The managing director informed him that in appreciation of his valued service, he was getting the highest bonus amongst their managers in 17 tea estates in India. So with this good news and after partaking of congratulatory drinks, Lewis went off to the birthday party in Sonada in high spirits.

Unfortunately as the jeep came to the last turning, the driver drove into the roadside ditch, resulting in Lewis having to stay indoors for a week recuperating from a whiplash. And it did not please Mylie that her husband had forgotten to collect Alfred's birthday present, a tricycle, from the toyshop.

It was during this week that Lewis decided to take leave and visit England. Mindful that this was the first time Lewis was going back since 1937, Mylie was all for it and encouraged him to go.

Lewis was given six months leave; and, in accordance with his employment contract, the employers paid for his passage.

There was much excitement in Brightside Cottage that the burra sahib was visiting his family, and there was the expectation that he would return with presents "Made in England", which were so highly sought after in those days.

Lewis left in mid-March 1948. He never returned to India.

Mylie and Alfred were abandoned with no explanation.

CHAPTER 25
Waiting
1948-49

There was no news of Lewis in the coming months.

Alfred believed his father was returning but did not know when. He did not keep a record of the time his father was away until one day his mother had a serious talk with him, so far as it was possible with a boy aged 5.

"Daddy has been away for nine months. He went to see his father and mother across the water. He is going to stay with them as you stay with me. You understand, Alfred?"

"Yes Mummy," he replied and went out to play.

It was only when he went to boarding school and saw the other boys with their parents that he realised his father would not be coming to see him. As he got older and his father's absence became more apparent, he did what most abandoned children do—he developed selective amnesia to protect himself from experiencing the abandonment. But the effect of this was that he was excessively fearful.

Mylie went to see Ferguson sahib regularly, but he had not heard from Lewis and could only assure Mylie that when he did, she would be told immediately. A year later Ferguson went on leave, and he too did not return.

Mylie could not arrange for a letter to be sent to Lewis, as she did not have an address for him. She went to see Major Mercy who said he would try to find out Lewis' home address, as he had heard Lewis saying at the Club that he was born in the town of Hove. Mylie had no idea how big or small the town was, but hoped it was the latter so Lewis could be traced. But working from a distance, Major Mercy was unsuccessful.

Mylie did not know why her husband had not returned, and therefore invented her own reasons when speaking to others. But a time came when she got tired of making excuses for him.

She thought long and hard, and decided that she had to let go of the life she thought she had with Lewis, and accept the life that was waiting for her.

Her first task was to find a school for her son.

Alfred would be six years old the following January. Mylie had no idea which school he should go to when he reached that age. What she did know was that Alfred should have a European education, and she that Major Mercy sahib was the right person to seek advice from.

So she went to see the Major at Sonada House. As was the custom, Mylie, being a native, waited in the porch till the sahib came out to greet her.

After listening to Mylie, the Major made a suggestion.

"I know that John from Roseneath is going to a boarding school in Darjeeling, and it would be a good idea if Alfred went to the same school. Let me find out; Mylie, come and see me tomorrow."

Mylie was worried that she could not afford the school fees, so she asked the sahib if he could find this information also.

When Mylie saw him the following day, the Major confirmed that John, who was attending a day school, were transferring to St Ignatius College in March, and that the school fees for boarders were Rupees 750 for a year.

"Can you pay, Mylie?" asked the Major.

"Major sahib, I will have to find the money."

The Major decided to raise the issue of Alfred's school fees with the Almoner at the next Lodge meeting as after all Alfred's father was a Freemason. This he did not tell Mylie, but he did tell her that he would arrange an appointment with the Rector of St Ignatius and accompany her. Mylie had no idea who the Rector was or what he did, but she decided to keep quiet as otherwise the sahib might think she was stupid as well as illiterate.

After the Christmas period, when the school was closed for the winter holidays, Major Mercy, Mylie and Alfred, in his European outfit of short pants, white shirt and sweater, went to see the Rector, who was the head of St Ignatius.

Darjeeling had been developed as a health resort, and one of the consequences was that European-type schools were established for children of expatriates who did not want to or could not afford to educate them abroad.

One of these boarding schools was St Ignatius College founded in 1888 by Belgian Catholic missionaries. There were nine standard and three infant classes. Foreign and Indian teachers, of whom most were priests and three were women, taught the students, aged between six and seventeen.

In addition to the expatriate children and the Anglo-Indians, there were students from Burma, Nepal,

Sikkim, Thailand, Tibet and also Indian students, although at that time the latter were in the minority.

On seeing the school, Alfred thought this must be the biggest building in the world.

They were told to wait in the school parlour for the Rector. Mylie introduced Alfred to the bearer in charge, who turned out to be one of his Mamas.

The Major started the meeting with the Rector, who was a Belgian, by saying that half the school fees for the first three year would be paid by the Freemasons and that Mylie, whom he introduced as a business woman from Sonada, would be able to pay the balance; and a deposit if necessary. She could afford to pay the fees thereafter. The Rector appeared non-committal.

He could not interview Alfred as the boy was illiterate and could not speak English.

"This is a problem, Major," said the Rector.

When Alfred was older he often wondered why his father had not taught him English, and this remained a mystery.

"Father," said the Major, "I should mention that John McIntyre who is also from Sonada is joining the school in March. We will speak English at home so that Alfred can start learning; and if you can give me the textbook for the English class, I will spend time teaching him. I should also mention that both Alfred and his mother are Catholics, and that his father is an Englishman."

"If I may, Major, I need a few days to come to a decision," said the Rector.

On leaving the school grounds, Mylie bowed down to kiss the Major's feet as a sign of respect, but he would have none of it. In later years Alfred could not remember the journey home other than that he ate the best cream horns in India at Lobo Restaurant in Darjeeling town.

In time for Alfred's Birthday, Mylie received a letter from the Rector and she took it straightaway to the Major for him to open it. He gave her the good news that Alfred was going to be a student at St Ignatius, and that the school would give a 25 per cent discount on the fees.

Mylie told everyone who would listen that Alfred was going to the famous St Ignatius as a boarder, much to his embarrassment.

"Mummy," he said, "do you have to tell everyone?"

"Yes, my son. I have to."

Alfred had no reply.

There were a few more outings to Darjeeling to visit the school outfitters and the Oxford Book Store in Commercial Row, as well as more cream horns at Lobo Restaurant.

CHAPTER 26

Open for business

1949-1960

"Did you not suspect Lewis was not coming back?" asked Kanchie.

"No," replied Mylie.

"Was he unhappy with you?"

"If he was, he did not show it."

"Is there anything that comes to your mind about Lewis?"

"When we had to move to Hopetown, I felt that he could get bored with me as we had nothing in common. Living everyday together, what could he talk to me about? I do not know anything other than to look after our home. That is why I suggested he move to the manager's bungalow on his own, and Alfred and I would spend alternative weeks with him."

"What did he say when he left?" asked Kanchie.

He just said that I should look after Alfred and myself, he expected the money he had given me would be more than enough, and that he would be back in six months' time.

"How do you feel?"

"He is a good man. I love him," said Mylie, "but that was not enough for him."

"Do you think he will come back?" Kanchie asked.

"I hope so," replied Mylie, "But Father Nigrelli says it is all up to God."

There were, of course, suitors for the beautiful and solvent Mylie after Lewis left, but she was not interested in such nonsense.

She had to chase the persistent petrol pump owner with a grass broom when he asked her to be his second wife.

Then there was a feeble attempt by a tea planter from Assam to seduce her, which resulted in him leaving Brightside Cottage soaked in sweet nimbu pani.

Once Alfred was in boarding school, Mylie had more time on her hands.

Although Lewis had left more than enough money to tide her over his six-month absence and she had followed her father's advice to save money for herself just in case, Mylie realised that her capital was diminishing.

She was worrying about paying her share of the school fees on top of the household expenses, which included the wages of her retinue of servants whom she found difficult to make redundant as they would have nowhere to go.

Therefore Mylie decided she would go into business.

She was aware that the richest man in Sonada had started off by owning a liquor shop before branching out to sell other merchandise.

The liquor shop was still open but, according to local gossip, in poor state of repair and supplies were short as the owner was no longer interested in it. She also found out from a relative, the local representative of Customs and Excise in Darjeeling, that profit was low now because of taxes and duties.

Mylie asked the illegal brewer from Neej Kaman to come and see her, and having been told by Mylie's bearer that it was in his interest to do so, he rushed over to Brightside Cottage. No one recorded the discussion that took place, but the brewer left Neej Kaman to reside in Sonada close to the railway station.

There was no grand opening of the new tea shop in Sonada, but it soon became very popular with local men who would come in empty handed and leave with a bag or two.

Whenever Mylie was informed by her helpful relative that Customs and Excise officials from headquarter were coming to catch those involved in brewing illicit brewing, the tea shop would be temporarily emptied of large cauldrons and other equipment, which would be buried in the nearby corn fields until the officials left. And whilst no allegation of bribery was ever made, did these officials not also visit Brightside Cottage to have a cup of tea with the memsahib?

They say that some people have a gift for business. Mylie was one of them. From the sale of illicit liquor she moved to opening a stall alongside the railway station selling churpee and supari for chewing, hot tea, milk, cigarettes and biris, Indian sweetmeats and potato chips. The travellers were also pleased to be able to buy magazines and stationery; and thirsty travellers were offered free drinking water.

In 1951 during the Monsoons season there was a catastrophic landslide just as you got to Sonada, which blocked the main road and the railway track. As this meant that there was no access to and from Darjeeling town and the surrounding area, the local authority gave priority to the re-building of the road and railway track, which meant railway workers and labourers temporarily moving to Sonada.

There's a silver lining to every cloud. As the contractor for the road repairs was her second cousin, Mylie was successful in getting the contract to supply food for the workforce.

But it was not only Mylie's businesses that were growing. Sonada too was expanding.

When in 1959 the Dalai Lama escaped to India from Tibet, some 80,000 Tibetans followed him into exile. A small group of them started buying plots of land in Sonada to build their homes, and this is why her road contractor cousin approached Mylie.

"Mylie didi, there is money to be made from the Tibetans. I know a farmer who will sell some land; and you could buy and then re-sell the land to Tibetans for a good profit."

"Who will deal with the Tibetans?"

"I will," said the cousin.

"What will you get out of this?"

"The farmer will pay me a commission; I will handle your sale and you can pay me a commission as well."

"Let me think about it," said Mylie.

"You have to act quickly before the Tibetans find out that there is this land for sale," her cousin replied.

The profit from the land transaction was more than the annual profit from the illicit liquor and the railways station stall, so it was not surprising that Mylie decided to go into another similar property scheme.

This time her cousin told her that the Tibetans were intending to build a monastery, and were looking for as big a plot as possible. He had met a farmer who was unaware of this fact and could be persuaded to sell his land. They had to act fast and there was a very big profit to be made.

To expedite matters, he asked Mylie to hand over the purchase price to him for onward transmission to the seller who would no doubt be impressed by the sight of hard cash. Mylie did not need time to consider and acted accordingly.

The cousin disappeared both with her money and the farmer's wife, much to everyone's anger. If only Mylie had known of the English advice: "If it sounds too good to be true, it probably is."

"You must be educated so not to be a fool like me," Mylie would say to Alfred and everybody else.

And this was unfortunately the time when Alfred was to go to St Ignatius; so when asked if she could pay the school fees, she could only reply, "Major sahib, I will have to find the money."

CHAPTER 27

THE BEST DAYS OF HIS LIFE?

1949-1960

In the first week of March 1949, Alfred joined St Ignatius College.

His proud mother took him around Sonada in his school outfit (in those days were a blue suit, white shirt, school tie and a khaki sola topee) to say goodbye to all and sundry.

Everyone commented on how smart Alfred looked.

"You look just like a young sahib."

When he entered the school ground with his mother and saw so many boys running round the playing field, Alfred had second thoughts of going to boarding school.

"What is the matter, Alfred?" said his mother.

"I do not know anyone."

"Don't worry. You will be alright as soon as you find John."

And he did find John, who knew English and was able to help him to understand the school rules that the housemaster was talking about.

Alfred managed to get through the first year at school without knowing English. He had the advantages of the school employees being mostly Nepali; there was John; and boys from Burma, Nepal, Sikkim and Tibet most of whom also did not know English. And then there was his Mama who provided him with the leftover biscuits, cake and sandwiches from the parlour.

Like others who lived in the Darjeeling district, Alfred was fortunate in that he was allowed to go home for the weekend every four weeks.

Whenever Alfred came home, everyone warmly welcomed him and told him how clever he looked.

"Alfred, you are speaking well, but you must improve your accent," Mrs Thompson would say.

It was when he met Major Mercy that Alfred would get nervous because the Major would grill him, and ask if he was at the top of his class as yet?

And as for his mother, Alfred noticed on his homecomings that she had started reading English magazines to the awe of the servants of Brightside Cottage.

"See burra baba, your mother is so talented, she can read English," they said as his mother pretended not to hear.

Sadly however, sometimes she was holding the magazine upside down, but Alfred did not have the heart to tell her.

Each time she came to the school to collect him, his mother would bring home-cooked roast chicken with stuffing (after all, was this not Father Nigrelli's favourite meal?) and fruits for his class teacher.

"Mummy, please don't bring anything for the teacher. It is so embarrassing. Nobody else brings food for the teachers," Alfred would say, and be worried as to what the teachers were thinking. Unknown to him, the teachers were very appreciative because their food was no better than that given to the students.

The school year lasted nine months, and then in November the winter holidays started. When Mylie collected Alfred at the end of the first year, she was even prouder of Alfred than before as he had started talking English, and been awarded the Class Prize for Good Conduct.

But she noticed that his ears were dirty so right there and then, much to Alfred's annoyance, she called Mama.

"Bhai, please bring some water and a small towel."

"Oh Mummy, what will my friends say?" said Alfred, "wait till we get home." But his mother was not listening.

The boys at St Ignatius College considered themselves to be part of an extended family, and they regarded their school as the best to provide them with tools for the future.

Most of the boys got on with each other notwithstanding that some might be from noble and royal families and others from lower middle class; some Europeans and others Asians; some Catholics and others not. But there were whispers amongst the boys that the Europeans got preferential treatment.

Alfred discovered this as a result of an incident that took place on Sports Day in October 1952.

St Ignatius had an excellent playground with a pavilion, which had limited space for the guests on Sports Day. Therefore some parents were directed to the pavilion where afternoon tea was served, whilst others were told to watch from the playground with no sustenance.

That evening the local boys were allowed to go home for the weekend. When Alfred came to join his mother, he noticed there was a heated discussion amongst the mothers.

"We're second class. We pay the fees but they will not invite us to sit in the pavilion or even give us a cup of tea. But the white parents are treated like royalty," said one irate Indian mother.

Mylie joined in with the other native mothers, speaking in Hindi (which is similar to Nepali).

"This is how we're treated in the tea estates. Inferior. I thought these people were religious and good men. I am not going to come again to be insulted."

And this is how it went on all the way back to Sonada.

The following year, Alfred spoke to his Mama who was in charge of the school parlour. Mama arranged for Mylie and one of her brothers, who amusingly was wearing Alfred's school tie, to sit in the pavilion that sports day.

But the preferential treatment given to European parents by religious men gave Alfred food for thought.

Another incident took place in 1960 also affected Alfred. He was given the responsibility of writing and directing a short play for a social with the girls of the local convent. To prepare for dress rehearsal, Alfred needed a few costumes from the Green Room in the School Hall, and he knew that Father Tee had the keys. He could not find him, so he went to see the Rector who suggested that he could enter the Green Room via the stage and there was a ladder that he could use. Alfred and his friends gained entry, and whilst they were shifting through the costumes, Father Tee arrived.

"Who let you in?" he shouted. "I certainly did not."

Everyone looked at Alfred, who admitted that he was responsible. Before he could say that the Rector had given permission, Father Tee became hysterical.

"Lord Mountbatten was right. You half-castes cannot be trusted. You want everything free and when you cannot get it, you steal. Return everything and make sure nothing is missing."

And he went on and on. Alfred was dumbfounded and every time he said "Father, but ___ "

"Don't interrupt me, you thief. I will make sure you do not get away with it."

Alfred was very hurt and decided the world was unjust. He was determined to fight for the downtrodden when he became a lawyer.

That evening the Rector came up to Alfred in the dining hall.

"I have spoken to Father Tee," he said. "There is nothing for you to worry about."

Alfred went to speak to one of his classmates, a Tibetan boy whose favourite book was the English Dictionary. The boy carried the Dictionary wherever he went and spent hours studying it. He was an expert on English sex words, but Alfred wanted to find something else.

Alfred told him about the incident and his classmate carefully studied the Dictionary and said: Prejudice, class or race. Alfred considered the definition in the Oxford Dictionary: dislike, hostility, or unjust behaviour deriving from preconceived and unfounded opinions.

Many decades later in London there was a gathering of St Ignatius boys and talk was about schooldays and teachers.

"Father Tee disliked me," said Alfred, and explained what had happened all those years ago.

"You know why Father Tee disliked half-castes like you, Alfred?" said one of the boys. "It was because he too was an Anglo-Indian, but as he had fair skin with blue eyes he tried to pass off as an Englishman. You reminded him that he was not."

Alfred could not say that the best days of his life were his schooldays.

CHAPTER 28

THE NIGERIAN INCIDENT

1961

In 1960 Alfred sat for his Senior Cambridge Examination. His school days were now over for him or so he thought. The class of 1960 (17 of them) bade farewell to the school and to each other that November.

As Alfred would later say, his time in St Ignatius College was unexceptional. He was neither good nor bad at sports, and, without really trying, he was in the upper half of the class so far as academic studies were concerned.

He was only interested in the subjects that his teachers told him were required for law studies; in particular he concentrated on essay writing, elocution, debating and Latin. If Alfred were truthful, he would say that he sailed through school without much effort.

Alfred came to realise that the real benefit of going to St Ignatius was the friends he made there were for life.

There was his best friend John from Sonada, who was the most handsome; and why is it that handsome boys and pretty girls have best friends who are not? He became a dean and student counsellor.

Kancha Pradhan became a world traveller, and living the life that others wished they could.

Sanjay became a distinguished professor in America.

Eddy, a Cambridge graduate, made his fortune in computer software.

Mahindra was always in the group at school that appeared to have more fun, were more worldly and never seemed to be studying, but he was the one from St Ignatius who was later awarded an honorary doctorate by a South East Asian university.

And what about Gerry? He became a media lawyer in London and had a galaxy of stars as his clients. On his first visit to Hollywood, Gerry sent a picture postcard to Alfred saying, "From Hollywood." Alfred replied by buying one from Woolworth on which he wrote, "From Brixton."

Alfred spent the winter of 1960/61 at Brightside Cottage.

There was no plan other than that Alfred wanted to be a lawyer, although the careers teacher had offered some other advice.

"Alfred, to be a successful lawyer anywhere, passing exams is not enough. You need contacts. You do not know anyone in England. Really, it will be a waste of time for you to study Law. You have an aptitude to deal with people—think about being a teacher."

Mylie had no idea what could be done.

Alfred had no one to depend on except Major Mercy.

The Major learnt that St Ignatius College was starting a new one-year course known as Higher Senior Cambridge for those wanting to go to England for further studies. The Major advised that Alfred should go back to St Ignatius for the extra year; the good news was that the Rector reduced the course fee by half.

Whilst Alfred was in his last year at St Ignatius, Major Mercy was looking into sea passages and legal training. And he was pestering the Almoner at the Freemason Lodge for a final grant.

This was also the year when Thomas Nkiruka (which means "the best is still to come"), an exchange student from Nigeria, arrived at St Ignatius.

Thomas was from the Igbo tribe found in the south eastern region of Nigeria. A Christian by religion, the student had lighter skinned than one would have imagined but he was still designated as black, was quite short and had curly hair.

"My father is in business and he wants me to join him. But first he wants me to learn English. He has a friend who is a Catholic missionary and your school was recommended," he said to Alfred.

Wherever Thomas went, people would gawk at him. Any attempt on his part to be friendly through greetings or smiles was usually not reciprocated.

"I am like a monkey in the zoo," Thomas would say and smile.

He was two years older than Alfred, and they got on well. Alfred learnt from him about Nigeria and the various tribes. According to his friend, the Igbo tribe were innovative and creative and liked the colour of money, so the Igbos usually owned the shops and businesses in Nigeria. But above all they were family orientated.

"A woman has no chance of marrying an Igbo man unless she is also committed to his family," he would say.

One of the few people in Darjeeling who spoke to the Nigerian in a friendly way, rather than just stare at him, was a Nepali girl working in a restaurant.

One Saturday in September, they started talking, and he casually asked her to go to the cinema with him.

The girl accepted his offer, but all hell broke loose when the film finished and they came out of the cinema hall.

The girl was taken away and was smeared with tar and covered with feathers as a punishment for failing to uphold Nepali purity, and her brothers beat the Nigerian.

Until Thomas left two months later when the winter holidays started, no one would serve him in shops and restaurants, taxi drivers refused to give him a ride, and the other students avoided him. Alfred felt that he had no backbone as he too had little contact with his friend, except that he would buy him momos, or chicken fried rice or noodles, which were the victim's favourite dishes.

Alfred was embarrassed and ashamed by the behaviour towards Thomas. His friend was looked down upon because he was a black man and considered to be inferior to Indians. If the disgraced girl had gone out with a sahib, no doubt she would have received Nepali society's approval.

The Igbos were the prime movers of the Nigerian economy, and years later it did not surprise Alfred to read in Newsweek magazine that Thomas had become a very successful businessman and was a leading candidate for a Cabinet post.

"Good for you," thought Alfred.

Looking back, Alfred could see that the behaviour of the labourers attacking the Muslims at Hopetown Tea Estate, his grandfather's behaviour in the kitchen episode, the Sports Day incident at St Ignatius, the ranting of the priest at school and the Nigerian incident could all be termed prejudice. Little did Alfred know then that he would be facing racial prejudice in England.

CHAPTER 29

THE LONG GOODBYE

1962

The day before his overseas departure, Alfred made sure to visit those who meant so much to him.

He first visited Mrs Thompson at Hillside. She was getting frail and finding it difficult to move around.

"Well, Alfred. Time and tide waits for no young man. I am sure you have lots of things to do before you leave, so I will be brief. I have seen you grow up and you are a fine young man. Work hard and make us proud of you. And one last thing, I have loved you no less than if you had been my son."

"Aunty," said Alfred, "I love you too. Thank you for everything. I will always remember what you have taught me, and you will always be the most elegant person in my life."

And so with a few kisses and tears, Alfred left to go to Sonada House.

Major Mercy had no tears to share with Alfred, but he gave him paperwork including a list of contact numbers and addresses to pursue his legal career; a chart showing the average weather month by month in London and a shopping list of bare necessities required, in his opinion, when Alfred settled down in London.

He also gave Alfred a schedule setting out his first air journey by Dakota, a fixed-wing propeller-driven aeroplane, from the Himalayan foothills to Calcutta, then a train journey to Bombay, a sea voyage on the Royal Mail Ship Circassia to Southampton, and by boat train to London.

Lastly the Major handed to Alfred his British passport and the travelling tickets, the costs of which were shared between Mylie, the Freemasons and the Major.

Alfred tried to say "Uncle ___" and broke down sobbing.

"I know," said the Major. There was nothing more to be said.

When Alfred got home and was sorting out the paperwork, he found an envelope addressed to the manager of a London bank with a handwritten note to him from the Major, which read:

"My dear Alfred,

As they say, onwards and upwards. You will see there is a letter to my bank manager in London. Please make an appointment to see him as soon as you get there. I have asked if an account could be opened for you, and I have requested him to transfer £50 from my account for you to use in an emergency. I wish I could have given you more, but you will one day find out that pensions are never generous.

I look forward to learning that you have qualified; and remember throughout your life: Blessed are the kind for theirs is the Kingdom of Heaven.

Yours etc."

Alfred visited the other residents, and made sure that the last port of call was the hut of the Burmese grass cutter.

Kancha said nothing, but just bowed his head. Bowju had made a garland of paper red roses that she gave him, and which Alfred kept throughout his life as his good luck charm.

"Burra baba," Bowju said, "I will keep an eye on the memsahib and you do what you have to do; and as we all have to, you must follow your destiny."

Alfred spent the last evening with his mother eating his favourite dishes, chicken curry and rice, fresh vegetable curry, dhal, homemade tomato and onion pickle and poppadum. However there was no deep and meaningful conversation with his mother as she was inconsolable now that the time had come to part. It was the plan for her to accompany Alfred down to the foothills to the airport, but both realised she could not make the journey as she was too distressed. So it was decided that they would part next morning at home.

"Surely your mother must have given you some advice on your leaving?" people often asked Alfred.

"My mother, being illiterate and never having travelled more than 40 miles from her home, did not," Alfred would reply. "But I do remember a few days previously she had told me to marry an English girl as this would open doors which would otherwise be shut."

Did Alfred listen to his mother's advice?

Alfred boarded RMS Circassia, a fine looking ship, at Ballard Pier, Bombay, not realising that his father had come on the same ship to India so many years ago.

As the Scottish ship sailed past the Gateway of India, a stone archway built in 1911 to commemorate the visit of King George V to India, the lament "Will Ye No Come Back Again" was played over the loudspeakers.

"Will I come back?" thought Alfred. "Will Mummy be there when I come back?" He broke down in tears as he leaned on the railings watching the Gateway of India disappearing.

The ship called at Karachi, which was busy; Aden, where passengers were allowed to visit on a day trip; Port Suez, where hawkers climbed the side of the ship to sell their trinkets; Limassol, which looked peaceful and Gibraltar, which was small. It went through the Suez Canal, which was narrower than Alfred had imagined; the Mediterranean, which was blue and calm and the Bay of Biscay, where there was a bad storm, which resulted in Alfred suffering from seasickness for the first time in his life and he was told to drink brandy and port.

The ship docked in Liverpool, where Alfred, just aged 19, disembarked with his tin suitcase on February 10, 1962.

CHAPTER 30

RETURN TO SENDER

1962

1962 was the year of the Cuban Missile Crisis while Elvis Presley had several number one hits including "Return to Sender."

It was also the year when our Anglo-Indian reached the shores of England.

When Alfred disembarked, it was a foggy and cold day. He was quite shocked at the dilapidated condition of the docks; and he saw that the Customs officers were somewhat hostile to the passengers.

Alfred was unaware that new immigration law restricting immigrants from the New Commonwealth had been passed by Parliament; but as the new law had not come into force there was a flood of immigrants from these countries coming to Britain.

"Young man," said an officer, "can you produce your visa?"

"Sir, I do not know what a visa is," said Alfred.

"Show me your passport," and he continued "Oh, I see you are a British Citizen by birth. No problem. By the way, why have you come to England?"

"Sir, I have come to study law," Alfred said.

"Good luck. Please move on."

Alfred caught the boat train from the Liverpool Dock to London, as the ticket price was included in his sea fare. He hoped his capital of sixty five pounds and ten shillings divided in his mind as fifty pounds from Major Mercy for rent and fifteen pounds ten shillings for extras, would be sufficient till he found employment.

On arriving in London, Alfred was met by his classmate, Gerry, to whom, at the suggestion of Major Mercy, he had written to asking for his help to find a place to stay.

Gerry, an Indo-Burmese from Burma whose father was a judge there, had come to London a year earlier and was studying law.

"I have found a place for you to stay with a family," he said. "They're a very nice couple, the husband is from Ceylon and his wife is a German. He is a bank official. I live about a quarter of a mile away in a boarding house run by a Burmese family. Unfortunately there is no vacancy at my place."

"Thank you, Gerry. I am sorry for all the trouble. I owe you one for this." Alfred thought it is true that a good friend is better than money in the pocket.

The two of them, accompanied by Alfred's tin suitcase, made the journey to Brixton lying to the south of the River Thames.

Originally the area was known as Brixstane meaning the stone of Brihtsige. These stones were identified as a meeting place for the local communities. As the years went by this was shortened to Brixton.

They arrived in a road of Victorian terraced houses, and stopped at 19 Hemberton Road, which was occupied by Mr & Mrs Fernando.

"So where were you living before?" asked the friendly landlord.

"Sir, I have just arrived from India," replied Alfred. "I have come from Liverpool Dock by boat train straight here."

"Helga darling, this young man has just come from India. He should have dinner with us." As a result, Alfred had dinner with them that evening and other evenings thereafter.

The attic room had been newly painted; there was a single bed, a bedside table, a double wardrobe, a writing table and chair and a paraffin heater.

The rent was £4 per week including breakfast, but the tenancy contract had been amended on arrival to include dinner also.

In the next few days Alfred walked around Brixton. He noticed that it was an ethnically diverse area of London.

After the end of the Second World War, Irish, Poles, Cypriots and Maltese migrants had moved into Brixton, but by the time Alfred had arrived many of the Brixton residents were Jamaicans. They had come in response to recruitment campaigns by British Rail, London Transport and the National Health Service. Alfred found it comfortable to be in their midst.

Once he had settled down, Mr Fernando took Alfred to Major Mercy's bank with the letter he had been given. The manager's assistant opened Alfred's Account and gave him a passbook that proudly read: Credit £50. Alfred withdrew the money to pay the rent in advance, and as he left his bank, the passbook now read: Credit £0.

An incident, which shocked Alfred, took place on the last Saturday of February 1962, when it became much colder and Mrs Fernando warned Alfred that snow would fall.

Alfred had heard stories from Mrs Thompson and Major Mercy that the friendliest place to go to in England was the local pub.

"Alfred, on a Saturday night there is nothing more pleasant back home than going to the local, drinking a pint and joining in the singing," said the Major.

As he had passed a pub in a nearby street, Alfred decided to go there for a pint on the coming Saturday evening.

So dressed in his school blue suit, white shirt and tie, Alfred entered the pub expectantly, but he heard no music.

"Get out—Pakis are not allowed," shouted the barman much to Alfred's shock.

Alfred was shaken and he returned to his attic room.

"Gosh, you are back soon. Do you drink that quickly?" said his landlady.

"Mrs Fernando, I don't know what happened. I went to The Alexandra but I was told to get out because I am a Paki."

"Oh dear, I should have told you. That pub will not allow you in as they only serve white customers. Poor you, come into the lounge and watch TV with us."

This is how Alfred saw his first TV programme; and this is how he learnt about racial prejudice in Britain.

No Briton in Sonada had mentioned racial prejudice in England to Alfred simply because they had not encountered this problem on leave, as they had gone to places in the country where this issue had not yet surfaced.

So Alfred was interested when Mr Fernando explained the next day that immigrants from the Indian sub-continent had followed those from the West Indies; seeking work and a higher standard of living. They were welcomed at first to work in transport, textiles and manufacturing because the pay was poor and there was shift work or long hours and therefore it was not the local inhabitants' cup of tea.

Gradually nurses and other domestic hospital staff had been recruited from the West Indies, and doctors from India.

Coloured immigrants had difficulty in finding accommodation due to the post-war housing shortage and prejudice, so there were only certain parts of London, such as Brixton, where they were welcomed; even then, many had to live in ghettos.

"At my Bank," Mr Fernando said, "I work in the back room as some customers do not like to be served by a coloured."

The effect of the incident on the last Saturday of February 1962 was such that Alfred completely lost his confidence, feared rejection and felt ashamed. He woke up some nights crying or shouting, "I want to go home."

He became adept at pretending to the Fernandos that he was ill.

For several weeks he remained in his attic room looking out of the window or writing letters home whilst snow fell on February 26 and there was sleet or snow during the first ten days of March.

CHAPTER 31

I AM SO SCARED

1962

It was the second week of March and the weather improved a bit. Alfred thought that he had to do something, and not feel fearful and ashamed. Had Eleanor Roosevelt not said: "No one can make you feel inferior without your consent."

Alfred's classmate Gerry explained the London Underground (known as the Tube) routes, and told him to go to Temple Station via the District or Circle Lines. From there, following Gerry's directions, Alfred found himself in Chancery Lane before the grand entrance to the Law Society, the headquarter of one of the two branches of the legal profession in England and Wales.

Gerry was a fount of knowledge.

"To become a lawyer here, you have to decide to become either a barrister or a solicitor." He then went on to explain the difference.

As far as Alfred was concerned, he needed a fixed income and he told Gerry that he would be too scared to speak in public.

"In that case, you should become a solicitor. Then you will have a salary and do not need to be an advocate in court unless you want to," said Gerry.

So Alfred was at the Law Society entrance to make enquiries about becoming a solicitor, but there was a barrier in front of him—the doorman in fine livery. Alfred walked up and down trying to get Dutch courage to approach him.

"Am I going to be thrown out again? I must be brave."

Alfred went up to the doorman "Sir."

"This entrance is for members and student only. Go through the back entrance in Bell Yard."

"Sorry, Sir."

Alfred turned back onto Chancery Lane. He did not know where to go until he saw a deliveryman who directed him to a narrow road at the back of the Law Society building, which turned out to be Bell Yard.

Having entered through the tradesman's entrance, Alfred went through a labyrinth of rooms; and more by accident than design, he found himself in the students' enquiry room.

"Ma'am, please could I have some literature about becoming a solicitor? Thank you."

The young Italian woman on the counter smiled and said, "Have you got Articles?"

"I don't know what this means. I have just come from India to become a solicitor."

She looked kindly at Alfred.

"I am busy now, but if you come back in an hour's time I will explain what you have to do before you can become a solicitor."

"Thank you, Ma'am. I will be back, that's for sure."

They both smiled and Alfred left.

He did not want to get lost, but had to occupy his time for another hour. So when he saw an archway opposite, Alfred decided to enter it. He found himself in a lovely and tranquil square in central London, known as New Square, Lincoln's Inn.

At the entrance of each office there were listed the names of the practising lawyers.

"Will I ever find my name listed here?" thought Alfred, and he remembered Mrs Thompson saying, "Alfred if wishes were horses, beggars would ride."

An hour later the nice young lady took him to a room and made him sit down.

"Young man, don't look so frightened. Now, to be a solicitor you have to be first a British Citizen. Are you one?"

"Yes, Ma'am. By birth."

"Good. Then let me explain. Before you can become a solicitor not only do you have to pass exams, but also you must work for a solicitor to gain practical experience. He will be your principal for a fixed period, and you will be his or her articled clerk. If you do not have a law degree, and you look too young to have gone to college, you have to be an articled clerk for five years. So really your first task is to find your principal."

As Alfred did not know anyone, the lady gave him a list of solicitors who were looking for articled clerks, and suggested that he wrote to each of them.

"You can also place an advertisement in our magazine?" she suggested.

"I am sorry, Ma'am. I do not have any money," said Alfred.

She took his details and promised if she heard of anyone looking for an articled clerk, she would remember him.

"Thank you, Ma'am, you have been very kind to me."

The next day Alfred wrote to the ten firms seeking articled clerks—the letter in his best handwriting read:

"Dear Sir/Madam,

I am 19 years old and have just come from India. It is my ambition to be a solicitor and be helpful to the community.

I am writing to enquire if there is a vacancy for an articled clerk. I am told that the period of articles should be for five years. If chosen, I will work very hard and be loyal to you.

I do not have a telephone number; my postal address is ___.

Thanking you,

Yours faithfully,

Alfred Stephens"

Every evening his landlord would come from work and ask if there was any news.

"No, Mr Fernando."

"Never mind, you may get a reply tomorrow."

But no one replied.

"Alfred, how are you financially?" asked the landlord.

"Mr Fernando, I am desperate for an income."

"I am not worried about rent. I ask because you need to plan your finance. If you have no income, what will happen to you?"

"You are right, Mr Fernando. Could I trouble you for some advice, please?"

"As you have not had a single reply, I suggest you find a temporary job whilst you are looking for Articles. There are local businesses that may want temporary employees. You should find a local job as in this way you will save on travel expenses."

Alfred decided that Mr Fernando was right, and he would take whatever job was offered until he found Articles.

Following his landlord's urging, Alfred went around to the local newsagents' shop where all sorts of advertisements were displayed from lettings to employment and even, dare it be mentioned, for sexual favours.

Alfred decided none were suitable, but Mr Fernando was quite adamant. "Alfred, you are not seeking a career, take any job which pays you. It is temporary."

So Alfred went back to the newsagents, and noted that there were vacancies for office cleaners.

He arrived at the address of one of the advertisers; it was a small employment agency with two women inside.

"Ma'am, my name is Alfred Stephens. I saw your advertisement for office cleaners."

"Have you got your National Insurance Number?"

Alfred did not know what she was talking about, and it was safer to say, "No, Ma'am."

"Ma'am. Ma'am, you make me feel like an old aged pensioner. Call me Mrs Evans," said the older woman.

"Thank you, Ma'am," said Alfred.

"There he goes again. Where are you from and how did you get an English name?"

Mrs Evans sent Alfred to the local Social Security Office to get his National Insurance Number; and once he had one, he went back to see her.

Alfred was employed as a temporary office cleaner at a mail order company within walking distance from his attic room.

He learnt that customers of his new employers were given catalogues from which one ordered and the price could be paid in instalments. Alfred asked for one, and he would spend hours at home looking through the catalogue, imagining which items he would buy when he had some money—his priority being a charcoal grey suit, blue shirt and red tie. After all he had been wearing his school outfit namely blue suit, white shirt and school tie for far too long.

"Yes Mrs Thompson, I know—if wishes were horses, beggars would ride."

CHAPTER 32

EARNING A CRUST

1962-63

The world of office cleaning welcomed Alfred. He became part of a team consisting of seven women and three men.

His first task was to polish desks and clear the office bins, but after a week or so he was designated to clean the Gents toilets. Was this a promotion?

Alfred became quite efficient at cleaning the toilets—after all, he had seen how the sweepers back home worked.

"You clean well," said his supervisor. Alfred kept quiet and did not say that his secret lay in the use of an old toothbrush and baking soda, which he bought cheaply in the corner shop near his attic room. In hindsight Alfred would have used plastic gloves also but he did not know then that such gloves existed.

Years later his girlfriends would sympathise, "Poor you. It must have been horrible."

"Not as bad as it seems," Alfred would reply. "After all, is not cleanliness next to Godliness, as Benjamin Franklin wrote?"

Alfred's supervisor was an Indian gentleman aged about thirty from Bombay. He was a Post Office telephone engineer, but as a result of his gambling habit, he had a second job.

"Call me Harry. I have anglicised my name, which is really Harinder. How come you have an English name?" So Alfred repeated his family history.

And Harry said he had married back home before coming. His wife did not work, as she had to look after their son, who suffered from rickets and had bendy legs. Harry was always buying cod liver oil for his son.

The team had a good relationship. Alfred looked forward to the women cleaners sharing their homemade food, and if Harry happened to be lucky with his horse or greyhound betting, which was infrequently, he would bring bottles of beer and stout to celebrate.

At the end of each week, Harry would distribute the wages in cash.

"Alfred, here is your pound of flesh."

Alfred would sit in his room and open the brown envelope containing his wage slip and bank notes, sometimes clean and crisp, other times dirty and tired looking. He was paid six pounds ten shillings, which meant that he had a surplus of two pounds ten shillings after paying for board and lodging.

Then there was better news for him.

"Are you there? Can I have a word with you when you come down?" said the landlord.

"I wonder what I have done," thought Alfred.

"Listen Alfred. These days you are working in the evenings, so why should you pay us for food that you do not eat? From now onwards you will pay three pounds instead of four and eat with us on weekends."

"Are you sure, Mr Fernando?"

"Of course I am sure. Now you have extra money to spend on a girlfriend. Ha ha," laughed the kind and jovial landlord.

The extra money meant that Alfred could indulge in small luxuries such as buying a daily packet of Smith's potato crisps with a small blue bag of salt or barley sugars that lasted longer than any other sweet. And even more important he could buy more aerograms, which were lightweight foldable and gummed papers for writing letters, cheaper than posting letters in an envelope.

When Alfred read in October that there were race riots in Mississippi because of the admission of a black American to University, he could not help but observe that the cleaners at the mail order company were either Indians or West Indians.

"Like the sweepers in India and the black Americans, perhaps we must be lower class too," thought Alfred.

In the meantime Harry was making him jealous of the employment benefits at the Post Office.

"Do you know Alfred, postmen get £20 per week? And tips from customers at Christmas. And when I retire there will be a Post Office pension. Think how much that would be worth in Indian rupees. I need one big bet to get the deposit to buy a house, and my wages will be enough to pay the mortgage. When I retire I can sell it too and go back to Bombay as a rich man."

Did Harry achieve his dreams? Alfred never found out.

"Don't waste your time," Harry went on. "You will never get a job with solicitors—you are coloured and the middle class don't know how to deal with our lot. Why don't you work at the Post Office? There are a lot of us coloureds."

But when he had a winning streak, Harry became an optimist.

"Alfred, don't give up. You will become a solicitor and be rich. Mark my word."

During the week Alfred was calling at the offices of solicitors in the neighbouring areas and delivering his letter in best handwriting, but there was never any response. He could see that the Fernandos were feeling sorry for him, and Mr Fernando even promised to speak to his solicitor. But this was of no avail.

Alfred tried to be optimistic which was not easy in the circumstances.

No one knew that he was living on one meal a day—weekday dinners at work due to the kindness of strangers, and weekends thanks to his landlady's cooking. At lunchtimes, he would go out.

Mrs Fernando would ask "Where are you going?" or "Are you going for lunch?" "Lunch, Mrs Fernando" Alfred would reply, or "Yes, Mrs Fernando. See you later"; but the truth was that Alfred would go to the local park and sit there for an hour or so; or in rainy weather, go to the public library and read the free newspapers and return.

"What did you have for lunch?" said Mrs Fernando.

"Pork pie, Mrs Fernando" or "Fish and chips" Alfred would reply.

"You must eat healthier," his landlady would say.

But Alfred was grateful for small mercies. There were benefits living with the Fernandos such as the landlady collecting his washing once a week, hoovering his room also once a week and offering a daily nightcap, in Alfred's case a cup of tea.

"Good night, Mrs Fernando. Thank you."

"Stop thanking me, Alfred. It is not necessary."

"Thank you."

Life went on, but whilst Alfred was ready to start his legal career there was no one there to offer him a chance to do so. Therefore Alfred considered the possibility of joining the Post Office.

"Harry, "he said, "I could not be a postman because a mail bag would be too heavy."

"You can get a clerical post at Mount Pleasant," said Harry.

"Thanks, Harry, but what is Mount Pleasant?"

"Ah, Mount Pleasant is one of the largest sorting offices in the world. Do you know the site is about seven acres and there are over 20 miles of train tunnels delivering the post? It is near Farringdon Street, not too far from the law courts. There are lots of temporary jobs available now that Christmas is approaching. I will get some information for you."

Harry found out whom Alfred should contact. So Alfred went to the Mount Pleasant site, which housed, amongst other departments, the Inland Letter Section, the London Returned Letter branch, the Engineering Department, the Supply Department and the Post Office (London) Railway.

When he got there, Alfred found a long line of mostly young people wanting work over Christmas. Many went to work either in the railway section of Mount Pleasant or nearby King's Cross railway station; but after interviewing Alfred, the recruiter allocated him to the Inland Letter Section for the Christmas rush starting from September 1 and ending on December 31.

Alfred had to attend an induction course; and then he started work in his section, which had a staff of several thousands. They dealt with junk mail, which in those days was bulk correspondence from publishers, businesses and advertising companies.

Alfred worked from ten at night to eight in the morning moving batches of junk mail from one location to another in freezing conditions, but the wages were good—£10 per week.

In the first week of December thick layer of fog enveloped London, which affected public health. BBC News reported that over 90 people died, including Gerry's landlord.

The Ministry of Health advised people to stay indoors, and if going out to use do-it-yourself masks such as a scarf around the mouth and nose.

The dense fog was followed by snow; it was recorded that for 62 consecutive days, there was snow on the ground. There were blizzards, snowdrifts and temperatures of minus twenty degrees, roads and railways were blocked and telephone lines were brought down. Alfred had never come across such cold weather in the Himalayas.

But this did not mean that he could stay in his attic room warmed by a paraffin heater. He had to fight Mother Nature and travel to and from Mount Pleasant—a journey that he could not take by a bus due to the inclement weather but by the more expensive Tube journey. He kept warm on his journeys and at the cold locations where he was working by wearing his mother's knitted jumpers and gloves; he wondered if he should change his priority in life from buying a charcoal grey suit with accessories to buying a warm woollen overcoat.

This did not mean that Alfred did not want to pursue a legal career, but he took what he could get until he got what he wanted. And how many rejections can a person take?

But in writing to his mother who would get someone to interpret the letter for her, Alfred said—

"My dear Mummy,

I am hoping this letter will arrive in time for Christmas. I miss you, particularly this Christmas time. I remember all the presents that Father Christmas or you gave me, and all the laughter and happiness. I am spending my first Christmas in London thinking of you and letting you know that I will not be alone. My landlord and landlady have invited me to have lunch with them, and after that I will go and see friends from work. Everyone has been kind to me. We have agreed that no presents will be exchanged. This is good, as I have started to save money for my plane fare to come to see you.

It has been very cold here—they say it is the coldest winter for more than 200 years. So I am happy that you knitted me the jumpers, scarves and gloves.

I am working hard; the pay is good and I am making more friends. I will let you know about my studies in my next letters.

All my love,

Your (handsome, according to you) son,"

CHAPTER 33

LUCK IS A LADY

1963

Alfred's temporary career at the Post Office ended on Monday, December 31. He went cheerfully home with his last pay packet.

Somewhat to his surprise the next-door neighbour, whom he had seen and sometimes said "Good morning" or "Good night" to but never had a conversation with, came up to him.

"Hello Son. Are you doing anything special tonight?" asked the neighbour.

"No Ma'am, Mr & Mrs Fernando are going out."

"Then why don't you come for a drink, say at midnight?"

"Thank you, Ma'am."

So as the midnight hour came, Alfred went next door and rang the doorbell.

"One minute," shouted the neighbour.

A few minutes later, the door opened.

"Happy New Year. Hold on to these things and come in."

Carrying the items, Alfred walked in and met a gang of strangers wishing him a Happy New Year.

After being given a drink or two, which was more than he had drunk before, Alfred left with a bag of ashes that he was asked to throw in the outside bin on his way out.

Next morning Alfred learnt about a custom called "first footing" from his landlord, who found the whole episode amusing. It appears that good luck would be brought to the occupiers of a household if as soon as the New Year started, a dark person carrying a piece of coal, bread, money and some greenery entered their home, and on leaving took with him with some dust or ashes.

"It is all right that the neighbours are going to be lucky this coming year, but what about me?"

His friend Gerry's Christmas gift was his textbook on Roman law, which he no longer needed. This was the book that Alfred was reading that first fortnight of January when he received a handwritten postcard addressed to him.

"If you have not found Articles so far, call at my office as soon as you can. Sophia Mezatta, The Law Society."

The next morning, Alfred went to Chancery Lane and sought out the sender of the postcard, who was the Italian lady who had been helpful on his last visit.

"Good you came. I have learnt that there is a solicitor in Lincoln's Inn who is looking for an Articled Clerk. He is involved in charity work and was in fact born in Africa. Let me ring his secretary and see if I can get an appointment for you."

This is how Alfred found himself in New Square, Lincoln's Inn at 9.30 the next morning to see Mr Ambrose Anderson.

"So young man, where are you from?"

"India, Sir."

"I have met Mahatma Gandhi. But you have Mongoloid features?" So Alfred had to repeat his family history.

"If you are part Nepali, you must be a Gurkha. They're hardworking, courageous and fine people."

"Well, Sir."

"Have you met the King of Nepal?"

"Sir, his sons were in school with me"

"Alfred here is a relative of the King of Nepal," Mr Anderson said to his secretary. Alfred kept silent.

"We must have a member of royalty in our staff. Go and see the accountant and you can start work next Monday, 8 sharp."

Alfred was flabbergasted. He heard the Hungarian accountant talking about pay, trial period and hours of work, but he could not take it all in either because he was too excited or he could not understand the accent.

"Come on Monday at 8, and start with helping to open the post," said the accountant; before he knew what to do next, Alfred was ushered out of the office.

Alfred crossed the road and went to see Sophia Mezetta to tell her of his probationary employment.

"Well done, Alfred. Let me know how you get on," said the kind lady.

Mrs Fernando was also overjoyed with the news and decided to cook a special German dish containing prunes, which she told Alfred her husband had liked very much when he had gone to meet her parents in Germany.

Alfred was happy to celebrate his good fortune eating this special dish, as he could not afford to celebrate with a bottle of champagne much as he would have liked to.

When Mr Fernando came home, Alfred was called for dinner, and with great ceremony, Mrs Fernando brought the piping hot German dish containing prunes.

"What is this rubbish?" said Mr Fernando.

"I cooked this speciality dish because you liked it when my mother cooked it for you."

"I pretended to like it. I hate prunes."

The result was that Mrs Fernando burst into tears and sulked, Mr Fernando went to fry his eggs and bacon; and Alfred went hungry to bed.

On the first Monday of April 1963, Alfred turned up at New Square at 6.30 a.m. as he did not want to be late. Since the gate to the Square was locked, he hung around the adjoining Lincoln's Inn Fields which is the largest square in London, laid out by Inijo Jones in the 17th century, at one time popular with duellists, but in 1963 a public open space with two tennis courts, a netball court and a bandstand. It was also a popular spot for office workers during their lunchtime break.

Alfred's first task was to open the post. The other clerk gave specific instructions, but as Alfred had never heard a Cockney accent he did not fully understand, so he opened all the post marked Private and Confidential and left the others unopened.

As the weeks progressed, Alfred had a variety of jobs to do. He was asked to make the tea and coffee for everyone after the post had been sorted. Alfred boiled the milk, as they did in the Himalayas, to add to the tea and not having seen instant coffee before and too terrified to ask, he put several spoonful of coffee into each mug. The result was so bad that he was never asked to make another hot drink, and he was moved to the filing section. Here he was a bit better, but was encouraged to move to reception. There Alfred was asked to man the switchboard during the lunch hour.

"Ambrose, where did you get that creature from?" said a posh client after speaking to Alfred.

Mr Anderson lent him vinyl records of Shakespeare plays, and requested Alfred to change his accent to that of John Gielgud, the actor. Unfortunately Alfred did not have a record player, but he did not tell this to Mr Anderson.

There was a kerfuffle because Mr Anderson wanted an old file for an important client and no one could find it. So Alfred was sent to the basement to go through the archives. The bad news was that Alfred had to shift through dusty files that had been untouched for years, but the good news was that Alfred found the file. This was his first success in the office for which he was much complimented.

"Alfred," said the accountant, who was also the office manager, "you are the right man to sort out the archived files. Bring some old clothes with you tomorrow and go and sort out the basement."

The end result of working for the next six weeks in the basement was, on the negative side Alfred became allergic to dust, while on the positive side the archived files were put in order for the first time in many years, and also Alfred hatched a plan.

He bought exercise books at the local Woolworths store; and as he went through the archived files, he made notes and copied by hand documents and letters that he found interesting. There were at that time no photocopiers.

Miss Rees was the solicitor in charge of the Matrimonial Department. She was a Welsh woman in her early 50s, buxom and short. She lived alone in a basement flat in North London.

Alfred learnt from other colleagues that she had wild pot-smoking parties on Saturday evenings to which he had never been invited; and if he had, Alfred was sure he would have made some excuse.

She was very popular with her matrimonial clients, and knew how to celebrate successes at the tiny Seven Stars Pub in Carey Street behind the law courts.

"Alfred, would you like to come with me to a conference with Counsel?" said Miss Rees. "You will meet a well known barrister and you will see how he advises clients." So Alfred accompanied Miss Rees and her client to obtain advice on a custody dispute.

The tall and impressive looking barrister listened to the client's opposition to custody being granted to her ex husband, and there was a lengthy discussion.

"Young man, what do you think about all this?" said the barrister to Alfred.

"Sir, why do we not get a paediatrician's report to support our client's claim?" said a timid Alfred.

"What a good idea. Miss Rees, this is what we must do."

"You are a sly one," said Miss Rees on the way back to the office.

"You know more than you let on."

If only Miss Rees knew that he had no idea who a paediatrician was, but he had read a report from one in an archived files.

Back at the office Mr Anderson spoke to Miss Rees.

"I got a call from chambers, and your barrister was saying that Alfred is a very clever young man and he should be encouraged to be a matrimonial solicitor, so you can be his mentor."

This is how Alfred started his legal career dealing with matrimonial cases under the supervision of Miss Rees.

However the first time Alfred went to court was on a criminal matter.

"Miss Rees, can you spare Alfred? I need someone to go to the Old Bailey. Everyone else is busy," said Mr Anderson.

"A barrister will deal with the advocacy," Miss Rees explained, "but there has to be a representative from the solicitors. So you are going to the Old Bailey. Go to Court Number 2 and ask the usher where to sit. Then there is nothing for you to do except to make notes of any important points, and record the times when the case started and finished."

Alfred was nervous but very excited. Had he not read about murder trials at the Old Bailey and had he not seen, in school, the film "Witness for the Prosecution" starring Marlene Dietrich and Tyrone Power?

Having reached Court Number 2, Alfred asked for the court usher, said he was from the solicitors and enquired where he should sit.

"Down there," said the gruff usher.

So off went Alfred and when he saw a group of people sitting on a bench, he went to sit with them.

The trial of a burglar carried on. Every now and then a barrister or two smiled at him, the people sitting on the bench smiled at him, the judge smiled also. Did the accused smile also?

"How friendly everyone is," thought Alfred until the lunch break came and the usher stormed towards him.

"You idiot, you are sitting with the jury." It must have been the first time in the Old Bailey's history that there appeared to be a jury of 13.

Afterwards whenever he came to the Old Bailey, Alfred would smile and think of how he had made a fool of himself on his first visit; and much to the amusement of his new staff, he had the habit of drawing a diagram showing where to sit in court.

CHAPTER 34

LEGAL LIFE

1963

Lincoln's Inn is situated behind the law courts in the Strand and alongside Lincoln's Inn Fields. The old buildings include one named New Square, which, notwithstanding its name, had been built in the seventeenth century.

Barristers occupied the buildings in the Inn, but during the poor economic times before World War II some were let to solicitors, including Mr Anderson. By the time Alfred went to work for Mr Anderson, the general opinion in legal circle was that prestigious firms of solicitors practised from New Square.

Alfred had been working for five months as a law clerk when one of Mr Anderson's two articled clerks, a female, approached Alfred.

"I complete my articles in a month's time. You must go and ask Mr Anderson to sign your articles, otherwise someone else will get there before you."

"I am too scared to ask Mr Anderson to sign my Articles. Could you speak to him for me, please?" said Alfred.

She did so, and that is how Mr Anderson raised the subject of Articles with Alfred.

"So you still want to be a solicitor?"

"Yes, Sir."

"You know it is going to be tough. There are two sets of examinations over the next five years, and in the Finals you have to sit for seven subjects. If you fail one subject, you have to sit all of them again," said Mr Anderson.

"I did not know that, but I will work hard to pass."

"I know you will. But how will you live? Articled clerks only get a nominal wage—say three pounds a week? In my days it was worse, my father had to pay a premium to my principal before I was taken in as an articled clerk, and there were no wages."

"Sir, I have an allowance from home," lied Alfred.

"I will think about it. Give me a day or two," said Mr Anderson.

The decision went in Alfred's favour. He signed his Articles with Mr Anderson with a weekly wage of three pounds, 15 shillings worth of luncheon vouchers per week, annual holidays of two weeks, and a month's leave without pay each time he had to sit for an Examination. The five years' Articles would end on October 2, 1968.

There was no leave given to attend daytime classes so Alfred enrolled for night school; and as no mention was made as to whether or not he could have a second job, Alfred decided to continue with his evening cleaning job until it was time for him to go to night school.

The Articles were registered at the Law Society, who in those days required a potential articled clerk to attend an interview to see if he or she was fit to be a solicitor. Alfred crossed the road from New Square to the Law Society to be interviewed by two officials, who seemed in awe of Mr Anderson, and were really only interested in how Alfred had met him.

There was no fanfare that he had become an Articled Clerk, except that Miss Rees' secretary Maureen baked him a lemon drizzle cake and Alfred went to buy his first textbook. This he could do from a nearby bookshop, which he entered with some trepidation.

"Sir, could I have the first law book that I need to become a solicitor, please? I can only afford a second hard copy."

"You want to be a solicitor?" said the officious middle-aged shop assistant, who turned to his colleague and said, "This Indian wants to be a solicitor," and they both looked at Alfred in an insolent way.

Having purchased a second hand copy of Kiralfy's The English Legal System (published in 1960), Alfred left. He decided that whenever he needed another law book, he would ask Maureen or another secretary to buy it on his behalf.

Winter was approaching and Alfred felt as gloomy as the weather. He was leaving for work at seven in the morning and working to six in the evening, the final task being to take the mail to the post office. Three times a week, he would rush to attend night school which started at six thirty and ended at eight thirty so that he would get back to his attic room in Brixton around nine thirty just in time to have some soup or a sandwich which had been kindly prepared by his landlady.

At night school, Alfred and a Chinese student from Hong Kong, which had the same system of lawyers as in England, were the only coloureds in their class. But even they did not bond, as students at night school were keen to go home after lectures, as they had to go to work the next morning.

Once night school started, Alfred stopped working as a cleaner. But a few months later, he went to see his cleaner friends. He found out that Harry was no longer supervising, and enquiries at Mount Pleasant disclosed he had left there too. No one knew why Harry had left or where he was working. Alfred hoped that he had given up his gambling habit, that he would buy a house if he had not done so already, and return one day to Bombay as a rich man.

Alfred also visited the employment agency where the proprietor, Mrs Evans was happy to see him and delighted that he was at last on his career path. When Alfred mentioned he needed additional income, Mrs Evans arranged for him to work in the weekends as a part time cleaner in Sanitary Steam Laundry, Coldharbour Lane, Brixton. After a short time the manager of the laundry, who had taken a liking to Alfred, offered to dry clean his suit and wash his shirts at no cost.

CHAPTER 35

TILL DIVORCE DO US PART

1963-1964

Alfred spent the first two years of his Articles supporting Miss Rees, who had for years ignored the advice that the devil is in the detail. So he would spend hours checking documents, taking down evidence from clients and their witnesses, preparing the paperwork for the barristers and representing the firm at court hearings whilst Miss Rees was entertaining prospective clients or celebrating with existing ones.

Alfred was also chosen to take confession statements from adulterers.

A ground for divorce was adultery, and it had to be proved in court that the adultery had been committed. This resulted in farcical incidents of private detectives tracking down spouses in hotel rooms with their lovers. But a cheaper way was for a solicitor's representative to meet the offending parties and have them sign a confession statement, which would be produced at the divorce hearing. So Alfred traversed the length and breadth of London and the suburbs, taking statements from couples who confessed to having sex in a hotel room, the matrimonial home, the lover's home, a friend's home, at work, in the back of cars, outdoors and even in a coal shed.

This is how Alfred learnt about sexual misdemeanours, and also he became an expert in the London bus routes.

However it was not always straightforward, and there were twists and turns before the evidence was complete and the divorce granted.

Mrs Marsh, a woman in her mid fifties and who would be described as a large woman no doubt due to a life of eating in expensive restaurants and drinking fine wines, came to see Miss Rees in a foul mood. She depended on her doctor husband for her status in society; and she could not get over the fact that her best friend, in a somewhat drunken state, had blurted out that the doctor had seduced her.

"Off you go to Harley Street and see Dr Marsh and his lover for a confession statement," Miss Rees said.

Harley Street is the street where successful doctors have their surgeries, so Alfred was quite looking forward to visiting one. Unaware the street was long, he arrived at the Tube station on one end of the road and the surgery was on the other end. The doctor, a short, bald and not good looking man in his early sixties, was not best pleased that Alfred was late as the waiting room was full of patients who could afford him.

"Come in, Mr ___ er Stephens. I hope this will not take too long," said the doctor and looked at Alfred in a familiar way—how does this man have an English name?

"Sir, sorry to trouble you but the lady must be present."

So the doctor pressed the bell and the attractive receptionist in her late twenties, wearing a rather short miniskirt and looking as if butter wouldn't melt in her mouth came in.

"Darling, please sit down. Mr Stephens needs you to sign a document."

It came as a considerable shock to Alfred that the lover was so young, she was not the client's best friend and the affair had been going on for some three years.

The shock was even greater for Mrs Marsh when she read the confession statement.

"Miss Rees, I want every penny from that serial adulterer. How could he make a fool of me? I now understand why that bitch smirked whenever she saw me."

In those days at a divorce hearing, the innocent spouse had to hand over to the judge (for his eyes only) a sealed envelope containing a short statement (known as the discretion statement) stating whether or not he or she had been unfaithful during the marriage. It amazed Alfred how he could not judge the clients—the flirtatious and sometimes glamorous spouse would have been faithful, while another person who looked meek and more often than not was below average in looks would list a string of sexual conquests.

"Do you remember Mrs Bryant who would not forgive her husband for a one night stand to which he confessed due to conscience, whilst she had seduced almost all his friends?" said Alfred to Miss Rees.

"There's nowt so queer as folk," she replied.

CHAPTER 36

LOVE THAT DARE NOT SPEAK ITS NAME

1964

In 1964, Alfred was told that he would be working for Mr Anderson as his personal assistant.

Mr Anderson had come from South Africa where his father had been a missionary to go to Cambridge University to study Law. After qualification, in 1934, he had started his own firm in the East End of London advising poor people and then moving on to New Square, Lincoln's Inn where he was advising both rich and poor.

From his contacts at University and involvements with numerous charities advising the aged, immigrants and the poor, fighting for pro-gay and pro-women rights and supporting free legal advice centres, Mr Anderson had built a very successful practice.

In contrast to lesbian acts not being considered to be illegal, male homosexual relations were still a crime.

One of Mr Anderson's friends from the 1920s was a woman who was the founding secretary of a penal reform organisation. The organisation was helping gay men charged with criminal offences, and supporting a campaign to change the law relating to them.

The secretary introduced many clients who were charged with committing gross misconduct, importuning for immoral purposes or being members of a gay ring.

At the time Alfred joined his firm, Mr Anderson had become well known for defending gays so that these clients would come to his office usually outside office hours, as they did not want to be identified.

The clients ranged from a well known actor, an MP, city gentlemen who picked up young soldiers near the barracks, artists, teachers who were fond of their pupils, married men; and to Alfred's surprise, the barber in Brixton who cut his hair and would whisper "Caro mio" to his handsome customers.

Mr Anderson personally handled these cases; and Alfred was selected to assist him.

"Sir, I have never heard of gays before, so I do not know how I can assist you?"

"You have become good at taking statements from clients and witnesses and both of us are early birds, so we can see these clients first thing in the morning before the office open," replied Mr Anderson.

Alfred wished he had the courage to say, "Actually I would like to come to work later like the other staff."

So Alfred spent the year helping these clients who would be arrested by the Police in places such as parks and public toilets where they met for cottaging, which Mr Anderson said was the term for picking up other gays.

Alfred had no knowledge of such behaviour; but as the year went by he became sympathetic to these clients as he could see that the police were unfairly targeting them, and that they lived their lives in fear of being outed or blackmailed.

"Every day I am frightened of being blackmailed. My life is hell," said a married stockbroker who was being investigated for gross indecency.

It was when he was working on one of these cases that Alfred realised that the truth did not always come out in court, even though an oath would be taken to tell the truth, the whole truth and nothing but the truth.

When Alfred arrived at the office on a Monday morning in late 1964 there was a somewhat agitated man waiting outside.

The Reverend Felix Hampstead, aged fifty-eight, was vicar of a West London parish, and unfortunate circumstances had led him to seek Mr Anderson's help.

"Vicar, have you come to see my principal, Mr Anderson?"

"Who are you?"

"I am his Articled Clerk."

"When is he coming? I have not got all day to hang around," said the Reverend as he looked around him.

"Please come in and I will make you a nice cup of tea. My father was a tea planter," said Alfred knowing he was useless in making tea.

The Vicar was getting impatient.

"So Vicar, the procedure we have is that Mr Anderson advises the client, and the client is passed to me to take a detailed statement. I have all the time to do so. As you are in a hurry, may I suggest we start on the statement?"

"So you know why I am here?"

"Yes Vicar. I am sorry that you have been charged," said a sympathetic Alfred.

"Where shall I begin?"

"Let's begin at the beginning."

So the Reverend gave his background details and carried on—

"I then arrived at Charing Cross Station, crossed over and walked down Long Acre, and when I saw the public toilet, I went in. Call of nature—you know. A young man saw me and smiled, so I started to talk to him when, out of the blue, two policemen arrested me, cautioned me, took me to the Station, accused me of loitering and charged me with importuning for immoral purposes and released me on bail. I have to appear at Bow Street Magistrates Court next Thursday at nine. I am totally innocent. When this is over I want to lodge a complaint against the two policemen."

"Vicar, why were you in Long Acre?" asked Alfred.

"Does it matter? When does Mr Anderson get to the office?"

"He will be here any moment. But coming back to my question, you will be asked what you were doing at Long Acre?"

"Why is this important, young man," said the Vicar.

"There has to be a reason why you were there. For example, there is a well known shop that sells maps and you could have been going there to buy a map and you needed to go to the toilet—that would make sense."

Mr Anderson walked in, apologised for his late arrival and asked Alfred to read out the draft statement.

"So Vicar, you walked down Long Acre. What were you doing there?"

"I was on my way to the shop that sells maps as I am planning to go on a walking holiday along Hadrian's Wall. I went to the toilet due to a call of nature." Alfred was flabbergasted but said nothing, but he did notice that the Vicar was looking away from him.

At the trial, the Vicar remembered that the name of the shop in Long Acre was Stanfords and that it had one of the largest collections of maps and that he went there regularly as his hobby was walking. However when Alfred had visited the shop to get supporting evidence and showed a Polaroid picture he had taken of the Vicar, no shop assistant in the map section recognised the parish priest.

As to the visit to the public toilet, the Vicar explained in the witness box that he had entered it because of call of nature, seen a young man in an agitated state, and spoke to him for pastoral reasons.

The Vicar was found Not Guilty and a small band of elderly parishioners cheered, complained about police behaviour, and took the innocent man to the pub nearby to celebrate. However the Vicar did not invite Alfred.

In 1967 Parliament passed the Sexual Offences Act decriminalising homosexual acts between two men over 21 years in private; and step-by-step gay relationships became acceptable in Law and in society.

In 1972 the first Gay Pride Rally took place in Trafalgar Square, and a retired vicar was interviewed on what it was like to come out.

"Bloody hell," said Alfred. "That's Reverend Felix Hampstead."

CHAPTER 37

WHATEVER WILL BE, WILL BE

1965

Whilst serving his Articles, Alfred lived from hand to mouth. His ambitions then were to qualify as a solicitor, and to buy a new suit as professionals had to dress the part but he could not as he had no money to spare.

When he was free in the weekends, Alfred liked nothing better than to walk around Brixton, particularly in Brixton Market (with its three market buildings, Reliance Arcade, Market Row, and Granville Arcade) where stalls sold rice, Jamaican patties, dried cod fish, dried pork and ackee, spices, beans, tinned yams, scotch bonnets, mangoes and avocados to the curiosity of the white customers; along Atlantic Road to see the brightly lit window of Stones Television and Radio and admire the consumer electronics such as Pye televisions and radios which he could not afford; and the men's clothes shop which occupied a cupola-topped premises on the corner of Electric Avenue, which was one of the first streets in London that had electric lights.

The good times for Alfred were when a case went well due to his good preparation, a client praised him or he passed the mock tests.

The good times were also when Miss Rees celebrated with her clients at the Seven Stars Pub in Carey Street where the Bankruptcy Court was also situated. Champagne flowed, but it was never clear as to who paid. There was talk that the payments came out of the office petty cash. No one enquired, but all who attended had a good time.

"Alfred, remember if you become a spendthrift you will end up in Carey Street [meaning the Bankruptcy Court]," Miss Rees' secretary would say.

"Do you mean at the Seven Stars [meaning the pub]?"

Maureen was 23, attractive with pure white skin, short brown hair. She was of average height and wore glasses. She came from the East End of London; her father was a customs officer in Surrey Docks, her mother a housewife.

"One thing about my secretary is that she always dresses well," Miss Rees would say. Maureen was proud that she stitched her own clothes.

Her main attribute, which attracted Alfred, was that Maureen had a mellow personality and did not get easily flustered. This was needed to work with Miss Rees, who would flare up every time she misplaced a document or even worse lost a file.

Alfred shared a room with Maureen; she seemed to like him and was interested in what he had to say. She would tease him.

"In India, was your house built on a tree? Ha ha."

"Definitely."

"Really, what sort of house would your family live in?" she asked.

"Well, when my father was running a tea estate called Hopetown we lived in a two-storey house on a land plot of about seven acres. It had a badminton court, flower and vegetable gardens and an orchard growing grapefruit, lemon, lime and oranges. The house had a service side entrance for staff and goods, and an entrance leading to the sitting room, a twelve seat capacity dining room, kitchen and offices on the ground floor: four ensuite bedrooms on the first floor. But the minus side was, according to my father, it was a cold house particularly in the winter months" said Alfred.

"And what about servants?"

"In that house, we had a bearer—the equivalent of a butler, the chota bearer that is to say his junior, the cook and his assistant the pani-wallah, an ayah or maid who looked after me and was my mother's companion, the sweeper, three gardeners who tended the gardens and orchard, a driver and his assistant, the day and night watchmen and the syce or groom. We also had a self employed dhobi or washerman, who did the laundry.

"Wow, you lived like a maharajah," said an impressed Maureen.

On the days when Alfred did not have to go to night classes, he used to work late. He noticed that Maureen too stayed behind. One evening he decided to ask her out, but he had to choose a venue according to his means. He did know that he could not afford to take her to a swanky restaurant.

"Maureen, what are you doing in the weekend?" asked Alfred shyly.

"Nothing."

"There is an Elvis Presley film on; would you like to see it with me?"

"I love Elvis Presley films," said Maureen much to Alfred's surprise, as he did not think others would think it was hip, as after all it was the swinging sixties and the first James Bond's film, "Dr No", was showing all over London.

So the couple decided to go to the Saturday matinee show. Maureen suggested that they meet at her local cinema, and then she would take him home to meet her parents and have dinner that she would cook.

On Saturday morning, after having got a day off from his cleaning job, Alfred went to Brixton market and bought two bunches of daffodils for Maureen and her mother. He would have preferred to get the colourful tulips but they were more expensive.

He was waiting for Maureen at the cinema entrance when she came wearing a bright shirtwaist dress. She found it touching that he had brought the flowers, although he had felt foolish carrying the flowers in the Tube with people looking at him.

Elvis sang his way through the film. Alfred was not interested in the storyline because, as soon as the lights went out, Maureen held his hand and just before the interval gave him a kiss. And as for the time after the interval, Maureen was only interested in devouring him, which he found enjoyable.

They walked to her home, but stopped holding hands as soon as they noticed passers-by were giving them filthy looks, and someone shouted "Bloody Paki."

"I am sorry," said Alfred.

"Do you get this often?"

"Not really. I have never gone out with an English girl, and I stick around Brixton where most of us are immigrants."

Maureen lived with her parents in a flat in a large sprawling council estate, in other words a public housing estate, built in the 1950s.

Her father was welcoming. As a customs officer, he had met people from various continents and knew a bit about India.

He opened a bottle of Mackeson stout and handed it over, and Alfred accepted it as he did not want to be impolite. After the first sip, he wished he had not.

Maureen's mother was unfriendly—in fact he could not remember her speaking, or for that matter putting the daffodils in a vase.

Maureen had cooked a lamb meat pie with a crust of mashed potato as well as boiled cauliflower and peas, which were overcooked.

"Do you know what this pie is called?" asked the father.

"Yes Sir, shepherd's pie, and if it had been made of beef, it would be called cottage pie. We have it in India."

"Lots of spices there I suppose," said her father and they both laughed.

After having strawberry jelly with pieces of fruit in it and then a cup of tea, Alfred thanked everyone and left. He was sure that Maureen's mother did not like him.

As for poor Maureen, she could not go to bed until her mother finished ranting that no one in her family had ever associated with a coloured man.

The result of her mother ranting at her was that Maureen was even more determined than ever to be seduced by Alfred. For his part, Alfred was willing to play ball.

The first hurdle that the potential lovers had to overcome was to purchase a packet of condom. Neither had ever bought a condom, and in fact Alfred had never seen one and he suspected neither had Maureen. They went to the local chemist, but on the three occasions Alfred attempted to buy a packet from behind the counter, he lost his nerve. The minute there was a customer behind him, he would pick up the item nearest to him, which was a toothbrush and buy it.

"You are hopeless," said Maureen.

Then one morning, Maureen proudly produced a packet that she had stolen from her brother.

There was no possibility of them meeting over the weekends because Maureen noticed her mother was bonding with her more than ever before.

On the evenings when Alfred did not have to go to night school, there was much anticipation, but then someone else was working late or the cleaners stayed on longer. It could be said that the couple had a frustrating time.

Maureen had heard that her brother took his fancies to the cinema where they could at least kiss and cuddle in the back row. This became the couple's next plan. They decided that Maureen would take a half-day off and meet Alfred, who would disappear on an outside appointment.

They went to a cinema hall nearby on the recommendation of a colleague. Alfred had been reliably informed that the cinema was small and rarely attended in the afternoons because there were only documentaries, in contrast to the evening when pornographic films were shown.

The excited couple were late, and to their horror the only seats unoccupied were in the front row. The result was that Alfred at least became an expert in the pesticide DDT, which was used to combat insect-borne human diseases and to control insects in crop and livestock production.

The possibility of a sexual encounter disappeared when Maureen's brother started calling at the office to take his sister home.

It was in early December 1965 that his classmate Gerry came to see Alfred in Brixton, and suggested that they spend the following Sunday together.

By now Gerry was in his pre-final year at law school and was living in the hip area of Chelsea, in Central London.

Alfred was feeling that there must be more to life than work, and therefore arranged to get another day's leave from his cleaning duty.

Gerry asked Alfred to meet him at a coffee bar named Corrillo, (which in Spanish means 'huddle') in Earls Court Road, Central London.

"Lots of girls will be there, and it is about time you found one for yourself," said Gerry, who was going out with a French nurse. So Alfred went to Corrillo in the hope of meeting someone, but with little expectation.

The pretty girls in baby-doll dresses with colourful bangle bracelets and pump shoes with two or three inch kitten heels were surrounded by young men with long hair loose or tied in a ponytail and wearing suits with narrow lapels and even narrower ties and drainpipe trousers. Alfred felt very orthodox.

Alfred with no experience of, in Gerry's words, chatting up the girls and not wearing the latest style, kept a low profile and just watched the passers-by.

This is how he saw a young woman walking down the road wearing a sari but having difficulty with it.

"Gerry, look at that girl in the sari—isn't she pretty?"

"She does not seem to know how to walk wearing a sari. You should go and help her," encouraged Gerry.

Alfred could not remember how he found the courage, but he got up and went to speak to the girl. Had he not done so, they would never have met.

On returning to Corrillo, he told Gerry what had happened.

"I told her I would be back at six."

"Good for you, be a man and take her out."

So Alfred steeled himself and went back at six to meet his date, but not until he had checked that he had sufficient luncheon vouchers to pay for dinner.

And this is how Alfred met Esme Chang, a Chinese coloured from Jamaica.

CHAPTER 38

THE CHINESE COLOURED FROM JAMAICA

1942-1964

Esme Chang was born in Jamaica on March 5, 1942 in the picturesque coastal town of Lucea in the parish of Hanover halfway between Montego Bay and Negril, built around a natural harbour surrounded by hills.

Lucea had once been the home of Captain Bligh of HMS Bounty. By the time Esme was born, there was a strong Scottish Presbyterian influence; Jewish immigrants from Europe had settled in the town; and there were also Asian immigrants, including the Chinese.

In the mid-1850s after slavery was abolished, the British recruited Hakka Chinese from Hong Kong area to work in the plantations. They came as indentured labourers; and at the end of their fixed term contracts, some remained in towns like Lucea and went into business, opening small grocery shops and trading in local produces such as sugar, banana, coconuts and yam.

It was the Chinese who were responsible for importing salt fish, rice flour and other provisions, which are now termed Jamaican food.

Esme's father was born in 1886 in a village in the Guangdong province outside Hong Kong. At the age of

30, he arrived in Jamaica via Hong Kong; and followed a family friend to the town of Lucea. As he had been a merchant back home, it was not surprising that he opened a small wholesale shop.

He worked hard to build up his business, opening his shop all hours and selling items in small quantities, which made him popular with the locals.

It was no surprise to the residents that Esme's father moved to a bigger building from where he sold petrol and kerosene in the front, household provisions in the shop and operated a bakery at the back. And he lived in the upper part of the building.

As he became more successful, he was able to build a holiday home in the north coast near Montego Bay.

By this time he had met a Jamaican girl and courted her. They married and had four children, of whom Esme was the youngest. The children were designated as Chinese coloured.

After Esme's father died, the business slowly deteriorated because there was no one experienced to run it. Therefore her mother decided to sell the business, and moved the family to the house near Montego Bay.

Esme started nursery school at the age of four, and three years later she went to the local primary school. Then at 13, she won a scholarship to Montego Bay High School (also known as Mobay High), which was the first Government owned High School for girls in Jamaica.

She finished at Mobay High at the age of 17, and having gained the required marks, she was admitted to University College Hospital in Mona Heights, Kingston the following year to train as a nurse.

"I like the idea of helping people; and why not the sick and dying?" said Esme on her choice of career.

Her mother fussed over her during her last weeks at home, whilst Esme was busy stitching blouses, dresses and petticoats on her mother's Singer 99K hand crank sewing machine.

"Let me tell you, Esme, there is no finer vocation than to look after the sick and needy," her mother would say. "Will the money I am going to send you be enough? Maybe, I should send you more?"

"Mum, don't worry. I will manage."

"Study hard," she would say at other times. "Don't be distracted from your studies. If you do, you will regret it later."

"Yes, Mum I will work hard."

"Don't forget your old mother. Keep in touch. Promise?"

"Don't be silly. How can I forget my beautiful mother?" Esme would say and they would both giggle.

The day came to leave home, and with some trepidation, Esme went to Mona Heights to live in the nurses' hostel in a campus between the Blue Mountain Range in the north and the Long Mountain in the south.

Esme did not know anyone at the campus so she was happy to share a room with Beatrice, who was of Scottish origin, until they both completed their nursing course three years later; but if truth be told, Esme would have been happier if her new-found friend did not share her clothes, shoes, handbag and makeup.

There were continuous social activities around the campus such as fetes, carnivals, sports days, parties and dances. At the nurses' hostel, the student nurses were expected to be back in their rooms by eleven p.m., otherwise they had to see the matron the next morning.

Fortunately for the girls the night watchman, who was responsible for the passbook where each student had to sign and note the time she had returned, could not read or write.

Esme remembers that the passbook recorded the arrival at ten forty five p.m. of nurses named Elizabeth Taylor, Brigitte Bardot and Doris Day.

"I never met any of them," she would say.

Esme graduated as a State Registered Nurse in 1963. The Graduation Ball that year was held at the Myrtle Bank Hotel in downtown Kingston, which had been rebuilt following an earthquake in 1907; until 1948, it had an official Whites only rule that meant non-whites could not register as guests or use the amenities just like in the Planters Club in Darjeeling until the early 1950s.

At the Ball, Esme came across a friend who had been her senior at University College Hospital and had just returned from England after completing her midwifery course. They arranged to meet for a coffee next day and following this meeting, Esme decided to go to London for midwifery and postgraduate studies.

At the campus and in town the young men would wolf whistle or say "You look lovely," "You look like Shirley Bassey," and the girls would say "Esme, I wish I had your figure," but being shy, she remained self-effacing and insecure. Therefore it came as a considerable relief when her roommate Beatrice had some news for her.

"My parents are sending me to Scotland for further studies, so let's travel together. It will be fun."

The transatlantic passage to England took over 12 days. The girls boarded the Spanish ship Montserrat, which sailed via La Guairá, the chief port of Venezuela from where the passengers were able to visit Caracas, and Tenerife.

Esme was 22 years old when the ship docked at Southampton, England in October of 1964. The sea journey ended, and it was the start of a new life for her.

CHAPTER 39

LONDON AND SUBURBAN LIFE

1964-1965

Esme had successfully applied for a place at Hackney Hospital in Homerton, East London after seeing an advertisement in a nursing magazine in Kingston for a midwifery and postgraduate course. It was one of the largest general hospitals in London, and was the first in England to accept male nurses.

The hospital arranged for a representative from the British Council (which assisted foreign students to study in Britain) to meet her at Southampton Dock.

"Welcome to the UK, Miss Chang," said the young man. "Please follow me."

The helpful man directed her to the waiting train. They travelled from Southampton to Waterloo Station in London, and then by cab to the nurses' home at Hackney Hospital.

Esme's priority was to get some warm clothes. So the next day, on the advice of some nurses, she took a bus and landed in front of a Marks & Spencer store, where she purchased an overcoat and a few woollies using part of the £50 she had brought with her.

She was always cold during her first winter, and she thought she had a novel idea when she filled an empty bottle with hot water and placed it inside her bed before lights off. If only someone had told her she could have bought a hot water bottle.

Esme marvelled at the fast pace of life in London, the double-decker buses and the architecture, which was so different from what she had seen in Jamaica. However she was surprised to see dilapidated houses around the Hospital area. She also noted how stern the people were with no one acknowledging you. She felt intimated and daunted.

She mixed with other Jamaicans who worked at the Hospital; they formed a group who met outside work, as there was an impression amongst them that mixing intimately with the white colleagues was socially frowned upon.

Esme was on nodding terms with a Lebanese nurse who had a white boyfriend who was also a nurse.

"You will not believe what happened this morning," said her colleague. "The matron called my boyfriend and told him that it was not in his interest to have a relationship with me. Bloody cheek."

Esme's course was in two Parts. She was at Hackney Hospital for six months until she passed the Part 1 examination; and then she was sent to All Saints Hospital in Gillingham in the county of Kent for another six months as a pupil midwife for Part 2 of her course.

The hospital found her a place to live. Her landlady was Mrs Skinner, a Yorkshire pensioner with two adult sons living with her. She had been taking on foreign students for some years.

Mrs Skinner was kind but had a watchful eye, and she was firm about time keeping.

"I am not on God's earth to wait for you. You must be on time for meals," was her credo.

Mrs Skinner cooked breakfast at eight thirty sharp and tea at five in the evening. The evening meal consisted of sandwiches, salads, beetroot, picked onions, cakes and biscuits with tea. Just before bedtime, which was around nine, Mrs Skinner would offer more tea and biscuits. The food was bland but as Esme would say when you are hungry, you can eat anything.

Esme was on call throughout the six-month period. She visited maternity patients and attended home deliveries, which was then the norm. She travelled everywhere by bicycle.

She also had to record the history of 12 mothers and babies from pre-natal to delivery to post natal for her Part 2 examinations.

She was working, studying and trying to cope with the different culture and lifestyle. So she was fully occupied.

After a three hour-written examination, and practicals when she had to examine a pregnant woman, describe the position of the baby, check the head was engaged, if the foetal heart was normal, and of course record the wellbeing of the mother, Esme passed and became a State Certified Midwife.

After this qualification, she had to decide which branch of nursing to pursue. She decided to be a surgical nurse in the operating theatre. So she applied to St Stephens Hospital in Chelsea, London, which had been in existence as long ago as 1664 when it was referred to as The Hospital in Little Chelsea.

Esme was accepted for the theatre course lasting six months; and she settled down in a bedsitter in nearby Warwick Road in Central London, which she shared with a colleague from her midwifery course.

At St Stephens, Esme met another nurse, a Goan named Gracie. They became good friends, and when not on duty, they would socialise on most Sunday afternoons.

One Sunday in early December 1965, Esme had nothing to do so she decided, on a whim, to go and see Gracie.

"Hi Gracie. I have come to try out a sari," said Esme; taking up a long-standing challenge to try and wear this Indian garment. Gracie fitted Esme with a sari and blouse in blue and gold, and teased her.

"Come on, go home in your sari, and let the men admire you."

They both laughed and Esme walked home.

She walked down Earls Court Road passing a coffee bar named Corrillo where youngsters hanged around.

Being shy, Esme looked straight ahead when she heard wolf whistles. Therefore she did not notice an Anglo-Indian watching her from Corrillo.

Shortly after passing Corrillo, Esme felt someone was following her. The young man came up to her.

"Very interesting face, but you are not Indian," he said. "I could see this because of the way you are fiddling to keep the sari on. Shall we meet for a drink later?"

Esme continued walking, and the man walked alongside till she reached her front door, so he now knew where she lived.

"I will be back at six," he said. "And by the way, my name is Alfred.

CHAPTER 40

KISMET

1965-1967

"I met a man who followed me," said Esme to her roommate. "He said he would be back at six."

"Lucky you," came the reply.

Esme thought he looked normal and showed genuine interest so as six o'clock approached, she changed into a black wrap dress, knee length hem, three quarter sleeves and a nipped waist. The doorbell rang on time.

"I am back," said Alfred cheerfully on seeing Esme, and took her to a local Indian Restaurant named Johnny Gurkha.

"What would you like to drink?" Alfred asked.

"Could you order for me, please?" Esme asked, as she had never drunk alcohol before. This is how she had her first glass of sherry.

"What would you like to eat—chicken, lamb, fish or are you a vegetarian?" enquired Alfred.

"No I am not a vegetarian. Do you know, I have never had Indian food."

"But surely there are Indians living in Jamaica?"

"Yes there are many, but I never had the chance to try their food."

So Alfred ordered. Esme ate little not because she did not like the food, but because she felt shy, the alcohol was affecting her and the lamb vindaloo was very hot.

Alfred was tucking in like a schoolboy. He was engaging and talked about films, the weather, what he was doing and what they were going to do when they next met. Esme wished she could be as confident as Alfred. He was talking non-stop as he too was shy.

The evening ended.

"I wonder if we will meet again?" Esme thought, as Alfred walked her home.

"How did it go?" asked her roommate.

"He is a real chatterbox."

"And what do you think of him?" enquired the curious roommate.

"As they say in Jamaica, every hoe ha dem tick a bush."

"Pardon?"

"In English, it means that there is that perfect someone for everyone."

And they both laughed.

CHAPTER 41
THE CHRISTMAS PARTY
1965

Alfred had heard of office orgies but he had not been a witness to any, let alone a participant.

Christmas parties at the firm meant Mr Anderson bringing his South African sherry, and sharing this golden nectar with the staff.

"Why does he like South African sherry?" asked Alfred.

"It is not real sherry, which only comes from Spain. But as he was born in South Africa, he likes to drink this fortified wine," replied someone.

"It's probably because it is cheaper," said someone else.

The Christmas office party in 1965 was a bit more interesting.

Miss Rees, worse for wear, had decided to be a cougar that evening.

Having spotted Alfred alone in one of the rooms, the dear lady attacked him, and started to take off her blouse and bra. The breasts were the first Alfred had seen since he played doctor and nurses in Sonada when the eldest Chinese girl was quite happy to display hers in exchange for his pocket money, but these were substantially bigger.

He was terrified.

"Miss Rees, someone will come in."

"Sorry Alfred, I am not going to stop."

"You will regret it tomorrow."

"Come here."

"I don't have any French letters," said Alfred as if he was a man of the world. He remembered friends at school talking about condoms, although they had never shown him one because he was a Catholic and the Church had banned this product.

Thankfully as she was lurching forward, Miss Rees slipped and hit a desk. The noise was loud enough for Maureen, her secretary, to appear and everything went back to normal.

"You had a lucky escape," said a laughing Maureen.

"You are not kidding," said a relieved Alfred.

When Alfred told Esme what had happened, she teased him mercilessly.

"You better be careful at the next Christmas party. In Jamaica there is a saying—old fire sticks are easily re-kindled."

CHAPTER 42

Sex discrimination

1966

Following the Christmas festivities, work started again. Miss Rees was sheepish when she saw Alfred, but nothing was said.

Mr Anderson told Alfred that to gain more experience, he would be moved to the Civil Litigation Department. This meant court work other than matrimonial and criminal cases. His new superior was an elderly solicitor named Miss Broome.

If he was asked to describe her, Alfred would say that Miss Broome was plain looking woman in her early seventies, and looked a bit like Miss Marple from the Agatha Christie novels. Her home was in a suburb of London, which she shared with a companion whom no one from the firm had met.

"Why are there all these older spinsters working in our firm?" thought Alfred. It was because Mr Anderson was against sex discrimination (he was also against noise and in particular the development of the Concorde, formal education, prison, religion, smell, war and all other forms of discrimination).

Mr Anderson liked nothing better than to form a charity, and his current campaign was to donate one's body for anatomical research. This charity was so successful that the Home Office wrote a formal letter asking him not to publicise it too much as they could not cope with the enquiries from the public.

"Tell me who your friends are, and I will tell you who you are," was a saying that Alfred had read and often repeated.

A friend of Mr Anderson instructed Alfred to form a limited company with a share capital of £100, and its main object would be to collect second hand clothes and sell them to the public to raise money for charities.

The client had chosen the company name Helping Hands Gift Shop Limited.

Alfred thought that this was a stupid idea.

"Who is going to buy second hand clothes in this country?" he said.

"There is no way I am going to wear someone else's clothes," said Mr Anderson's secretary.

Little did they know that a decade or two later, there would be charity gift shops in every high street in the country selling second hand or vintage clothes, and even books, CDs and DVDs, furniture and household accessories.

Unlike his previous superior, Miss Broome was a meticulous worker—her room was clean and tidy, her files were in pristine condition and everything on her desk was in place.

"Alfred, let's start working on a case just given to me by Mr Anderson. She is one of his odd friends. We will probably get nowhere, but it is interesting."

So Alfred sat with Miss Broome when she interviewed a 71 year old widow, who told her story.

"My name is Florence Nagle. Besides being a dog breeder and judge of Irish wolfhounds and Irish setters, I have for some forty years been breeding and training racehorses. In fact the first horse I bred, Sandsprite, came second in the 1937 Derby. I am now, what they call, a jobbing trainer as most of my horses are also ran, rather than winners.

"I now have 15 racehorses that I train, but the governing body for horse racing, the Jockey Club, will not licence women to be trainers. So my head lad, Alfred Stickley is the licensed trainer for my stables.

"I do not see why a woman cannot be a licensed trainer, so I want to challenge the Jockey Club's decision in court as being unfair to women."

There were no sex discrimination and human rights laws at that time.

"Mrs Nagle," replied Miss Broome, "I can see the unfairness, but I cannot see what law the Jockey Club has broken. Let's get advice from the experts. But it will cost you."

"I can afford it, so let's go ahead."

Barristers were instructed to advise. The legal opinions obtained were divided except that everyone agreed that the restriction seemed morally wrong.

But Mrs Nagle was determined; and proceedings were issued in the High Court for a declaration that the refusal to licence women trainers was against public policy and for an injunction prohibiting it.

In the first round the Jockey Club succeeded in striking out Mrs Nagle's claim on the ground that there was no cause for legal action.

On the way out of court, Alfred was walking alongside her.

"Young man, what can one do now?"

"We can appeal," replied Alfred, and Mrs Nagle right there and then decided.

"That is what we have to do."

Alfred was so frightened he had said the wrong thing that he went straight to Mr Anderson and told him what had happened.

"Florence is no one's fool. She is not relying on your advice. The decision to appeal is her decision."

The appeal day arrived and whilst the professionals were little apprehensive, Mrs Nagle seemed more confident.

The presiding judge on the appeal was Lord Denning, a famous liberal judge. He upheld Mrs Nagle's claim by making a novel decision that those having governance of a trade or profession cannot make rules that reject an application arbitrarily or capriciously, a ruling that was subsequently followed in courts all over the world.

Following this decision, the Jockey Club relented and allowed women to apply to be trainers. Mrs Nagle became the first woman trainer in Britain to saddle a runner under Jockey Club Rules in 1969.

After the appeal, there was no champagne celebration at the Seven Stars Pub, but there was a celebratory party in the House of Lords to which Alfred was not invited; it was limited to women, including Miss Broome.

But Alfred did learn at an early stage in his legal career how it feels to make a difference.

In Britain the sex discrimination law came into force in 1975.

It did not surprise Alfred that when her application to become a member was rejected by the Kennel Club in 1978, Mrs Nagle was ready to go to court again, but this time she was financially supported by the Equal

Opportunities Commission, which had been set up by the Government to tackle sex discrimination and promote gender equality.

On the threat of going to court, the Kennel Club changed it's rules and allowed women to become members.

CHAPTER 43

GETTING TO KNOW YOU

1966-1967

It was the Swinging Sixties. As the editor of Vogue magazine said, "London is the most swinging city in the world at the moment."

It was the time of the hippy movement, people experimenting with LSD and marijuana for mind-expansion, new music and art as well as the arrival of the birth control pill.

But for Alfred and Esme it was the time when on weekends, apart from the times either was working, they would meet up and explore London.

They went everywhere it was free—Hyde Park, Clapham Common, Brockwell Park, the galleries, museums and churches. They would also join their few friends for a cup of tea or a homemade meal, or attend house parties together. And once a month they would try a new restaurant after checking the menu displayed outside the entrance, and making sure that Alfred had enough luncheon vouchers.

They would meet in Victoria, Central London and go to Sunday Mass at Westminster Cathedral, the mother church for Roman Catholics in England and Wales.

Alfred spoke about his life in India, and asked Esme about her own past.

"Darling," he said, "You mention your mother all the time. If you do not mind me asking, what about your father?"

"My father died seven months before I was born."

"Oh I am so sorry. I do not know what to say."

"There is nothing to say. These things happen in life."

"Esme, I am sorry for prying. Can I ask you another question?"

"Of course, I don't mind."

"How did your father die?"

"My Mum told me that in 1941 a hurricane started in mid-June," said Esme. "There were heavy storms in quick succession. The weather was foul, but my father had to go to a neighbouring town to sort out problems regarding delivery of supplies. When he came back a few days later he had a fever. Mum said he was sweating and shivering and had pain in his chest. He did not recover and died of pneumonia."

"I am so sorry," said Alfred.

"I know. My father was 55 years old when he died. I was born seven months later. I do not know what it is like to have a father."

They both remained silent, and Alfred was determined to love her more.

Esme had promised her mother that she would return home when she completed her further studies and got some practical experience for a short time in a London hospital. It was now a year since she had completed these studies.

"Alfred, I do not want to leave you, but I should visit my mother. It has been a long time."

"You must. I will be here when you come back. But you do not have enough money, so let me give you what I have saved."

"Thank you darling, but I cannot take your money. I will write to my eldest sister, who is not short of money and let's see what happens."

Esme was pleased to hear from her sister who offered to pay the airfare, but she said that half would be enough.

The couple discussed the best time for her to leave London (temporarily), and they decided that October of that year was best. In her absence Alfred could concentrate on his Law Finals as the examination was set for the following February.

On October 22, Esme left London on a cold and foggy day. She was travelling on a plane for the first time.

The couple missed each other and corresponded almost every other day.

"Do you know I am spending more money buying aerograms than on food?" Alfred wrote in one of his letters.

It was time to buy more textbooks and to pay for the Law Finals, but he had insufficient savings. The only way Alfred could find the money was by selling one of the six gold bangles that his mother had given him. When he discussed the sale with Mrs Fernando, she suggested that he could pawn it, as he would then have the possibility of getting it back.

Alfred went to the local pawnbroker in Brixton Road, and was surprised to see there was a queue of people either pawning items or paying the dues.

He was sad to hand over the gold bangle for cash but desperate times call for desperate measures.

He was given three months to repay the money owed together with the high rate of interest. When the period expired, he lost the bangle. He felt he had betrayed his mother.

On January 24, 1967 Esme made an international call at some expense.

"Happy Birthday, darling. Are you missing me?"

"Oh my God I cannot believe it is you. Why don't you come back and settle down with me?" said Alfred.

"Do you really want me to come back?"

"No question."

"Then I will come back," replied Esme.

"Hurrah. I love you."

CHAPTER 44

THE LAST LAP

1967

The main work for the Civil Litigation Department had to do with recovery of money. The firm were either acting for creditors chasing debtors or for debtors fighting their creditors off.

When acting for commercial lenders, the firm was to collect arrears mainly from debtors who had borrowed money to buy goods on hire purchase as credit cards were just being introduced in the late 1960s.

Alfred defended allegations of misrepresentations or faulty goods, obtained judgments for the debt, took enforcement proceedings to recover the judgment debt or negotiated an instalment payment arrangement.

He had also to field the telephone calls from debtors who would curse the shops or lenders, or plead for time to pay giving a variety of excuses for falling into arrears. He learnt all the excuses for non-payment; the most common being that there was a cheque in the post.

However, Alfred preferred to fight for debtors as how could he forget the dishonourable conduct of the Afghan moneylender in Sonada?

He also did not forget his English Literature classes at school, and Polonius' advice to his son in Hamlet.

"Neither a borrower nor a lender be;

For loan oft loses both itself and friend,

And borrowing dulls the edge of husbandry."

In the last year of his Articles, Alfred was moved to the Property Department, where the work consisted of buying and selling, letting and mortgaging commercial and residential properties.

Business was carried out at a more sedate pace; above all, he learnt that this was the work where there were no bad debts, as solicitors would not complete the transactions until payment; and cash flow was regular which were important if one day he was to start his own firm.

Alfred had received no pay increase since he had entered into Articles, and he was now in the last year. The accountant bullied him to ask Mr Anderson for a rise. This was granted and his wages were increased to twelve pounds per week, which made his life easier.

It also meant that he no longer needed a second job and his cleaning days were over at last.

CHAPTER 45

COMETH THE HOUR

1968

The Law Finals took place in February 1968 at Ally Pally (the nickname for Alexander Palace). It is a North London venue, which was used as an examination hall.

Alfred had taken a fortnight's leave to study and felt reasonably confident until on the bus route to the venue, he saw students reading law books that he had never seen before. He had a panic attack until he remembered someone had said that the more you read the less you know.

But it did not help his nerve that at Ally Pally he went accidentally to the Ladies Toilet, and frightened the few female students that were there.

The examination took place over four days with seven subjects being taken, all of which had to be passed in one go.

The first paper was on Land Law.

"I have gone through so many hurdles, perhaps more than my fair share. Please God, give me a chance," prayed Alfred.

The first compulsory question was on easements and quasi-easements, which he had researched on a land development file at work a few months previously. Things were looking up.

He took a day off work after the examination when all he did was sleep.

Exactly two months after the Law Finals, the results were published in the Times and Daily Telegraph newspapers. Alfred promised Mr & Mrs Fernando that he would bring the papers from the newsagent and check in their presence.

"A. Stephens—1,2,3,4,5,6,7."

"Well done, Alfred" said the landlord.

"Has he passed?" asked the landlady.

"Of course. I told you he would," was the landlord's reply.

Alfred had a lot of emotions. He felt so happy; he had to tell his mother who would be even prouder; he realised his poverty days were over; he did not know if he should tell Esme now—perhaps he should keep a secret and announce his success when she returned, and this is what he decided to do. And when he got his new pay, maybe he could also buy a new pair of black shiny shoes?

Alfred sent an aerogram to his mother saying that her son had become a lawyer. By the time it arrived, celebrations in Sonada had already taken place as Major Mercy had received his copy of the Daily Telegraph and checked the results.

Alfred's mother told all and sundry that the English newspaper had reported that her son was now a lawyer. The news spread throughout the hamlet that his qualification was the headline news in England.

And when he subsequently visited St Ignatius, Alfred learnt that an announcement had been posted in the school notice board that he had become a Solicitor of the Supreme Court of England and Wales. Much to

Alfred's embarrassment, many had believed that he had received a legal honour from the Queen, when in fact there were some 22,000 practising solicitors that year. However as his mother looked so proud, he remained silent.

At work, the firm's accountant told Alfred that Mr Anderson had increased his salary from twelve pounds per week to one thousand pounds per year but he was not longer entitled to luncheon vouchers; and that afternoon, a further two hundred pounds per year was added as a result of Mr Anderson appointing Alfred as an authorised signatory to the firm's bank accounts. To cap it all the sign writer came and added Alfred's name to the entrance door in New Square, so dreams can come true.

After work, he took all his colleagues to the Seven Stars pub for celebratory drinks, and this time petty cash was not used.

"I now know how it feels to be in Heaven," said Alfred as he sipped a glass of champagne.

CHAPTER 46
Almost living together
1968

When he had returned to work after his Law Finals, Alfred noticed that Maureen had a beau, who was now faithfully coming to the office and escorting her home.

Five months later they married and some of the staff went to the wedding, but he did not get an invite.

The newlyweds had gone on a fortnight's honeymoon to the Norfolk Broads, where they had hired a boat and sailed along rivers and lakes, which are known as the Broads. Alfred could not help but notice how happy Maureen looked, and hoped that one day he too would feel the same.

In the coming months, Maureen was even happier as the newly married couple found a house to buy outside London, where prices were cheaper; and she had no problem in finding employment in a local solicitors' office.

At the farewell party, Alfred gave Maureen another wedding present. It was a toothbrush.

"Are you sure you will not need it?" said a mischievous Maureen.

"No, I have two more."

They laughed hysterically.

"What are you two laughing about?" asked a colleague.

"Nothing."

Once Esme agreed to return, Alfred had the task of finding a place to live together, but in correspondence it became clear to him that she, being a devout Catholic, did not want to live with him until they had married.

'Darling, we cannot live in sin," she wrote.

So he decided to find two single rooms in the same building or near to each other at the lowest rents possible.

Mr Fernando suggested that he buy the London Weekly Advertiser, a weekly paper, which came out on Wednesdays and had nothing but advertisements, and he should look for the columns headed: Rooms to let. Alfred had also noticed similar advertisements in the local newspaper shop, which he would check.

Every time he went to see an accommodation to rent, Alfred was told "Sorry, the room has just been let."

"I am a very unlucky man, Mr Fernando. The rooms are let just before I arrive. Maybe I should get up even earlier."

"Show me the advertisements you were interested in," said the landlord.

Having seen them, the landlord continued, "Alfred, you must read the advertisements more carefully, then you will not waste your time. Have a look again."

Sure enough he had not paid attention to the sentence that read: No coloureds; No coloureds and Irish; No coloureds, Irish and children or No coloureds, Irish, children and pets. At that time there were no racial discrimination laws.

"Mr Fernando, I am not unlucky. I am an idiot."

This discovery led to Alfred seeing a smaller number of rooms. Unfortunately most of them were situated in less than salubrious areas of Brixton.

Up until the Industrial Revolution, which began in England in the 18th century, Brixton had been undeveloped and mainly agricultural.

The area underwent a transformation between the 1860s and 1890s when railways and trams linked Brixton to the centre of London. Large, expensive houses were constructed and the middle class moved in.

In the twentieth century the middle class moved out of Brixton. A growing working class population, including those working in theatres, replaced them. They rented flats or boarding houses that had been converted from the large family houses.

By 1925, Brixton had a popular market, pubs, cinemas and a theatre as well as the biggest shopping centre in South London.

The imposition of Government rent control after World War I resulted in a decline in private rented accommodation, and falling unearned income meant that landlords were not keeping the properties in proper repair. Then the bombing of the area in World War II escalated the housing crisis.

The local authority had no alternative but to impose slum clearance and to build public housing. This was the time (1950s) that many of the West Indian immigrants who came to England settled in Brixton because accommodation there was cheaper. And for the same reason, Alfred was looking for accommodation in Brixton.

It was five weeks before Esme was to arrive that Alfred knocked at a door of a terraced house in Brixton, and was surprised to see an attractive Cypriot woman in her late thirties.

"Can I help you?" she asked.

"Yes Ma'am, I am looking for two rooms to let, one for me and the other for my fiancée."

"Please come in. I am Mrs Kang."

"What?" thought Alfred, until she said, "My husband is an Indian."

There were two single rooms and a double room (unfurnished) on the top floor, one double and one single room on the first floor both of which were let. It was also on the first floor that the communal bathroom and separate toilet for all tenants were situated; on the landing of each floor there was a gas cooker and a stainless steel sink to be shared. The owners lived on the ground floor, which had a rear yard.

"You will save two pounds a week if you take the double room" said Mrs Kang.

"Thank you, Mrs Kang. But we will live separately until we get married."

"And when will that be?" asked Mrs Kang.

"In about eighteen months' time—as soon as we have some savings to rent our first home."

"You seem sensible. Come this evening to see my husband. As the English say—he is the lord of all he surveys," said Mrs Kang.

That evening, a tall and slim Sikh in his early forties wearing a white turban and a herringbone brown suit, cream shirt, brown tie and black shoes interviewed Alfred, or rather spent an hour or so talking about his background, with his wife frequently rolling her eyes.

"Kang, the young man must go home before it gets too dark. Are you going to let the rooms to him?" said Mrs Kang, who also seemed keen to eat her dinner.

Mr Kang and his new tenant agreed the rental terms, and the landlord laid down the house rules:

1. One month's rental deposit.
2. No other occupier in the room.
3. No noise.
4. One front door key for each room. If lost, must pay for replacement of lock and sets of keys.
5. No electric heaters in room, but a paraffin heater provided and tenant to pay for the paraffin; and it must be unlit when the room is unoccupied.
6. A pre-paid electric meter in each room. (Alfred would find out later that all the meters had been tampered with, and the tariffs had been illegally increased.)
7. Use of bathroom to be agreed with other tenants, and bath must be cleaned after use.
8. Time to use the cooker to be agreed between tenants.
9. No curries to be cooked to avoid the smell. (This surprised him as the landlord was an Indian, and surely the ground floor accommodation had a distinctive butter chicken curry smell?)
10. Rent payable in cash on Saturday at midday. (Alfred assumed that the landlord did not trust tenants, but in fact it was for him to avoid paying income tax.)
11. No Africans. (It appears that they had given Mr Kang a hard time when he was growing up in Uganda.)
12. Behave as gentlemen and ladies.

It was time for Alfred to give the four weeks' notice to quit his attic room. With a heavy heart, he spoke to Mr and Mrs Fernando about his intended departure.

"I am sure she is a nice girl. Bring her when she comes back as we would like to meet her," they said, and he promised.

The day came for Alfred to leave and it was not easy for the parties to say goodbye. When Mrs Fernando went to clean the attic room, she found a vase of roses, a bottle of Tweed perfume for her, pair of black leather gloves for her husband and a note that read:

"Dearest Mr and Mrs Fernando,

You gave shelter to a stranger. I found a home. I will never forget your kindness and friendship; and I will do my best to act like you when I meet strangers along the way."

Accompanied by his tin suitcase that he had brought from Sonada, Alfred left his first home in England to move to Mr and Mrs Kang's lodgings.

CHAPTER 47

NEIGHBOURS IN BRIXTON

1968

Esme intended to come back to London once she had enough money to buy a one-way trip back to London. She worked for four months at Nuttall Memorial Hospital in Kingston to raise the funds.

With a fortnight to go before she returned, Alfred had to prepare Esme's room as well as his own with bare necessities. To do so, he needed money so he used his little savings for an intended trip to see his mother.

From a second hand shop in Acre Lane, Brixton he bought a single bed, a bedside table, a formica table and two chairs for Esme's room, and a table and chair for his own room as he had already bought a single bed from the shop. The only new item he bought was the cheapest mattress he could find for Esme's bed.

During this period Alfred also met his new neighbours.

Mr and Mrs Albert and their two small daughters occupied the first floor double room. The husband was a postman and came from St Lucia, whilst his wife, who was from Barbados, worked as a shop assistant. They were always teasing each other as to which island was better.

The Albert daughters' pastime after pre-school was to run up and down the staircases creating as much

197

noise as possible much to the annoyance of the other residents.

"Where are your Mum and Dad?" they would be asked, and one of them would reply, "They're playing."

If Alfred had to choose a happy couple, he would have chosen the Alberts. But Mr Albert did confess to Alfred that he was still bitter about his half brother's behaviour.

Mr Albert had come to England on his own, found employment, brought over his family; and hard as it was, sent small sums of money to his mother. Instead of using it for herself, she had saved the money so that she could send his half brother to England.

The half brother lived in a hostel, ate his meals with the Alberts and contributed nothing.

When he saw Mr Albert playing the weekly football pools, the half brother decided to do likewise. Mr Albert won nothing, but his half brother won the jackpot.

Mr Albert was excited when his half brother said that he was returning to St Lucia, and to meet him the next day at London Waterloo Station as he had something to give him before catching the boat train.

Mr Albert was awake all night dreaming of what he would do with the money, whilst Mrs Albert slept soundly as she had no expectations.

At the railway platform, the half brother handed over an envelope, and Mr Albert wished him a fond goodbye. As soon as the train left, Mr Albert opened the envelope which contained a note which read, "Have a drink on me" and a £20 note.

A single man in his early 20s occupied the single room on the first floor. He kept to himself. As he never cooked at home, the other residents were puzzled as to what and where he ate.

Over time he started speaking to Alfred. On one such occasion, Alfred asked the neighbour what he did.

"I am an accounts student."

And when Alfred asked him where he came from, he replied "Jamaica."

Mr & Mrs Malcolm, an Anglo-Indian couple from Park Circus, Calcutta, occupied the double room on the top floor. Their full story was unknown except that it was said they had once owned a house, which they had to sell because they had lost a court case instigated by Mrs Malcolm. The husband had retired, but the wife was working, according to her, as a manageress at Clapham Junction Railway Station. Sadly for her, a resident had seen her at the station where she was in charge of the Ladies toilets in four of the platforms.

As for Mr Kang, he would proudly say, with his wife rolling her eyes, "We're a league of nations—Caribbean, Europe and India."

What Mr and Mrs Kang had not mentioned to Alfred was that, according to Mr Malcolm, in 1907 a young woman was shot three times in a room on top floor of the house. When the other residents went to see what had happened, she was found bleeding profusely from the wounds with her boyfriend standing over her with a smoking revolver. The girl had received such terrible injuries that it was impossible to take her to a hospital, and she never recovered consciousness.

Alfred decided not to tell Esme about the murder, and chose to occupy the scene of the murder.

CHAPTER 48

THE ARRIVAL

1968

Esme arrived at the Oceanic Terminal of London Airport.

Alfred was excited and was waiting for her with a wide grin. He was proudly wearing a new charcoal grey suit, a blue shirt and a red tie with shiny black shoes.

"You look very handsome."

"Wow. Welcome home, darling. I have passed and I am now a solicitor," were the first words that Alfred spoke on her arrival.

On the journey from the airport to Brixton by taxi, Alfred explained briefly how he had qualified, how he had found the two rooms to rent which he had furnished, and that there was a local hospital where Esme could apply for a post. He also gave her information about the neighbours in the house and Mr Kang's house rules.

"Thank God, I am not an African," said Esme as she laughed.

Mr and Mrs Kang's house was in Speenham Road, which had suffered damage from flying a bomb raid in July 1944. The houses and the area were run down, but it was walking distance to the bus stops, Stockwell Tube Station, the town centre in Brixton Road, and most important to Esme who had tremendous faith, the local Catholic Church.

She met the residents. When Alfred introduced her to the accounts student, Esme whispered, "He is not Jamaican."

She was right as sometime later the young man confided in Alfred.

"I am from Ghana, but don't tell Mr Kang."

As for Mr Kang, he was most charming when he met Esme. Alfred was convinced that Mr Kang would have reduced her rent if his wife had not been present.

He was expansive, and Esme had to listen to the long history of his life when all she wanted to do was to go to bed as she was suffering from jet lag.

"He likes the sound of his own voice," she later said to Alfred.

Esme liked her room.

"I will buy some material and stitch curtains," she said having already noticed Mrs Kang's electric sewing machine.

When Esme was sewing, other residents asked her to shorten the length of a trouser, widen a skirt waist or stitch a blind hem.

"Darling, you must stop taking on this work—they will never pay," said Alfred.

However her nature was such that she had never thought of asking for payment She just wanted to help everyone.

Besides spending time sewing, she was house-proud and kept the two rooms nicely clean and tidy. As the weeks passed by, she added personal touches. The landlord was impressed.

"You are my best tenants," he would claim.

Esme also took steps to apply for a post as a theatre sister at South London Hospital in nearby Clapham Common, whilst Alfred was working as an assistant solicitor with Mr Anderson.

She was called for an interview at the hospital, which was one of the few women only hospitals at the time in Britain. She was offered the post, which she accepted immediately.

With both of them working and being paid decent salaries, the couple could discuss their future positively. They agreed to save as much as possible to rent their first home; but Esme was keener to send Alfred to see his mother after a break of seven years.

This was also the time when there was a sea change in respect of racial discrimination. The Race Relations Act 1968, which came into force at the end of October, promoted harmonious community relations and made it illegal to refuse housing, employment, or public services to a person on the grounds of colour, race, ethnic or national origins. So it became illegal to place advertisements like the ones that Alfred found when he was looking for accommodation earlier that year. In 1974 the discrimination law extended to the fields of provision of goods and services, education and public functions.

As far as Alfred was concerned, the consequence of the changes in the law was that he no longer felt he was racially prejudiced, although this was not the opinion of all coloured people.

CHAPTER 49

AN INNOCENT COUPLE

1968-1969

The two of them were together all the time outside work.

Alfred and Esme slept in their own single rooms in Speenham Road, but shared everything else. Alfred would have been happy to live together in one room; however he did not make the suggestion knowing that Esme was a devout Catholic.

At the instigation of Esme, every evening they said the Rosary.

"A family who pray together stay together," she would say.

On occasions, they would lie together in one bed or the other. As a result, both would go to confession the following Saturday evening at their local Catholic Church.

"Father, forgive me for I have sinned. I made my last confession a fortnight ago. I have once this week slept with my girlfriend. And I am sorry also for all my venial sins such as swearing, grumbling and being selfish," confessed Alfred.

"Did you have sex with your girlfriend?"

"Did you fondle her?"

"Did you have sexual thoughts about her?"

To all these questions, Alfred said "No, Father."

"Then what did you do?" said Father Confessor.

"We slept side by side last Sunday afternoon and held hands," the penitent replied.

"Then what happened?"

Alfred thought the Father was very inquisitive.

"We fell asleep."

"Then there is no question of committing a sin. But try not to do it again so you do not fall into temptation. For your other sins, say three Hail Marys."

Besides the Almighty, the other person interested in whether or not the couple would fall into temptation was their landlord.

Taking into account the house rule that there should be no other occupier in a room, Mr Kang would walk up and down the staircases checking.

"Hello, Miss Esme, how are you; and where is Alfred?" he would ask.

And when he had the time, Mr Kang would stand outside her room and speak about his past.

"I met Mrs Kang on the bus." he said. "Do you know I am a bus conductor, and she was trying to get on with her shopping and I helped her. Every time she came onto my bus I recognised her, and one day I asked her out and she accepted. The rest is history."

Mrs Kang's version given to Esme was slightly different.

"After he helped me one day to get on the bus, he started to pester me. I got so fed up that I changed to travel by Tube but this was more expensive. So back I went to travelling by bus. He wore me down and I agreed to go out with him. The next thing was that we were at the Marriage Registry. Now my family are not speaking to me."

The landlord would also talk about the couple's inability to have children.

"Mrs Kang cannot have a baby—it is a medical problem."

And when medical tests showed that he had a low sperm count, he had a ready answer.

"It is Mrs Kang's fault. She forces me to have hot baths before she will allow me to come to bed. She has caused the problem because hot baths kill your sperms."

As for Mrs Kang, she had no time to spare to listen to her husband. She spent her days typing on her Remington Rand portable typewriter addresses on envelopes for advertising mail for which she was paid on a piecemeal basis.

CHAPTER 50

ORDINARY LIFE

1969

When Esme was on day shift, she could use the cooker on the top landing from 7.30 p.m. onwards after Mrs Malcolm had finished.

When Esme was on night shift, she had access to the cooker during the day whilst Mrs Malcolm was at work.

She had not been taught how to cook back in Jamaica, so that initially it was hit and miss as far as the food was concerned.

The first proper meal Esme cooked was rice and dried shrimp with potato curry, and this became the staple dinner for the young couple. Alfred vowed he would never eat this curry when he became prosperous, but he did regularly as it reminded him of happy times.

Once Esme learnt to cook, she had time to prepare more substantial meals, which she would leave for Alfred to heat up.

As time went on, Esme discovered that she had an aptitude for cooking, and she was able to cook meals that she had tasted in restaurants and at friend's homes—Jamaican foods such as rice and peas, ackee and salt fish, curried goat, fried dumpling, and jerk chicken.

Mr Malcolm also benefitted as she cooked him lunch when she was at home during the day, which was far preferable to the soup that his wife left for him.

"I know the mulligatawny soup comes from India, but don't you think it is too much to expect me to have the same soup every day?" asked Mr Malcolm, to which Esme would reply, "Tell her," but he never did.

When both were at home in the weekends their routine was worked around going to see a Saturday matinee film at the Classic Cinema, known locally as the fleapit and where the tickets were half-price, instead of the ABC and Odeon Cinemas which were more luxurious and ticket prices more expensive. They could also not afford the tickets for the Beatles, Freddie and the Dreamers, Roy Orbison and Rolling Stones concerts at the Odeon, which was around the corner from Speenham Road.

They would go to confession on Saturday evening, and fortnightly they had dinner at the local Indian or Chinese restaurant no longer paid by Alfred's luncheon vouchers.

On Sundays they would go to church in the morning (sometimes still to the Westminster Cathedral); and the rest of the weekend was taken up by household chores, Alfred working on a case file, Esme studying some branch of medicine; and meeting friends who like them were careful with their earnings.

Anyone could see that the couple took enormous pleasure in each other's company.

The good news for the Almighty and Mr Kang was that the young couple had not succumbed to temptation. The couple were waiting for their wedding day, which they thought was getting nearer.

They had seen the parish priest and discussed the documents that were required, which were to give notice to the local register office and for the wedding banns to be read not only in their church but also in the churches in Montego Bay and Sonada, and they had looked at dates for the wedding.

However first, as far as Alfred was concerned, it was necessary to have enough savings to rent their first home; and as for Esme, she wanted Alfred to visit his mother before committing to married life.

CHAPTER 51

GOING HOME

1969

One morning Alfred got up and decided that to progress in life he had to leave Mr Anderson's firm, otherwise he would be always working as an assistant.

He made some half-hearted attempts to find other employment, but he knew what he wanted which was to start his own firm in Brixton helping the underprivileged. So he went to see his bank manager for a start-up loan, but was turned down because he had no security. The two other banks in Brixton also declined his request; and the moneylending company, who charged high interest like the Afghan moneylender of Sonada, was unable to help because he had no credit history.

Alfred was disheartened and wondered if it was his destiny to always be disappointed. But did someone not once write: "Never give up, for that is just the place and time that the tide will turn."

"Never mind, darling. Why don't you go and visit your mother before you start your firm?" said Esme. "I have checked the bank balance and we have enough money saved. Go now."

"But that money is for our first home."

"No, my priority is for you to visit your mother," said Esme, who then went to see the travel agent to book a cheap charter flight.

On March 2, 1969 BOAC's first flight of Concorde took place; two months later Alfred flew on his first intercontinental flight from London to Bombay by a propeller-driven aircraft owned by a charter company named Bosco.

Alfred felt important as he boarded. There were then no security procedures, and smoking was allowed on the plane although Esme had the foresight to book him a non-smoking seat.

Unlike flying non-stop and quietly by Concorde, the journey that Alfred took was noisy and bumpy. There were re-fuelling stops, including at Kuwait where the passengers were stranded for three days until some spare part was delivered.

Alfred was thankful that he had bought life insurance for a few pounds at the airport whilst he was waiting for his flight, and that he had posted the insurance policy in a pre-paid envelope to Esme.

From Bombay, Alfred he went by train to Calcutta and then onto Siliguri Station where one of his cousins was waiting to greet him.

"Mummy could not come so she sent me. She has been excited for weeks."

The road journey from Siliguri to Sonada, which took four hours, was by an old Land Rover. Whilst the scenery was the same, Alfred noticed that during his seven years absence the villages along the way had expanded, so it did not come as a surprise that Sonada looked different.

The first thing he noticed was that Sonada had electricity, and then that it was no longer a hamlet but a small town. The population had risen from 250 in 1938 to about 15,000.

As the Land Rover approached Brightside Cottage, there were numerous make shift huts built on either side of the main road, and the meadow where Alfred had flown his kites was now the location of a cinema hall with no roof as the proprietor had run out of funds. If there was rainfall for more than half an hour, a notice stated that the owner would refund the tickets.

Brightside Cottage looked about the same—no, the gardens looked different. Vegetables were no longer being cultivated for sale, the rose garden needed more attention, there were tall dhuppi trees shading the cottage, and even a small palm tree near the front door surprisingly growing in the cold and mist of Sonada.

At the front door Alfred saw his mother looking older and weak; and as old people do, looking a little shorter than he remembered. Alfred thought he should not have left her alone.

As the day passed, visitors called to see the lawyer sahib from England, and it was a happy day for Alfred to see his mother looking at him with pride.

The next morning Alfred spoke to his mother.

"Mummy, you do not look well. What is going on?"

"Son, there is nothing to worry about. I am taking medicines from the dispensary. It is my heart. Everyone is saying I have eaten too much red meat, so I have stopped and become a vegetarian."

"You need to be examined by a consultant. I will make an appointment at the Planters Hospital in Darjeeling."

"You are here one day and you are behaving like the man of the house" she replied, and both of them laughed as they used to do.

After a good lunch, Alfred went to the dispensary accompanied by his mother, the old bearer, the ayah and her four children.

Alfred discovered that the dispensary provided information on hygiene and nutrition, and prescribed herbal and homeopathic medicines.

Since the changeover from Mrs Thompson's English bungalow, the dispensary looked the worse for wear. The red corrugated roof was rusted; in fact the whole building was badly in need of repair and a coat of paint. The living room was now the waiting room, and the dining room was the consulting room. The bedrooms had been converted to offices for the two nurses and a pharmacy, and the kitchen was the storage area. The surrounding ground was unkempt, and Alfred was sad to see that the tennis court and croquet green were no longer in existence.

He spoke to a nurse about his mother, and he realised that she needed more specialist attention.

Three days after his arrival, Alfred took his mother and her retinue of family and servants in two Land Rovers to Darjeeling on an outing; and whilst the others were eating and shopping at his expense, the consultant examined his mother.

"The nurses have checked her diet and this can be improved. She is having too much salt and fatty food—these must be cut down," he said and continued, "Your mother is complaining about shortness of breath and tiredness. As these can be symptoms of heart disease, she will need to be regularly checked."

Alfred arranged for his mother to be checked every quarter, and left sufficient funds for the coming year, although his mother protested as she had a good rental income from the properties she now owned in Sonada.

"Mummy don't worry about the money. If you do not pay attention to your diet or go for the check ups, you will have a heart attack and die. And then where will I be?"

Besides dealing with his mother's health and spending time with her, Alfred also took the opportunity to visit his relatives in Neej Kaman and to go to Hopetown Tea Estate to trace the doctor's brother who had so impressed him during the Muslim incident.

And Alfred did not forget to spend time also with Major Mercy, by now aged 79. He owed so much to his old friend and he regretted that he had not been able to repay his kindness as yet.

Alfred was able to tell the Major about his life in London, his legal training and qualifications, the work he did and would do, as well as the social changes that were taking place in England, such as manufacturing industries closing down, more building in the countryside, the influx of immigrants, the lack of respect for authority, which his old friend could not quite accept.

On his last visit to Sonada House, Alfred left for the Major a large box of Black Magic chocolates which his old friend had told him were his favourite, and a white envelope containing a new and crisp £50 note in repayment of the money that the bank manager had credited his newly opened account. He also left a letter.

"My dear Uncle,

All that I have and will have is due to you. I will never be able to repay my debt to you. In your memory, I can only follow your example and do my best to be kind to others.

With much love,

Yours,

Alfred."

As to the other neighbours in Sonada, Mrs Thompson, Mr and Mrs McPherson of Roseneath and the Burmese grass cutter had died.

Mr Hunt (of the bungalow with no name) had also died following an altercation with a Tibetan who had trespassed onto his property. In the ensuing argument the Tibetan had thrown a small boulder at the Englishman and cracked his skull.

John McPherson was abroad doing his Master's degree in counselling, and Alfred was determined to track him down. Roseneath Cottage was now owned and occupied by a Nepali merchant and family.

Mrs Nicholls of Azalea Cottage, aged 77, had moved to Siliguri in the foothills of the Himalayas with her toy boy, now aged 52, as she was suffering from arthritis and the hotter climate was more suitable. The Church of Scotland owned the cottage, and the resident was the headmaster of their local secondary school.

Kancha had left Sonada, as had the Afghan moneylender, who had retired to his home country very much richer than when he left it.

And the Chinese family had immigrated to Hong Kong, where the eldest daughter was known as Madam Can, and she ran a very successful escort agency. Alfred was not surprised as after all she had always been willing to display her breasts in exchange for his pocket money; so making money from sex was something she had known since childhood days.

CHAPTER 52

THE NEW FIRM

1969

The 1960s brought a freedom which had not existed before.

At home, parents were less strict and youngsters decided one did not have to conform—you could let it all hang out.

Flower power was on the ascendency, and peace and love was talked about. It seems sex and drugs were in abundance in London, but such opportunities passed Alfred and Esme by.

Popular music was revolutionized by rock music (Beatles, Rolling Stones); folk rock (Bob Dylan, the Mamas & The Papas and Simon and Garfunkel); psychedelic rock (The Doors and the Grateful Dead); and surf rock (Beach Boys).

It was also a time when young solicitors decided to practise on their own, rather than work for fuddy-duddy employers.

Before he had gone to visit his mother, Alfred had decided that the way forward for him was to set up his own firm. But he had been unsuccessful in raising start up funds.

"You will never make money helping the underprivileged. If this is what you want to do, you should work for a charity," was what one of the bank managers had told him.

With Esme working and able to pay their household expenses, Alfred could afford to lease a room or two at a reasonable rent for a few months, and then he would require a fee income.

The Greeks said: "luck is when talent meets opportunity." The manageress of the local launderette in Brixton Road, just near the Oval Cricket ground, mentioned to the young couple that there were empty rooms above which had been used as offices but were now unoccupied due to disrepair.

A Jewish landlady of a certain age showed the young couple around. There were two habitable rooms on the first floor and three more rooms on the top floor although these could not be occupied as the roof was leaking. There was a large broom cupboard on the first floor, and in the mezzanine there was a toilet, which was not working.

"If you take the rooms for three years and carry out the repairs yourself, I can give you one month rent free and the rent after that will be ___ "

Alfred could hardly believe what he heard, but Esme interrupted his thought and spoke to the landlady.

"Mrs Cohen, can you give us a day or two to think about your offer?"

"Why did you not let me take the rooms? It is so cheap. Someone else will beat us to it," said Alfred to Esme.

"No one has rented the rooms so far. Don't worry about it. Let's speak to Mr Kang—he knows all about properties."

Mr Kang was very happy to help. This may have been because he was considered to be a property expert by his tenants, but more likely because Esme had asked him so sweetly that he had to be a gentleman.

Mr Kang accompanied Esme to see Mrs Cohen. He found every fault possible with the property, and spoke to Mrs Cohen in such an authoritative manner that the tenancy was increased to five years, rent-free period was extended to three months and the small rent reduced by a third for the first year. Mr Kang was on a roll, and took Esme for a pot of tea and jam doughnut at the local ABC tearoom.

"Kang, when have you ever taken me to tea? All I am required for is to clean your bloody house and obey your orders," said his annoyed wife when he returned later than expected.

In October 1969, a year after he had qualified as a solicitor, Alfred took possession of his first office and was ready to start his new firm with no capital, but with a new office bank account (credit £1,000). Alfred had sold three more of his mother's gold bangles so he could get his office ready for business.

Alfred gave his month's notice to Mr Anderson, who seemed quite excited that his protégé was going to help the underprivileged.

"This is how I started in East London when I qualified, and where I met Gandhi," he said and went through the office pointing out which furniture and equipment Alfred could take with him. As the firm had just purchased IBM Selectric typewriters, Alfred was told he could take any of the manual typewriters, and he selected two.

There was a farewell party at the Seven Stars Pub, and yes there was champagne in abundance paid from petty cash.

Mr Anderson, with a glass of South African sherry in his hand, said that Alfred had been his best articled clerk and faithful employee, as he would have expected of a Gurkha and member of the Royal family of Nepal.

"I did not know you were a prince," said Miss Rees.

"Nor did I."

During the first three weeks at his new firm, Alfred did no legal work but was busy with mop and bucket cleaning the office.

Whenever they were not at work, Esme was decorating the first floor rooms with a little help from Mr Malcolm, and Mr Albert (a DIY enthusiast and another kind neighbour) installing a kitchen sink in the broom cupboard and replacing the toilet cistern, both of which Alfred had bought from the second hand shop in Acre Lane, Brixton.

But Mr Kang was of no help. His wife had reined him in as she had come to the conclusion that he had an unhealthy interest in Esme.

The day came when a telephone line was installed in the office, and the sign writer wrote in gold lettering Alfred's name and occupation on the window of the first floor overlooking Brixton Road and around the corner from the house on Hackford Road, where the Dutch artist Vincent van Gogh lived in 1873.

The next day Alfred came into the office, and noticed that the window with the signage was looking dirty. As he started cleaning the window, a young woman looked up from the road.

"I did not know there were solicitors here," she said, and this is how Alfred got his first client.

CHAPTER 53

THE FIRST CLIENT

1969

Mrs Barbara Smith was Alfred's first client. She lived in Vickary Street, Brixton in a small house in disrepair along the same side as St Savior's Church Hall, which was named Ambrose Chapel in Alfred Hitchcock's film, "The Man Who Knew Too Much" starring James Stewart and Doris Day.

She wanted a divorce and a custody order for her baby son. She would also have liked to claim back her youth, but no court could grant such an order.

Mrs Smith did not apply for a maintenance order because her husband had been on unemployment benefit for some years, although the 1960s had seen a very low rate of unemployment (around three per cent on average) as a result of the postwar boom.

"This just shows what a lazy and no-good husband I have," Mrs Smith said.

As Alfred had no other legal work, he was able to concentrate on Mrs Smith's case, personally attend the law courts in the Strand nearby to Lincoln's Inn to file the court documents, hand deliver correspondence and documents to the husband and his solicitors. He had informed the court staff that this was his first case so that they pushed forward Mrs Smith's case at every stage. Before she knew it, Mrs Smith was divorced and had sole custody of her baby son.

"You are great, Mr Stephens," she said, and baked a Victoria sponge cake for him when she found out this was his favourite.

But more than that, Mrs Smith told her friends, neighbours and the local advice centres how good her solicitor was. So before he knew it, more and more matrimonial clients came to instruct Alfred, and five months later he decided he needed to employ a helper.

CHAPTER 54

THE DIZZY BLONDE HELPER

1970

The work was increasing, and Alfred realised that he needed help.

As the fees for the matrimonial cases came from public funding (then known as Legal Aid), payments were slow. So he had no alternative but to sell the fifth gold bangle belonging to his mother so he could employ a helper.

He could not afford to employ anyone legally trained, but this did not worry Alfred as he had a plan.

He decided to employ a 21-year-old confident, extrovert, flirty and bubbly blonde girl named Linda who came to work for him with no legal experience.

"Are you mad? Why did you do that?" asked Esme.

"Darling, I have a plan. Trust me."

The plan was hatched when Alfred was attending the lower level magistrates' court in nearby Camberwell Green. Whilst this court dealt with separations, custody and maintenance cases that Alfred was doing, the main reason for the existence of this court was that it had jurisdiction to deal with criminal cases. At that time Camberwell Green Magistrates Court had the highest number of criminal cases in London.

As almost all of these cases were paid for by Legal Aid, Alfred went to see the chief clerk who allocated the cases to solicitors once the magistrates granted Legal Aid.

"You are the first solicitor to ask for work. Most of them are arrogant, and treat my staff as low class," the chief clerk said.

Within the next eighteen months Alfred was one of the top six solicitors dealing with criminal cases in Camberwell Green.

But things did not go well with the first three criminal clients allocated to him. All three were in custody in Brixton Prison, which was a short bus ride from his office.

Following his interviews with the three prisoners, Alfred was upset that they changed solicitors.

Alfred thought he had explained the law properly, took statements patiently and gave sensible advice. The only reason for the change was that the prisoners did not want to be represented by a coloured solicitor as they thought they had a better chance with a white one—this was the explanation given to him by a friendly prison warden in charge of the solicitors' interview rooms.

So when he was given the fourth case, Alfred took Linda with him. From then on, she would visit the clients and take their initial statements, followed by a second visit from Alfred.

It can be said that if there had been a poll for the most popular visitor in the solicitors' interview rooms, the prisoners and wardens would have voted for Linda.

This was the plan Alfred had to expand his criminal practice.

CHAPTER 55

WANT ALL, LOSE ALL

1970

As 1969 ended, the firm was more successful than Alfred had ever imagined. The money, whilst paid slowly by the Legal Aid fund, was nevertheless flowing.

His relationship with Esme was also on a high, and the talk between them was of marriage at the end of the year and a home. They were even talking about the number of children and their first names.

But she would say that they should not wish for everything, as there was a Jamaican proverb that said if you want everything you see, you will eventually lose all.

It was towards the end of June when Esme received a telegram from her oldest sister in Jamaica: Mum is ill. Please telephone.

As the young couple did not have a telephone in Speenham Road, Esme booked a call to her sister from the hospital.

"Mum has been suffering from shortness of breath, dizziness and headaches for some years," said her sister. "I am worried as she is now complaining about sudden pain throughout her body. Her doctor has not diagnosed the illness as yet. All she is given is painkillers. I think you should come home, as I cannot cope."

"What about your other siblings?" Alfred asked Esme.

"They have all moved to Florida."

"Darling, you must go and see what you can do for your mother. You will never forgive yourself if anything happens to her."

Esme explained her problem to her employers who agreed to give her leave on compassionate grounds, and with Alfred's encouragement she travelled back to Jamaica on an open-ended air ticket.

CHAPTER 56

SICKLE-CELL ANAEMIA

1970-72

On arrival in Montego Bay, Esme found her mother in great pain, the cause of which was unknown.

Following the advice of friends she had made when studying at Mona campus, Esme travelled with her mother from Montego Bay to Kingston to see a hematologist at University Hospital.

After the tests were carried out, a doctor at the Sickle Cell Unit saw the two of them.

"Mrs Chang, I am sorry to say that your symptoms and test results show that you have, what is known as, sickle-cell anaemia. The sudden pain you suffer is known as sickle-cell crises. Do you know about this disease?"

"Not really, other than some of us Jamaicans can suffer from it."

"What about you, Miss Chang?"

"I did learn a bit about it when I was doing my nursing training. But that is all," replied Esme.

The doctor explained that sickle-cell disease was a blood disorder characterized by red blood cells assuming an abnormal sickle shape, which reduced the flexibility of the cells. He went on to say that Esme's mother had to accept that the disease was life-long, and as sickling reduced the cells' flexibility, various complications could arise.

He then gave the bad news.

"At the present time, I am sorry to say that all we can do is to relieve your pain from crises, do our best try to prevent infections and control any complications," said the doctor, much to the disappointment of mother and daughter.

Esme was worried for her mother as she had been taught that frequent crises damaged major organs such as lung, liver and kidney. And her mother could get strokes or infections, which would be life threatening.

The doctor concluded by saying that Esme's mother should remain in hospital for a few days so the present crises could be monitored and controlled.

"In the meantime, drink plenty of fluids," was the advice given.

As soon as it was possible, Esme telephoned Alfred and gave him the up to-date news.

"I am sorry darling. You will have to remain with her. But please keep in contact with me," said Alfred.

"I agree. Don't worry and make sure you eat properly, and don't work too hard. I will let you know as soon as there is any real news."

Esme stayed on and looked after her mother who had to be given pain medicine, folic acid and fluids. She arranged for her mother to have flu shot and other vaccines to prevent infections, took her to the dentist to prevent infection and teeth loss, as well as to the optician for tests, as sickle-cell disease could damage the eyes.

Esme made sure that her mother followed a healthy diet, and the two of them would go for their daily walks whenever possible; she also insisted that her mother had afternoon siestas.

But her mother continued to have sudden pain. Sometimes it lasted for a few hours, but other times the pain went on for days.

Her mother could not do much on her own when she had these crises, which made her even more depressed.

As her mother was not getting any better, Esme had the arduous task of taking her monthly to the Sickle Cell Unit, Room 3, Rippel Building in University Hospital until a sickle cell clinic started operating every six weeks at the country hospital in Montego Bay, much to Esme's relief.

During any spare time she had, Esme attended church, and her parish priest asked her to help with the flower arrangements for the altar. She found that being at church was peaceful and took her away from the daily worries. And speaking to the parish priest about their religion also comforted her.

"Hi darling, it's me. Are you all right? I have written four letters to you, but you have not replied," said Alfred a fortnight before Christmas.

"I am so sorry. I have been so busy with Mum, and the parish priest has asked me to help with the Christmas festivities."

"I thought you were only doing the flower arrangements."

"No, Father has asked me to help arrange the Christmas dinner for the parishioners who are living on their own."

"How is your mother?" asked Alfred.

"Mum has now got jaundice so we're in and out of hospital. By the time I get home, it is too late to telephone you. Are you OK?" said a guilty Esme.

"I am. Off to court now. I will book a call to you on Saturday. Love you," and Alfred put the phone down.

By the end of the day Esme would be exhausted, and the consequence was that she was no longer writing letters to Alfred as often as she had the previous time she had come to Jamaica. Her thoughts were also turning to Jesus.

What was happening to Alfred? He had become a workaholic just like both his grandfathers.

CHAPTER 57

DEATH KEEPS NO CALENDAR

1972-1973

Esme spoke to her two siblings in Florida as well as her oldest sister who lived with her family close by.

The whole family decided that after many years they should be together for Christmas of 1972, and that this was the best present they could give their mother.

The family had expanded with the addition of in-laws, nephews and nieces so Esme booked hotel rooms nearby for the American side of the family.

Besides being responsible for Christmas dinner for the lonely parishioners of her church, Esme prepared the meal for her family with a little help from her oldest sister. She was not seeking any reward for her efforts, and only hoped that the participants would enjoy themselves. The best reward for Esme was to see her mother happy surrounded by her family.

"How time flies," said her mother and the adults concurred.

And in the kitchen whilst washing up, the oldest sister commented, "You know, this may be the last Christmas we're all together." Everyone hearing this felt sad and hoped that this would not be the case, but death keeps no calendar.

After New Year's Day, the family separated again, and Esme and her mother went back to their daily routine.

Esme could not help but notice that the Christmas get-together had raised her mother's spirits, and that she appeared to be more energetic and positive about the future.

But alas, shortly after Esme's birthday in March, her mother had an infection and the anaemia worsened. As they say in Jamaica, when chicken merry, hawk deh near.

Esme rushed her mother to the local country hospital.

Alfred received a letter from her. He felt a little abandoned, as it was the first letter in which she did not enquire after him—

"Darling,

I am rushing to catch the post. I am with Mum in hospital where she had a blood transfusion two days ago as a result of an infection. I pray that this is a temporary blip and she will get better soon. I am staying with her in hospital.

Hope the church can soon get a replacement for me as I have been helping Father with the Confirmation classes.

How is your mother?

Take care.

Love."

On Maundy Thursday, Alfred came to the office and was given a telegram by Linda, which read: Mum in intensive care following stroke.

On Good Friday, Esme telephoned the Kangs' number to speak to Alfred.

"Darling, I am sorry I have not called before."

"Sorry seems to be her favourite word now," thought Alfred, but he said to Esme, "What is happening?"

"Mum had trouble walking and had falls. I could see that she had loss of balance. She then said she could not see in one eye, and her speech was not normal. All of a sudden she also had a severe headache and was confused. So I called an ambulance and the medics brought her to emergency. As I suspected, she had a stroke."

"Esme, thank you for calling. Now go and have a rest. Please keep me informed as and when you can. Don't worry if you cannot. I love you."

On Easter Monday, Esme's mother passed away according to the telegram that Alfred received. She was aged 67.

Alfred booked calls to Esme but the line was either engaged or not answered. He was desperate and was planning to go to Jamaica when she called.

"Do you want me to come over? I can," said Alfred.

"No, there is no need to. The rest of the family are here or on their way. Just pray for her. I will telephone you again after the funeral, which is taking place tomorrow."

Alfred was upset as he was beginning to feel surplus to requirement. He did what he did best—he opened a new file.

In Sonada, the monsoons started in July that year. Incessant rain blocked the roads nearby and the residents were running low on food supplies.

At Brightside Cottage, Alfred's mother was wondering if she should go to the Planters Hospital when the roads were repaired as she had been suffering from a hoarse voice for over a month. Her other worry was that she had not heard from Alfred for over two months, which was unusual.

"Bearer bhai, go to the Post Office and ask the postmaster to send a telegram to burra baba asking him if he is alright and to write a letter."

When Alfred received his mother's telegram, he felt guilty and immediately wrote a long letter telling her what was happening in Jamaica (he knew his mother had no idea that there was a country of that name, so he referred to it as being far way from England and near America). This reminded him that during the War, American soldiers used to come to Darjeeling for rest and recreation, and he had been the beneficiary of their generosity in the form of bubble gum.

When his letter arrived at Brightside Cottage, the bearer travelled to Darjeeling to deliver it to the memsahib. She had been admitted to the Planters Hospital diagnosed with throat cancer.

CHAPTER 58

FAITH KEEPS THE WORLD GOING

1973

"Were you surprised?" his friends would later ask Alfred.

"Yes and no. I knew Esme was getting more involved with the church especially following her mother's death, and that this gave her solace. But when you are in love you are blind, and I was just waiting for her to return.

"In fact, I had been viewing houses and shortlisted three for her to see; and I had attended interviews with building societies for a mortgage loan. In those days you had a problem getting a loan if you were coloured, unless you had a guarantor or substantial deposit. I had neither, but I had some hope that as I was a professional this could tip the balance in my favour."

The fateful news came in a letter on a day in August, and it was not one that Alfred was expecting.

"My dearest Alfred,

I am sorry that I have not been in communication with you recently. I am finding it very hard to write this letter but I must, as I do not want to keep you waiting any longer for my return.

Following the advice of our local parish priest, I began an eight day retreat of silence, which provided me with the opportunity to think about Mum's death, my relationship with you, my deep religious feelings, my belief that I should put other's needs ahead of mine.

I have decided to choose a religious life. I think that you will understand. You wanted to be a lawyer at a very young age and you stuck to your guns. I believe that choosing a religious life is the right decision for me. Therefore I will not be returning to London.

After I have helped my family administer Mum's estate, I propose to join an Order here in Montego Bay as a postulant nun, which means a trainee nun.

I am sorry for all the hurt I will cause you. I pray that one day you will forgive me.

As for me, all my memories of you are happy ones. Please take good care of yourself.

You will always be in my prayers."

The first thing Alfred did after reading the letter was to give a month's notice to vacate Esme's room in Speenham Road.

Thankfully Mr Kang was at work, as Alfred was in no mood to have a long discourse with his landlord.

Mrs Kang seemed to have understood what was happening.

"So, she is not coming back?" said the landlady.

"You are right, Mrs Kang."

"I am sorry. If you want to speak to someone, you can always come to me."

"Thank you, Mrs Kang."

Alfred went back to his room and stayed there till he could cry no more.

CHAPTER 59

STOP MY TEARS

1973

The office could not run by itself, so Alfred had no alternative but to continue to work.

Alfred often thought that if Esme had found another man, he could have a chance of winning her back. But how can one win against Jesus?

The occupants of the Kangs' lodgings were shocked.

"She is such a lovely lady," said the accounts student (who had told Mr Kang he was a Jamaican but was in fact from Ghana). "Your loss is the church's gain. This is the will of God, and Alfred you have to accept it."

Mr and Mrs Albert could only express their sympathy.

"We're sorry, Alfred. You were so good together. Religion causes problems everywhere."

Mr Malcolm had nothing to say, but did Alfred see tears in his eyes?

Mrs Malcolm was adamant.

"You should find an Anglo-Indian girl. We must stick to our own race."

As for Mr Kang, Alfred got the distinct feeling that if his landlord had not been trying to be a gentleman, he would have said: "What a waste."

Mrs Kang was the most practical of the lot, and she took on the task of cleaning his room every other day and leaving cooked meals most evening at the door to his room. And one evening, as he was passing her on the staircase, she gave him a sympathetic kiss.

At the office, Linda was censoring the prospective new clients because she did not want Alfred to be overburdened, and she seemed to know when he should be left on his own. Alfred now realized that his dizzy blonde helper had a wise head on young shoulders.

What about Alfred? Could he be blamed for thinking that his future looked bleak? His dream of happy married life had been crushed, and his mother, the other woman in his life, was in the Planters Hospital.

As usual, Alfred buried himself in work until he felt so tired that he would fall asleep. He stopped going to church. He was lonely, and felt even more strongly that he was meant to be disappointed.

Alfred wanted to spend Christmas that year in his room on his own. He did not feel like celebrating. He felt tired and depressed. Therefore he was quite annoyed when Mr Kang knocked at his door.

"Alfred, Mrs Kang asked me to call you down. Please come immediately. She said she wants no excuses from you." So reluctantly he went to their residence.

Mrs Kang was looking attractive, dressed elegantly in her light blue woolen dress which she had bought with her own money as Mr Kang did not celebrate Christmas.

She insisted that Alfred join them and their guests Mr & Mrs Malcolm.

It was three o'clock, but the Christmas lunch was not ready, as Mrs Kang had forgotten to light the oven for over an hour because she was so angry with Mr

Kang for buying the cheapest Christmas crackers from Woolworths.

Mr and Mrs Malcolm were looking glum and sipping their apple juice as Mr Kang had banned alcohol (and Africans) from his residence.

"Do you remember our Anglo-Indian Christmases, Alfred? Do you remember the food that we ate— biryani, tandoori and mughlai chicken, koftas and kebabs and mother's Christmas cake? And there was lots of alcohol. There was singing and dancing. We Anglo-Indians know how to have a good time," said Mrs Malcolm sarcastically.

Alfred doubted if the Malcolms had ever drunk, sang and danced and had a good time, but who knows?

Everyone enjoyed the hearty Christmas lunch when it was served, except that Mr Kang complained there was no rice and that Christmas was a pagan festival.

"Let Kang sulk" said his wife; and as it appeared no one was paying attention to him, Mr Kang decided to go for a walk. To the surprise of the guests, Mrs Kang immediately took out a bottle of what was then sold as Cyprus sherry from the laundry basket, and the participants had a drinking spree.

The effect of drinking the sherry in haste resulted in the Malcolms' dozing off; and whilst Alfred was helping her wash up, Mrs Kang confided in him.

"Alfred, I know how you feel. When I was a teenager in Cyprus I fell in love with a boy and thought he felt the same about me. My friends told me that he had other girls also, but I did not believe them. When I found out I was heartbroken. I felt my world had ended, and this is why my parents sent me to London to stay with my aunt. You will not believe it now, but

239

a time will come when you will feel better and you will fall in love again. You are a lovely gentle man."

"And handsome?"

"Of course, Alfred" and he laughed with her, and she gave him a kiss.

CHAPTER 60

BEAST IN OUR MIDST

1973

Alfred was working seven days a week dealing with a continuous flow of matrimonial and criminal cases. He was also doing property work known as conveyancing. He thought he could not go on working like this, and sooner or later he would make a mistake.

Because the local advice centres were impressed that he acted quickly, Alfred was getting cases from them involving battered spouses, where immediate legal action was required.

The usual orders sought from the court were non-molestation order and an ouster order, which prohibited the abuser from remaining at, entering or attempting to enter, or be within a specified distance of premises (usually the matrimonial home) named in the order. It had been Alfred's experience that judges considered an ouster order to be too excessive in most cases.

Although the victims were almost always women, there were cases where the client was a husband.

Mr Russo was of small stature and aged around 60.

"Mr Stephens, can you save me from my wife who beats me," said the soft-spoken Italian.

"Of course, Mr Russo. I will help you," said Alfred not quite believing him.

"Tell me your story."

Mr Russo's affidavit in support of his application for an order restricting his wife from assaulting him set out various incidents, the most recent of which had taken place the previous day.

When Alfred received the wife's affidavit in reply denying the allegations, he wondered if his client could succeed, as it seemed unusual in his opinion for a wife to be the abuser. However when Alfred saw Mrs Russo at the High Court, his opinion changed slightly as he watched her speaking to her solicitor in a most aggressive manner.

The application was successful after the wife's solicitor cross-examined Mr Russo.

"I do not see any bruises on your face?"

"There are none, Sir."

"What about your body?

"No bruises."

"Your legs?"

"No, Sir."

"Were there any witnesses to these incidents?"

"No, Sir."

"So it is all a figment of your imagination," said the solicitor.

The husband took off his wig to display slash wounds.

"Never ask a question if you do not know the answer," is what Alfred would tell his juniors.

The judge granted a non-molestation order preventing Mrs Russo from attacking her husband. Alfred never saw Mr Russo again and hoped it was because the wife was behaving herself but he was not confident.

Domestic violence involved preparing multiple court claims against the abuser on an emergency basis—asking for non-molestation and ouster orders, seeking custody order for the children, restricting the abuser's access to them and claiming maintenance, and in most cases filing the divorce petition also. This work took priority and meant that Alfred had to work unsociable hours.

Working in this fashion resulted in more of these cases being sent to Alfred, but he was troubled that other court cases were being put on the back burner. So he was never amused when victims failed to turn up in court or an abuser was given another chance; and in one case the couple came to court holding hands, laughing and joking.

"But Mrs Brown yesterday you were terrified your husband was going to kill you?"

"Oh Mr Stephens, I exaggerated. I just wanted to frighten him. He is alright."

When she came back accusing her husband of another assault, Alfred politely told her that he was too busy to take her on.

Mrs Harold was aged 44 years, had been born in Guyana and worked as a nurse at a local hospital. Her Jamaican husband was of the same age and had been working as a guard on the London Underground. They had no children.

She came to see Alfred as the office was closing. He heard her story of domestic violence.

"My husband is very jealous. Everyone says how lucky I am to have such a charming husband. But in the privacy of our home he is a monster. He is frustrated with his life, and as I am not giving him all my attention and enjoying my work, he is always angry. He keeps on accusing me of having an affair with a work colleague, which I am not.

He started by going on and on, and I kept on telling him that we must sleep, as we have to go to work. Then he started slapping me, but it has now got worse. He uses his fist. Once he hit me so hard in the face that I had minor whiplash. This has been going on for over a year.

Two days ago I was late from work because I had to look after a patient. As I walked in, he started shouting that I was a whore, and hit me on the base of my spine. I was unconscious for a moment. When I got my breath back, I screamed for help but no one came. I managed to call the police, who advised me to come and see you.

Each time he promises it will not happen again, and that I am the only person who can help him. Time after time I have given in, but I cannot carry on like this."

"Mrs Harold, you do not have to put up with this," said Alfred. "From what you have told me, you are in danger. You need to be protected. We will go to court tomorrow."

Alfred remembered that Gerry had invited him to a party that evening, so he telephoned his classmate to say that he would be late because he had to prepare for an emergency application the next morning.

"But Alfred, it's my birthday. Remember you missed it last year because of your work," replied Gerry. "Can't you get someone else to work on the case?"

"I am sorry my friend. Everyone has gone home. I must protect this woman. She has been badly beaten," said a contrite Alfred. "I will come as soon as possible."

But he did not go as the drafting of the documents took some time, and by the time he got home it was not a question of missing a party but being too tired even to eat dinner.

The next morning, Alfred made an emergency application in the High Court for non-molestation and ouster orders. The judge granted the non-molestation order, but ordered a full hearing for the ouster order in three day's time.

On the way back from court, Alfred went to the Harolds' flat to serve the court orders on Mr Harold. He was charming and offered the visitor a cup of tea, and spoke in the most loving terms about his wife. He walked with Alfred to his car, and promised that she was safe from him, and there was nothing to worry about.

"Sir, she is the one person I love," he said.

Alfred was aware that the fact that a man was charming did not mean that he would not have assaulted his wife. So when speaking to Mrs Harold, who was staying with a friend, he advised that she should stay away from her husband until the next hearing, which she promised to do.

Alfred was feeling tired and half-heartedly telephoned the local refuge centre for battered wives and the police to see if they could help Mrs Harold. But as both numbers were engaged when he called, he did not pursue the matter further.

Two days later Alfred was glancing through the Times newspaper on his journey to work when he saw a short article stating that a housewife had been killed by her husband; and to his utter shock, he saw that the address was that of the Harolds.

The police told Alfred that Mr Harold had traced his wife to the friend's home, and she had returned to their flat with him. That night a neighbour had called the police when she heard Mrs Harold screaming for help.

The husband admitted that there had been a heated argument in the kitchen, and he had in a moment of madness picked up a knife. The police found his wife had died from stab wounds in the heart.

Alfred was so distressed by this news that he went home, and went for a long walk along the River Thames.

"Why did I not continue trying to get hold of the refuge home and police?" "Why did I not take her to a refuge home?" "What more should I have done?" Alfred felt responsible for failing to protect Mrs Harold.

But Alfred also thought that he had grown up feeling unreasonably responsible, wanting to rescue others, and suffering from excessive fear that he would let people down. He needed to do something about this behaviour.

The next morning he wrote to his clients and the advice centres to tell them that he was no longer doing battered spouse cases due to shortage of staff, and he never worked on this type of case again.

CHAPTER 61

DELAYS HAVE DANGEROUS ENDS

1974

The New Year started with Alfred receiving a much delayed letter from Major Mercy. The date stamp on the envelope read: 30 November 1973, but he received the letter in early January.

Major Mercy gave some news about Sonada, and went on to inform Alfred that his Mother had throat cancer and was undergoing surgery at the hospital. Alfred booked a call to the Planters Hospital.

Finally he was able to speak to a doctor.

"Mr Stephens, your mother will be pleased that I have spoken to you.

"She came to see us as she had been suffering from a hoarse voice for some time and she also had some other ailments. She was referred to me, as I am the ear nose and throat man.

"I carried out the initial assessment, ordered a biopsy and concluded that she had a type of throat cancer, known as squamous cell carcinoma of the larynx.

"I graded the cancer as intermediate, and carried out surgery to remove the tumor.

"But until the wound is healed she has a temporary stoma, that is to say a hole in the neck, so she can breathe. The other news is that her speech has been mainly preserved."

Alfred thanked him and asked how long his mother would be in hospital, and was told that it would be a few more weeks. The doctor recommended that when she was discharged, she should recuperate in a convalescent room of the hospital.

Alfred agreed and asked the doctor to inform his mother that he would be coming from London to see her, but it would be a little while before he could come, as he had to sort out his office first.

When Alfred asked about the hospital bills, he was referred to the accountant who said his mother had deposited a large wad of cash on her admission. This was more than enough for the time being. Alfred assured him that there would be no problem paying any shortfall, and offered to deposit some more money but this was declined.

Being self-employed, Alfred could not abandon his clients and leave immediately. So he concluded the procedure to employ a solicitor, a secretary and an in-house bookkeeper.

He also went to the Passport Office to enquire about a British passport for his mother. The official said this was possible provided his mother could produce her birth certificate or an affidavit of her birth as well as her marriage certificate to a British citizen.

Alfred had viewed a small mock Tudor terraced three-bedroom house in the leafy suburb of Kingston upon Thames in the county of Surrey for Esme to see. As it was close both to the river and the local hospital that had a cancer wing, he renewed his interest when he learnt it was still on the market.

His initial offer was refused as he later found out the owners did not want to sell to a coloured, but they gave in because no one else matched his offer. Alfred bought the house for £5,250 with a mortgage loan of £3,000 payable over 25 years, and he moved out of Speenham Road.

Alfred had been practising on his own account long enough for the lender to take a risk on a coloured, and to his amusement the branch managers of the three banks in Brixton, who had declined to help him when he wanted to start his new firm, were now offering him not only a mortgage, but business expansion loans and overdraft facilities at favourable interest rates at a time when he did not need these loans.

Alfred did not have Mr Albert to help him. However he had builders who assured him that they could quite easily convert, whilst he was away, a ground floor room and the conservatory into a bedroom with a bathroom annexed for his mother. And they could start immediately to repair the leaking office roof and decorate the top floor rooms for the new employees, and Alfred gave the go ahead.

Having recruited his three employees and purchased his house within three months of speaking to the doctor, Alfred ordered his air ticket to go and bring his mother back with him.

But as Shakespeare wrote: "Delays have dangerous ends."

CHAPTER 62

GOD DISPOSES

1974

Alfred was due to travel in a week's time, when the telegram arrived at his doorstep.

"Your mother died today (12 March) at 1 p.m. Funeral to arrange. Telephone hospital for instructions."

Alfred's world collapsed. God had taken away the two women in his life—Esme to serve him, and his mother to rest in peace.

Alfred spoke to the hospital administrator who tried to explain what had happened. Alfred asked that Major Mercy be contacted, and to follow his instructions as he could not get there in time for the funeral. He also telephoned the local undertaker, whose son had been at St Ignatius with him, and asked for his help.

When the British Airways flight took off from London a week after his mother had died, an airhostess could not help but notice that there was a sad looking man on the flight who seemed oblivious to what was going on.

"Are you alright? Can I help you?" she asked.

"Thank you for asking. There is nothing I need."

"My name is Maggie Arthur. If there is anything I can do for you, let me know," said the airhostess.

Alfred saw an attractive English girl, about to be 24, a redhead of medium height and size with brown eyes. She had a South London accent.

On arrival at Dum Dum Airport in Calcutta, Alfred rushed to get his suitcase, and proceeded to check in for his short flight to the foothills of the Himalayas.

About five hours after leaving Calcutta, Alfred reached his final destination, Brightside Cottage in Sonada.

It was nighttime, and the cottage was empty except for the grieving servants. Meaningful exchanges could take place another day, but for the moment Alfred thanked them for their loyal service to his mother and told them to go to bed, saying that they would speak in the morning.

Alfred went to his mother's bedroom and drifted to sleep looking at the picture of the Sacred Heart of Jesus hanging on the wall opposite the bed.

CHAPTER 63

ACT OF GOD

1974

Alfred woke up at nine, which was late in Sonada where by seven the shops opened and the farmers were working in their fields.

He was having his chota hazri (a pot of Darjeeling tea and an apple) when he had his first visitor. Major Mercy, aged 84, looking feeble and supported by his faithful bearer was waiting for him in the living room.

"My boy, I am sorry that you missed your mother's funeral but it was not possible to wait for you."

Alfred knew that funerals in India had to take place immediately, and was again grateful that his old friend had come to his aid in time of great need.

The Major described the funeral arrangements. He had decided that the funeral service would not take place at St Teresa because Sonada did not have a cemetery, and his mother a Catholic he did not believe a funeral pyre by the bank of the khola was appropriate.

So the service took place in the parish church adjoining Loreto convent in Darjeeling, and his mother was buried in the European cemetery.

"I can say that the funeral was well attended, the church was full. There was a cross-section of society there to pay tribute. For example, there was a group of

Muslims who had walked seven miles from Hopetown before catching the train to Darjeeling to attend. Your Mother was much loved and respected."

Alfred went to Planters Hospital to find out how his mother had died.

Darjeeling town seemed eerily empty.

In November, schools and colleges in Darjeeling District closed for the three months' winter holidays. The children from the boarding schools, like St Ignatius, went to warmer climates.

In those days the town was also void of tourists in winter. As the years went by, tourists did not differentiate between seasons and the town would be flooded with their presence throughout the year, but not in 1974.

The doctor and the hospital administrator were waiting for Alfred.

After offering their condolences and following an awkward silence, the doctor explained what happened.

"As I told you when we spoke before, following the removal of the tumor your mother had a temporary stoma. She used to have coughing fits and there was a lot of phlegm. We decided to leave a phlegm suction unit in her room.

"I had the day off. I was told that there was an emergency operation and unfortunately a similar unit in the operating room failed to work. So they took your mother's unit intending to return it later.

"Your mother had a bad coughing fit, and there was a blockage due to the phlegm. She could not breathe. By the time the unit was recovered from the operating room, your mother's heart gave in and she passed away. Mr Stephens, there was nothing anyone could do."

"So you are saying it was an Act of God?" said Alfred.

"Mr Stephens, if you put it that way," commented the administrator.

After offering their condolences again, Alfred asked for an account. There was a surplus of his mother's cash, which Alfred donated to the hospital so they could use it towards buying another phlegm suction unit.

The European cemetery was situated close to St Ignatius. It was a flat piece of land with an uninterrupted view of the Mount Kanchenjunga range and surrounded by huts occupied by squatters.

As Alfred's mind was on a tombstone, the first thing he noticed was that most of the tombstones were missing.

"People steal to use them as chopping boards in the kitchen and as scrubbing boards to wash clothes by hand," said the chowkidar, who was the only full time employee at the cemetery.

After some confusion, the chowkidar identified his mother's grave. Alfred asked to be left alone.

Alfred did not know if he should be angry at the hospital, but he was certainly angry with God.

CHAPTER 64

LIFE CHANGES

1974

Alfred noticed that in 1974 there was still no influx of tourists coming to Sonada. But there were a few foreigners who had come to seek a well known monk, who resided at the Buddhist monastery.

These new types of foreigners, who were known as hippies, puzzled the local residents. They looked scruffy, took drugs and were quite happy to share their food and humble lodgings.

The older generation was used to seeing the foreigners and their families living in style in Sonada in contrast to the hippies, so they would shake their heads and comment.

"You should have seen the sahibs who used to live in Sonada—these are not real sahibs."

Notwithstanding the lack of tourists, Sonada had expanded and what was agricultural land was now housing colonies. Alfred's mother owned three of these (one of which was built on land once owned by the Chinese family) as well as Brightside Cottage.

Major Mercy recommended a local Nepali property agent, and Alfred instructed the agent to collect the rents and to find buyers for all the properties. He also left instructions that his Mother's three servants should be paid until such time as he gave contrary instructions.

After a month in Sonada, Alfred returned to England. He said farewell to dear Major Mercy.

"I am proud of you," said the Major, kindness written on his face.

Alfred would not see him again. But he would repay later a little of the debt he owed his old friend.

"Hello, did you enjoy your holiday?" said the airhostess.

When he looked up, Alfred recognized Maggie who had been kind to him on the outward journey.

"Hello, nice to see you again. No, it was not a holiday. I went home because my mother had died."

"I am so sorry," said Maggie. She knew now why this passenger had looked so sad on the earlier journey.

It was a night flight so the airhostesses had less to do, and Alfred found it pleasant to have a conversation with Maggie.

When she learnt that he was a solicitor, she said that she was thinking of buying her first house and Alfred said if there was anything he could do, than all she had to do was to contact him. They exchanged telephone numbers.

Alfred arrived in London on a foggy day, which resulted in delay in landing, but the weather was no colder than in Sonada. He went to his home in Kingston upon Thames, and then to his office where he was relieved to find, on first sight, that the office was running as smoothly as it was possible with the owner absent.

He told Linda what had happened. She was shocked to learn how his mother had died, and she seemed very pleased to see him back as she was waiting to give him some of her news, but now was not the time.

A month later, Linda suggested they had lunch together at the Golden Egg restaurant, where in the early days they went when there was something to celebrate and their meals always ended with deserts, banana split for her, and Eton Mess for him.

"Alfred, I do not want to add to your problems. But Ian (her fiancé) says that I should work locally as the journey to work is getting more difficult by the day. He thinks also that it would be better for me to have a local job, especially as we're preparing for our wedding."

Another woman in his life was leaving Alfred.

"You know I am going to miss you. But Ian is right. When do you want to leave?" After some discussion, the employer and his first employee agreed that it would be in two months' time.

So the day came when Linda was leaving. She had been with Alfred from the beginning, and had been his guardian angel. She made Alfred promise to attend her wedding, and the last words exchanged between them that day were, "I love you."

CHAPTER 65

NEVER FORGET KINDNESS

1975

Confucius had said: "Forget injuries; never forget kindness." Alfred had never forgotten this quotation.

He had arranged on his previous year's trip to Sonada for the Major's bearer to send a telegram in the event that his employer became ill or was too frail to live on his own. He had also given instructions to the Planter's Hospital to notify him if the Major was admitted and he would take responsibility for his bills.

When he heard from the bearer and the hospital that the Major had been taken ill, Alfred spoke to the hospital administrator and deposited funds from the proceeds of sale of his mother's properties so that the Major had a private room with a window from which he could see the Mount Kanchenjunga range, and the bearer could sleep on a mattress on the floor.

Ten weeks later, Major Mercy died peacefully in his sleep with his faithful bearer at his side.

"The Major knew you were helping and was very appreciative. He was always boasting about you," wrote the hospital administrator when he sent the receipted invoices to Alfred.

The one thing that gnawed Alfred was that it had not occurred to him that the Major was penniless towards the end of his life, just like Mrs Thompson.

The property he owned, Sonada House, had been mortgaged to the hilt to a local merchant. He felt he had let the Major down.

All Alfred could do now was to instruct the undertaker to bury him in the same cemetery as his mother; and the tombstone, which no doubt would be stolen one day, should have an inscription fitting for this good man: Blessed are the kind, for theirs is the kingdom of heaven.

CHAPTER 66

A NEW FRIEND

1976

The Camberwell Workhouse Infirmary in South London had opened in 1875, and was renamed the Camberwell Parish Infirmary in 1911. During World War II it was damaged by a V1 flying bomb.

In 1948 the Infirmary joined the National Health Service and was renamed St Giles Hospital. It was in this hospital that Maggie Arthur (nee Hardy) was born on September 24, 1950.

Maggie's family lived in Bermondsey, South London, which was close to St Giles Hospital.

Bermondsey lies along the River Thames so locals found work on the riverside, and in particular in the docks and wharves where imported goods were landed. Therefore it was not surprising that the men on her mother's side worked as dockers, although by 1976, more and more inner-city docks were closing and the number of dockers had decreased by two thirds during the previous two decades.

The mother's side considered the father's family to be snobs. Maggie's paternal grandfather had worked in the City of London in a shipping company, and went on to own a popular sweet shop in Bermondsey.

Her father was the regional manager of a well-known butcher's shop, and her mother was a housewife.

Maggie went to the local primary school from age five to eleven, and in the final year of primary school she had to sit for the 11-plus examination. Based on her results, Maggie was selected to go to a grammar school, which suited those who were academic.

When she was 14, her mother was diagnosed with breast cancer, the most common cancer in England. All she was told by her parents was that her mother had cancer and needed treatment—that was it, and life was supposed to carry on.

As her parents had not been open about her mother's diagnosis and options for treatments, believing it was not in her best interest to be told about these things, Maggie found it difficult to cope with her mother going in and out of hospital.

She was on tenterhooks every time her mother underwent treatments, and had to wait for the results. The worst thing for Maggie was that she felt bad for her mother, but there was nothing that she could do.

When Maggie came home from school on November 7, 1969 she was told that her mother had died. Maggie was 15 years old.

It was all very difficult and Maggie buried herself in her studies to forget that her mother had died; she passed her examinations.

At the age of 18, Maggie left school and rather than to go to college whose fees her father could ill afford especially as he had re-married, she went to work as a junior secretary for a shipping company.

A year later she went for an interview for a job with the Queen's bankers and was successful, but she had also seen an advertisement for airhostesses, and was tempted to apply.

She worked for British European Airways (BEA) as an airhostess until March 1974, when it merged with BOAC to form British Airways.

Four months after they had met on the British Airways sector between London and Calcutta (he had gone to Sonada following his mother's death), Maggie telephoned Alfred.

"It's Maggie. Do you remember me?"

"Of course. How nice to hear from you. Are you coming to see me?" said Alfred.

"That's why I called. We need you to help us buy our first home."

So Maggie and her husband, Joe Arthur, a fireman in the London Fire Brigade, came to see him. Alfred did the legal work on the purchase of a house by these first time buyers.

"Why don't you come and work with me?" Alfred suggested to Maggie on an occasion when she had called at his office.

"Thanks, but I am quite happy at British Airways," she replied.

"What about you—have you a girlfriend?" teased Maggie.

"No, I am still on the market. I am looking for someone rich."

"I have a friend who I think you will like. She is not rich, but she is pretty, nice and an Anglo-Indian" said Maggie, and a few days later she told Alfred that she had arranged the blind date.

This is how Alfred met the girl from Ajmer.

CHAPTER 67
THE GIRL FROM AJMER
1975

Founded in the seventh century, the city of Ajmer is in the state of Rajasthan, India on the border of the Thar desert and the Aravali hills.

The city was a popular pilgrimage centre for Hindus and Muslims; it had a school built exclusively for Indian nobility, but children from other walks of life, such as Anglo-Indians, attended less prestigious schools; and since the start of the railways it had been a busy junction connected to Bombay, Delhi, Calcutta and other major cities of India.

Many Anglo-Indians lived in Ajmer, and worked either for the railways or the post and telegraph.

Mr Barron's grandfather had been an Irish soldier who had married a Rajput girl, and continued to live in India after leaving the Army. His father had worked in the railways and married an Anglo-Indian.

Like his father, Mr Barron had married another Anglo-Indian and worked for the railways. He had done a little better, and he was a senior foreman at the Ajmer's railway workshop.

The Barrons occupied a bungalow in the railway colony rented from the employer, although they owned the furniture.

The whitewashed stone bungalow had drawing and dining rooms, two bedrooms, two bathrooms with thunderboxes and a kitchen. There were verandahs all along the front and back, electricity and running cold water. Behind the oleander bushes there were two servant quarters.

Mr and Mrs Barron had three children, of whom the youngest and only daughter, born in 1945, was Angelica Severina. The siblings called her Angela and that is how she was known throughout her life.

The defining date for Anglo-Indians was August 15, 1947 (Indian Independence Day). They believed that in independent India there would be problems for them as members of a minority community, and in any case they felt culturally aligned to the West. So after Independence it was not altogether surprising that there was an Anglo-Indians exodus to foreign shores.

Most of their extended families had already left India, but it was in May 1952 that the Barrons decided to leave as well for the sake of their children.

They travelled by train from Ajmer to Bombay, and sailed on the SS Strathmore (carrying 1,100 passengers, of which 665, including the Barrons, were in the tourist accommodation) to the final destination, being Tilbury Docks, London's major port.

From there the Barrons went by train to Bermondsey, South London to occupy a furnished small terraced house that had been found for them by a distant relative. It had a living room, kitchen, two bedrooms, an outside toilet but no bathroom.

Maggie's parents were welcoming, but the other neighbours ignored them.

Angela went to the same schools that Maggie would later attend, and her parents were proud that their daughter passed her 11-plus examination and was admitted to grammar school.

Angela was unhappy at grammar school where she was bullied because she was one of the few coloured pupils; she looked forward to finishing school at the age of 18. Unlike Maggie, Angela went on to college and obtained a degree in teaching.

"My daughter is the first in our family to get a college degree," her mother would boast.

Whilst Maggie and her father continued to live in a small terraced house with no mod cons until they were re-housed when the area was cleared for new development, the Barrons bought a house in Putney, also in South London once Angela's father saved the deposit from his employment as an engineer for British Rail. Her mother got a staff mortgage as she was working as secretary to a bank manager.

The bank had recruited her on the basis of her obtaining certificates with distinction for secretarial courses from Pitman and her experience as receptionist/typist in Ajmer (which she had reluctantly given up as her husband said no senior foreman's wife should be working). She was considered by her employers to be valuable as affluent immigrants were moving to Putney.

When Maggie arranged the blind date, Angela was a class teacher in a Catholic primary school in Kingston upon Thames, not too far from Putney and coincidentally in the town where Alfred was living.

When Alfred met Angela she was thirty years old, five feet two inches and slim. She had olive skin and long black hair; she was graceful, smelt modern

(Revlon's Charlie perfume) and was stylishly dressed in a Tiffany blue jersey wrap dress, knee length with long sleeves and she wore large gold loop earrings.

On their first date, Alfred was interested to know how Angela had come to England.

"I was too young to know the reason for leaving or when my parents decided to leave. But later my father told me that almost all his family had left after India's Independence in 1947, so he thought we should leave as well because there was no future for us Anglo-Indians.

"It seems my parents' first preference was to go to Australia but their application was turned down because of the White Australia policy.

"They thought of going to Ireland because we held Irish passports, but relatives advised we would be better off in England, and that is how we came here."

Australia had implemented the White Australia policy in 1910. Nine years later the Prime Minister, William Morris Hughes, proclaimed that "it is the greatest thing we have achieved." It was only in March 1966 that the first steps were taken to abolish this policy.

There were some Anglo-Indians who found a way around this policy and were able to immigrate to Australia. They relied on their British names, were fair skin and had blue eyes, and they could pass the dictation test, which was given in English only. Unfortunately for the Barrons, they could not meet the second requirement.

"What about you. Why did you leave?" asked Angela.

"My story is slightly different. As my father was English and I wanted to be a lawyer, the natural step was to come to England to study. At that time I knew nothing about immigration laws or the Anglo-Indian dilemma."

"Do you remember your life in Ajmer?" asked Alfred.

"Not all of it. I remember my ayah, how hot it was in the summer, sleeping in the verandah with mosquito nets, the Monsoons, lizards on the wall and ceiling, eating mangoes, travelling on a tonga. I remember the Railway Institute where my parents would go for the dances or watch sports, and feeling sad when I had to say goodbye. I cannot remember much about school, which was near our home, except that the nuns were strict. I was there for only a year. And you?"

"I remember everything. One day I am going to bore you with my stories," replied Alfred.

"You can bore me as much as you want."

Following the first date, he telephoned Maggie.

"How did you get on?" asked Maggie before he could speak.

"Very well. I like her."

"Good. She likes you too. Make sure you keep in contact with her."

"Maggie, does Angela have anyone else?" asked Alfred.

"I know she has gone out a few times with another teacher in her school. But as far as I am aware, there is no romance in the air," she replied. "By the way, Angela is a devout Catholic." Alfred thought, "Surely history would not repeat itself?"

He telephoned Angela and made a second date.

It was a sunny Sunday when Alfred took Angela to Kew Garden, described as the world's greatest garden. She was pleased with his choice.

Although Kew Garden was just a few miles away from her home in Putney, she had never been there before. Alfred did not tell her that he had not been there either.

They visited the Palm House, the most important surviving Victorian iron and glass structure. It had suffered from lack of maintenance during World War II and been closed to the public, but in the bicentennial year (1959) it had been restored, and was now open again.

They walked around the Arboretum that had a large collection of hardy trees, and the Rhododendron Dell.

"In the 1850s a Sir Joseph Hooker went to Darjeeling and made it a base for his plant-collection expedition. He brought back orchids and rhododendrons to Kew from the Himalayas.

"He is considered to be one of the great English botanists and explorers, and even today in Darjeeling there are Hooker's paperbark and oak trees in the botanical gardens, as well as a Hooker Road," said Alfred impressing Angela with his knowledge.

"Did you know that several of the original tea planters in Darjeeling were gardeners from here?" and pointing to some tall evergreen trees, Alfred went on, "And those are dhupiis that grow in the Himalayas. The English, I think, call it Japanese cedar. Can you smell the fragrance of the wood? It reminds me of home."

As they walked around Alfred gave a summary of his life, which interested Angela but she did think affectionately "How can a man talk so much?"

"Did you always want to be a teacher?" asked Alfred.

"I wanted to be a nurse, but my parents were against it. So I decided to teach. I like my job," replied Angela.

Alfred hardly spoke about his firm, but Maggie had told her about it and how hard he worked for his clients.

"Alfred does not talk a great deal about his firm. I suspect he just wants to get away from work and relax in the weekends," she said to her parents whenever they asked what he had said about his prospects.

They were enjoying their lunch at a local restaurant in Kew when Alfred took the bold step to ask Angela a personal question.

"Would you be offended if I ask if you are seeing someone?" said Alfred.

"I have a man friend who is also a teacher in my school. Sometimes we go to the pictures and shows. There is nothing going on, but my mother says what a nice man he is, and I should be more interested. I keep on telling Mum that if she likes him so much, she should go out with him." They both laughed.

And so the two of them started seeing each other, and the time came for Angela to introduce Alfred to her parents. He would also meet her two brothers, both of whom lived with their families outside London.

Alfred and her family got on like a house on fire, according to Angela's father, and it did not come as a surprise that he became a regular weekend visitor to the Barron residence where her mother would cook Anglo-Indian food such as curry puff, meat balls, brain chilly fry, salt beef, corned beef, masoor dhal and fish head curry.

Angela's father liked talking to Alfred about the good old days in India, life in the railway colony, his exploits playing hockey; and, like all other Anglo-Indians, they would listen to Jim Reeves records.

Angela's mother was charmed by the attention that Alfred gave her, and thought he was a real gentleman as he brought her flowers, chocolates and little trinkets.

Although her parents had hoped Angela would marry a white Englishman, they could not help but notice that their daughter was relaxed in Alfred's company, and she was moving towards a loving relationship.

The two of them would see other mostly during the weekends as they were both busy at work during the weekdays: they would go to see films (full price tickets) and live shows, enjoy shopping together, walking around Richmond Park and along the river.

Alfred had told Angela about Esme, and one day when they were sitting in Richmond Park gazing at the sky and looking at the cloud formations, she in turn told him about the betrayal.

Angela had graduated and started as a pupil teacher at a primary school in East Sheen, South London, which is near to Putney.

At a social function for teachers in the area she was introduced to the deputy headmaster of the junior school. Eric was a good looking Englishman, tall, confident, muscular and a decade older than her.

There was no doubt that he was attractive to the women around him. Somewhat to Angela's surprise, Eric asked her out for a drink. She was flattered, as she knew many of her colleagues fancied him.

Thereafter he would sometimes pop over to her school to see her, and on occasions give her a lift to her home. Once her parents heard about him, they insisted that Angela bring him in for tea the next time that he dropped her.

Angela's father was quite taken up by Eric, and he could see his dream of his daughter marrying an Englishman coming true.

As for her mother, she was quiet as usual, but she was the first who noticed his odd behaviour.

"Have you noticed that he never stays late, eats little and never comes to see you in the weekends?" she said.

"But he does telephone me on the weekends. And Mum, he is a deputy headmaster and has a lot on his plate," replied Angela.

"There's more to it than that."

Unfortunately for Eric, Angela's parents from the top of a double decker bus saw him one day walking with a woman and a child.

"He is married. Why are you going out with a married man?" asked her irate father.

"I did not know he was married, and it is not that we're friends [the Anglo-Indian expression for being in a relationship]."

The consequence was that Angela telephoned Eric, accused him of having a wife and child, and as he did not disagree this developing relationship ended. Angela was now not trusting men.

Alfred smiled.

"Why are you smiling?" asked a puzzled Angela.

"I was just thinking of what Oscar Wilde wrote: "I like men who have a future and women who have a past."

"Take that back. I do not have a past," replied Angela, and started ticking him.

CHAPTER 68

COMMITMENTS THAT STOOD THE TEST OF TIME

1977-1978

Bells rang out and gun salutes were fired on February 3, 1977 to herald the beginning of the Queen's Silver Jubilee.

It was also the year when Alfred received a letter at the office from British Honduras, which lies on the Caribbean coast of Central America between Mexico and Guatemala, and later that year would change its name to Belize.

The letter was from a Sister Martha whom Alfred did not know, but the handwriting was familiar.

"Dear Alfred,

I know this letter will surprise you.

I wanted to write to you many times before, but I did not know if it was right to do so. However as I approach the time to take my vows, I decided to write this letter, and once more to ask for your forgiveness and understanding.

It has been over three years since I made the decision to serve God. I have gone through the various stages of my vocation, and I take my vows on the feast of St Francis of Assisi on October 4.

Once it was known that I had trained at University College Hospital, my superiors told me that I would be needed in British Honduras where the Sisters of Charity of Nazareth are involved with health care. I have been missioned here working at a local hospital.

I hope you will let me know how you have got on, as I am very interested. I have always felt that you will have succeeded, and are the same kind and lovely person I knew.

Yours in Christ,

Martha

PS. You will see that I have taken a new name— Sister Martha.

Alfred went back to Speenham Road to remember Esme, and how he had fallen in love for the first time.

It came as a surprise that the road was no longer there. Following slum clearance, it was now part of the site of a large public housing estate.

"Be careful, man," said a young resident. "Anyone from outside the area will get robbed here. Enjoy yourself."

"What do you mean?" Alfred asked.

"There is a big gang in the estate who terrorise outsiders. Don't stay here longer than you need to."

Alfred left with no intention of returning.

He must not forget to reply to Esme's letter. But he had something else to do first.

Angela was leaving the school where he worked. She was looking attractive: her hair was tousled and she wore a blue and white spotted drawstring top complemented by a full dirndl skirt and wedge shoes.

"Alfred, what are you doing here?"

"I thought we could take a walk along the river?" replied Alfred.

"That would be nice."

They went a stone's throw from the school to the Fairfield Recreation Ground along the River Thames and sat on one of its many benches.

"Angela, I think we should talk about the future. Will you marry me, please?"

"What? I don't know what to say."

"Say, yes" replied Alfred.

"Yes, yes."

They kissed, and that is how they got engaged on April 7,1977.

"You are behaving like a lawyer. What about acting like a human being? Have you bought her an engagement ring?" said their mutual friend Maggie, when Alfred telephoned her to give the good news.

And that is why the newly engaged couple went to a jeweller in Hatton Garden, famous for being the centre of the UK diamond trade.

The couple did not want a big wedding particularly as the bride's parents insisted on paying.

"It is traditional in our Anglo-Indian community for the bride's parents to pay, and it would be an insult to us if you refused," said the prospective father-in-law.

In early August, during the school holidays, Alfred and Angela married at St Simon's, the local Catholic Church in Putney, in the presence of the bride's family and friends of the couple.

The honeymooners went on a road trip in California; and on their return three weeks later they moved to their large house in Kingston upon Thames as Alfred had sold his old one.

Kingston upon Thames lies on the east bank of the middle stretch of the River Thames.

In the 10th century West Saxon kings, such as Edward the Elder, Athelstan, Edmund and Edred were crowned on the coronation stone, displaying outside the town hall.

The town had become a London suburb with good schools and easy access by train for commuters travelling to the capital.

When the time came to give vacant possession to the buyers, Alfred asked Angela to give him a few moments in his house.

As he walked around the house, Alfred realised, with a wry smile, that his neighbours had not been in anyway friendly; that not a single one of them had said hello or knocked at his door or invited him for a cup of coffee (which he did not drink). He was an outsider, but this may have suited him as he was used to being socially isolated.

He remembered Esme; the things they did; the laughter; how he had found this house for them, and she had never seen it. How different his life would have been if they had got married.

No, it was not right to start married life with Angela in this house. One door had closed, and he saw another door of happiness opening for him.

"Are you OK? I love you," said Angela.

"Yes, let's go to our new home."

Did they live happily ever after? No—but they were very happy together for fifteen years.

CHAPTER 69

Bringing up husband

1978

The newly married couple bought their house from an elderly couple, who were downsizing.

"Well, we have a lot of work to do," said Angela as she looked around their first home, which had not been improved for many years.

The builders carried out the major works, such as new roof, damp treatment, re-plumbing, re-wiring and installation of gas central heating.

Alfred remembered how cold the winters were when he was on a low-income and fuel-poor, and how the heating of his rooms by wick paraffin heaters had put him off the smell of paraffin forever.

Angela decided that they should decorate their home. Alfred would have acted otherwise.

But on his wedding day, Alfred concluded that Angela should make all the minor decisions in their married life, and he would make the major ones. Although it has to be said during their marriage, Alfred did not make a single major decision.

Instead of Alfred working on files in the weekends, he now had to learn interior decorating, and help Angela paint and wallpaper the house.

He found it funny to remember that Esme had painted his office, and perhaps he must be attracted to women who liked DIY?

"Darling. You are not very good, are you?" said Angela.

"You are right. I am too much in a hurry to be an artisan. But I am an expert at cleaning," Alfred replied, laughing too.

Angela and one or other of her brothers worked away. Ceiling by ceiling, door by door, flooring by flooring, wall by wall their home took on a new life; but it was amusing that her girlfriends would say how lucky Angela was for having a husband who could do DIY.

In reality Angela had consigned Alfred to the garden to get him out of the way.

Alfred was not entirely happy that the first task for him in the garden was to tidy up a major part of it, and he came to the firm conclusion that gardeners must be masochists. He wished Kancha was around to help him.

However Alfred had many hours of enjoyment going around the gardening shops testing and buying tools and equipment, the more complicated and newer model the better.

"Alfred, you really know how to waste money. What is this, darling?" said Angela.

"That is a gas-powered leaf blower," said a contrite Alfred.

"The noise is so loud, you will drive the neighbours mad. Why don't you use a rake?" said a helpful Angela.

"I'll see if the shop will take it back," was Alfred's reply.

After reading gardening books (which now equalled the number of cookery books that he owned although it should be said he did not cook), Alfred ventured into the discovery of plants.

He bought plants such as cacti, yukkas, cordylines and flaxes, many of which were surplus to requirements. Remembering his mother, he made sure that he also planted roses, and a palm tree outside the front door.

As they say, Rome was not built in a day, and it took several months before their home was modernised and looking good.

Thinking of his mother's venture into the property market, Alfred wondered if now was the time to sell their house for a quick profit, but he remained silent when he thought that there might be more backbreaking gardening chores if they moved.

Alfred and Angela lived the whole of their married life in their first and only home.

Angela was a fair cook thanks to her mother's training. Alfred was now eating Anglo-Indian curries with strange names like baradoo, buffadoo and richadoo, as well as tongue roast and rolled mutton.

"But I cannot bake," said Angela.

"No one is perfect."

CHAPTER 70

LIKE THE GODFATHER

1979

Like all young lawyers, Alfred liked dealing with criminal cases because each accused was interesting, you were fighting for justice, and, for Alfred, the payments out of the Legal Aid fund were quicker for criminal cases than for matrimonial cases.

Criminal cases were varied. Alfred acted for clients who were charged with robbery, burglary, violence against the person, rape, gang rape, as well as motor vehicle thefts, religious and hatred cases. There were five murder trials, an IRA accomplice had to be defended as well as a restaurant waiter from the Indian sub-continent who had been successfully practising as a doctor using his brother's qualifications. Then there was the case of a kidnapping.

The client came to see Alfred.

"Mr Stephens, I have been charged with a serious crime. Demanding money with menaces."

"How did this happen?" asked Alfred.

"Well, about a fortnight before Christmas, I lost my wages betting on the horses. My wife was mad at me and threw me out of the house. I had a few pounds so I went to the pub.

"I was blind drunk and as I passed the high street, I saw a parrot in the pet shop staring at me. So I smashed the front window, stole the parrot and took it home.

"A few days later I saw an advertisement in the local newspaper offering a reward for the return of the parrot. So I telephoned the shop owner and said, 'I have your parrot and I want £200,' to which the reply was, 'Get lost. This is the fifteenth call I have had this morning.'

"I had just seen the film the Godfather and remembered the mafia placing the head of a racehorse in a Hollywood producer's bed to pressurise him. So I plucked a few feathers, put them in an envelope with a note to the shop owner saying that here was the proof, and I would call him.

"I did telephone and an arrangement was made to meet at an open area, Clapham Common.

"I put the parrot in a shoebox and went to meet the owner. He handed me the £200, and as I was taking the parrot out of the shoebox the Police pounced on me and the bird flew away.

"My hearing date is next Monday morning at Camberwell Green Magistrates Court."

So Alfred went to court with his client; and in view of the unusual circumstances the local press also attended the hearing. The client pleaded Guilty. However the magistrates decided that because of the seriousness of the charge, sentencing would take place at the Old Bailey—to the delight of the press, as this story would roll on.

The Central Criminal Court has been the most well known of the higher criminal courts in England, and is commonly known as the Old Bailey after the street in which it is located.

Murderers, spies, terrorists and traitors have stood in its docks, and guilty prisoners have heard the judge's verdict to take him down or take her down to serve at her Majesty's pleasure.

The Old Bailey had witnessed all human emotion so it was not altogether surprising to see a graffito on the door that read: A boy's best friend is his mother.

The client stood in the dock and waited sentence. His emotion was not one of penitence, but of stupidity as the national press waited to report the story to the outside world.

On the client's behalf, the judge was told that his action was out of character, he apologised for the waste of public money, and accepted the distress caused to the parrot's owner. The judge seemed unimpressed, and handed down a prison sentence of six months suspended whilst he was of good behaviour during the next two years.

Four months later the client's wife dialled 999 and called the police for help.

The client was charged with assaulting a policeman, and his defence was that it was all an accident. But unfortunately for him, the policeman had remembered the words that the man had shouted as he passed out.

"Here's one for you."

This time the sentence was nine months imprisonment calculated on the basis of the six months' suspended sentence and three months for the assault.

CHAPTER 71

THE FRENCH WIDOW

1979

When Alfred employed Linda in the first year of the firm he had told her that they should be different from other solicitors by not giving clients the impression that time was at a premium, and one way this could be done would be to offer every client tea or coffee and biscuits on arrival. This practice had continued.

On the week in question, two prospective clients had come asking for advice on divorce, and both had eaten the biscuits and enjoyed the hot drinks.

When Alfred's receptionist was passing through the garden of nearby St Marks Church, where in 1887 Viscount Montgomery of Alamein (Monty) had been born as his father was the vicar, she noticed the two of them were sleeping rough on the benches.

"Obviously they heard we hand out free drinks and biscuits," thought Alfred.

"There is another one of them here," said the receptionist.

Alfred went to see the intruder and found an elderly woman with a stooped posture, unkempt hair, a dirty raincoat and not smelling of perfume. She was leaning on a very old pram filled with her belongings.

Alfred felt sorry for her and offered tea and biscuits. She turned down the biscuits, but sipped the hot tea.

"How much do you charge for selling a house?" She spoke with a slight foreign accent.

"Oh, I would charge you a fixed fee of £110 all inclusive," replied Alfred in jest, meanwhile thinking how to get her out as soon as possible as the smell was becoming unbearable.

She shuffled her belongings and handed over an envelope to Alfred.

"Will your fee be the same?" she asked.

Alfred opened the envelope and read an estate agent letter confirming the sales commission and valuing a house in Hampstead, North London (a premier location). Had he known the sale price, the fee would have been at least five times more.

"Yes."

"Good, I have found an honest solicitor," she said, and took out a large and bulky file containing her title deeds.

On checking her other papers, he noticed that she was 72 years old and a widow. She had a bank account, so Alfred spoke to the manager, who confirmed her identity.

The house was sold, and the client asked Alfred to keep the net sale proceeds for her.

When a buyer was found for a second property she owned, Mrs Rosalinde Drummond, which was her name, said that she had checked fees charged by solicitors in the Hampstead area and that if Alfred did not charge more, he would end up in Carey Street. She said a fee of £600 inclusive would be acceptable to her.

"Are you sure? It is too much." As she nodded, Alfred went on to say, "Thank you Mrs Drummond. It is much appreciated and not taken for granted."

In the next 18 months she sold another four properties and there was a substantial sum of money kept by Alfred on her behalf.

Mrs Drummond would visit Alfred at least twice a week, but unfortunately the cash in the bank did not improve her attire or her smell.

From snatches of conversation, Alfred learnt about her past.

Mrs Drummond was French. She had fled her country with General De Gaulle and the Free French, and came to live in England in 1940. She was then 37.

She went to live in the town of Brighton, close to Hove where Alfred's father was born, and there she met an ambitious bank manager. They fell in love and married.

Her husband was posted to London where they lived till his death in 1960. By then he had become a regional director of the bank. He had also built up a property portfolio as a result of which they were wealthy.

Just before he died, Mrs Drummond was told by her husband to be careful of the Inland Revenue, and to try and avoid as much tax as possible.

By the time she met Alfred, she had become somewhat of a recluse, and was obsessed with the idea that the Inland Revenue was after her. Therefore she moved around and was a person of no fixed abode.

"What are you doing with your money, Mrs Drummond?" Alfred would ask, and she would say that there was no rush to decide.

On one of her visits, she mentioned that she had a sister in Paris, and that they had not met for over 30 years. Alfred persuaded her to contact her older sister by a letter addressed to her last known address. To their surprise a reply was received.

The letter was from her nephew, who explained that his mother had died and that he was a married lecturer with two children. He went on to say that if at any time she wished to visit Paris, he would be pleased to open his home for her.

Alfred suggested that she should go, and after much persuasion, she agreed. The two of them went to a second hand shop in Brixton where she bought some clothes, a handbag and a pair of shoes. Alfred lent her a small suitcase.

Alfred saw her off at Victoria Railway Station in London. The train left for a station called Dover Marine where she got off, and then she travelled by ferry to Calais from where she caught the train to Gare du Nord Station in Paris.

Five days later she came to see Alfred.

"Mrs Drummond, why are you back so soon?" said Alfred.

"I would have come a day earlier but I was too tired," she replied, and explained what had happened.

"My nephew was waiting for me at the station, but I got the idea that on seeing me he was not pleased, probably because he was ashamed of me and thought I needed money.

"Anyway he did not take me to his home as I expected, but to a small bland hotel opposite the station with the promise he would come to see me again after his lectures finished the next day.

"He did not come back, and here I am."

"I am so sorry Mrs Drummond. I cannot imagine how you must have felt," Alfred said.

"I am not bothered, and I am certainly not going back."

But what Mrs Drummond did do was to make a Will appointing Alfred as her sole executor and, after discussing the issue over several weeks, she made the decision to divide her estate between three charities chosen by Alfred.

Two years later Mrs Drummond died peacefully in a hostel.

They say that in this world nothing is certain other than death and taxes.

Mrs Drummond's estate was able to avoid paying capital transfer tax (later re-named inheritance tax) on her death because charities inherited.

However Alfred had to negotiate with the tax inspector regarding arrears of income tax and capital gains tax (payable on the profits from the property transactions) to which were added interest for late payments and penalties for failure to disclose. Only after paying these taxes could Alfred, as the sole executor, distribute Mrs Drummond's estate.

It gave Alfred great pleasure to write to the nephew to inform him that his aunt had died, and that her very substantial estate had been distributed between three charities. Alfred hoped that the nephew's day was spoilt when he read the letter.

Did Alfred profit from his choice of charities? Yes and No. Yes as he received calendars from these charities each year, and No as he received deluge of begging letters for more donations.

And there was a surprise for Alfred too. The matron at the hostel came to see him, and said that Mrs Drummond had left a large envelope to be given to him on her death.

The note read—

"Dear Mr Stephens,

You are a stupid man. Use your talent and make some money.

Your friend,

Rosalinde Drummond (Mrs)"

And inside the envelope there was also £4,000 in cash of which £300 was no longer legal tender as they were old notes and which Alfred had to exchange at the Bank of England.

When Alfred got home, he gave Angela the good news.

"What are you going to do with the money?"

"We could pay the mortgage off. Let me think about it."

One morning at four Alfred woke up. His mind was clear as to what he wanted to do with the money. After listening to him, Angela did not disagree.

Alfred contacted the overseas development and mission office, and through them Sister Martha was told that her friend had made a generous donation, and the money should be used as she wished.

It was not long before Sister Martha wrote a letter.

"Dearest Alfred,

I cannot thank you enough for the money, which you have trusted me with.

Since I have come here, I have been helping with the care of geriatric and chronically ill patients.

Accommodation is always in short supply, and therefore I will use your money to build another ward, which I intend, with your blessing, to name after your beloved mother.

I hope to hear from you with all your news.

I want you to know that I continue to be happy in my vocation, that I do worry about you, and you are always in my prayers.

May God bless you."

As the years went, people visiting the Mylie Ward would ask, "Who is Mylie?"

The explanation given was that someone in England had donated the money to build the ward in memory of his late mother, who had lived and died in India. This was very appropriate as the country prides itself as a melting pot of many races.

CHAPTER 72

THE PARENTS-IN-LAW

1980

The 1970s had been a disturbing decade for Britain. It was often said that the country was the sick man of Europe, as its economic policies were not working.

In 1979, Margaret Thatcher and the Conservative Party won office and she remained in power until 1990.

One of the Thatcher government's most popular policies was the Right to Buy scheme introduced in 1980, under which longstanding local authority tenants could purchase their homes at discounted prices.

As Brixton and the surrounding areas had large-scale council estates, Alfred's firm enjoyed a substantial increase in workload, added to which during the Thatcher period divorces increased twentyfold and the prison population increased sevenfold.

Since Alfred had come to London in 1962, there has been only four White Christmases. In 1979 it was cold, but those gamblers who bet there would be snow in London on Christmas Day were losers.

Angela's parents, siblings, nephews and nieces came to spend Christmas day with the couple. Just like the gamblers, the nephews were disappointed with the weather, as they could not use the toboggans that they had brought with them on the hills of nearby Richmond Park.

But they and their sisters were certainly not disappointed with their Christmas presents as Alfred and Angela had gone over the top, according to their grandfather.

The New Year Party of 1980 was larger in number than at Christmas as friends also came to enjoy Alfred and Angela's hospitality.

Everyone was affected for years to come by what happened.

Dinner had been served and everyone was ready to party. As they sang "Auld Lang Syne" minutes after the clock struck midnight, Mr Barron was standing next to Alfred. They could not hold hands because his father-in—law was holding a glass of champagne.

Suddenly Mr Barron fell and hit his head on the floor. Those who saw what had happened thought Mr Barron would get up, but he did not.

There was hysteria, and one of the guests, a nurse, started to administer CPR, whilst someone called an ambulance.

Everyone started complaining about the delay in response from the Ambulance Service. It seemed an eternity, but it was twelve minutes after the emergency call that a single responder and an ambulance crew arrived.

They assessed that Mr Barron was in cardiac arrest, and was taken as a priority to Kingston Hospital. He died that morning aged 63.

Florence Barron was aged 59 at the time of her husband's death.

As Angela lived closest compared to her brothers, she would visit her mother every other day after school; and, with Alfred's encouragement, she stayed overnight on occasions. Alfred even spoke to Angela about the possibility of her mother moving in with them, but Mummy preferred to stay in her home.

On becoming a widow, Florence, a portly woman who was seen but not heard during her marriage except when she was scolding one of her sons, found a fresh lease of life.

She started inviting bank colleagues and neighbours for a curry or a roast, and they readily accepted. All had a good time. But she reduced her invitations over the course of time as she noticed that she was never invited back, the common complaint of most immigrants in England.

Mrs Barron decided to go further afield. Her children were astonished when she started going on Mediterranean cruises, and even flew to Australia to visit relatives. And for the first time since she had left India in May 1952, she dipped her toe in the water and spent a winter holiday in sunny Goa.

"It is so cheap there" is all you heard her saying.

But the shock to her children happened just after the second death anniversary, when their mother asked them to come for Sunday lunch as she had an important announcement.

When Angela and Alfred entered her home, they found a stranger sitting in her father's chair. He was introduced as Aidan, my boyfriend.

"How did you meet him, Mummy?" asked Angela.

"He is an engineer, and he came to set up my VHS recorder."

When her children asked for his background, Mummy gave them short shrift.

"I do not wish to discuss it," and that was the end of the matter as far as she was concerned.

On the way home, Angela raised the subject with Alfred.

"What do you think?"

"There goes your inheritance," said Alfred.

"Thank God I have got you," Angela jokingly replied.

Six months later the mother in law asked Alfred to see her on his own on a private matter.

Aidan, eight years younger than her and twice divorced, had moved in with her. His income was less than that of his girlfriend, but he did not seem to mind and enjoyed the fruits of her income coming from various pensions, as well as bank interest from a fixed deposit account containing the proceeds of her late husband's life policies.

Unfortunately for Aidan, he was seen by one of Mrs Barron's friends in a local pub kissing a girl wearing the shortest miniskirt, leg warmer and a sweater in electric neon colours. This information was mischievously passed onto his girlfriend.

Alfred was asked by his mother in law to get him out of her home. He approached Aidan but he refused to move out, and in any case why should he not kiss whomever he wanted to?

Alfred attended Wandsworth County Court to represent his mother in law in her application to seek an eviction order. It was a relief to both of them that Aidan did not defend the application, and an order was granted for him to vacate within 28 days.

As the ex-boyfriend was homeless, he went with the court order to the local authority, which was legally obliged to re-house him as a homeless person. He was given a one bedroom flat to rent, where a young person of the opposite sex promptly moved in with him.

As for Mrs Barron, she never trusted another man.

She died in 1996 at the age of 76. According to the eulogy given by the Nigerian assistant parish priest (by now there was a shortage of home-grown priests in Britain), she had lived a life devoted to her family. She had been much admired for her strong resolve not to burden her children in her later life. She suffered ill health (arthritis in her hands from years of typing) stoically. She had been a loving grandmother (from a distance according to her two boys and their wives), and proud that her children had done so well. She had returned to the Lord and was together again with her beloved husband.

CHAPTER 73

THE WAY LIFE TURNS OUT

1980

"What are you thinking about?" asked Angela.

"I am thinking of getting someone to run the administration side, as it is too much for me to do on top of the legal work," replied a tired Alfred.

This is how the topic arose when Angela met Maggie and her son aged seventeen months to go on a shopping trip.

"I am getting bored at home, so if Alfred needs some part-time help, I am game," said Maggie when Angela told her Alfred was looking for a helper.

Angela passed on this message to Alfred who met up with Maggie, and told her that he needed someone to deal with the administration and finance side under the supervision of the outside accountants. Maggie explained that she had no experience, to which Alfred replied she could attend a few courses and learn on the hoof.

Maggie came to work part time initially for a maximum of six months, but eventually took over running the practice for the reminder of Alfred's career. Thanks to her good husbandry, Alfred had no financial worries in later life.

Meanwhile eighteen months had passed since Alfred and Angela's wedding. One thing that Angela was told by her mother was to watch out for a missed period. So when this happened and in addition she felt sick, nauseous and had sore breasts, she went to see her doctor for a urine test. She was given good news, and she told Alfred that their baby was expected to arrive in mid January.

Angela was about seven and a half weeks pregnant when she slipped as she was getting off a bus and fell on her stomach. As this happened close by, she went home and lay on the sofa until Alfred arrived.

"Darling, what's the matter? You look as if you are in pain," said a worried Alfred.

"I fell when I was getting off the bus, and I have a back pain. I will be all right soon. Let me know when you are ready to eat."

However as far as Alfred was concerned, eating was out of the question as soon as he learnt that Angela was bleeding continuously. He took his wife straightaway to Emergency at Kingston Hospital, where the doctor who checked her gave the couple some bad news.

"I am so sorry. The pregnancy is miscarrying, and nothing can be done to stop this."

Angela started crying, and Alfred could only console her and tell her that he loved her.

In the next few weeks, Alfred was walking on eggshells as Angela was very angry with the conductor rushing her out of the bus, and she was having difficulty sleeping. There was no way that he could suggest that when she wanted to they could start planning another pregnancy.

At school half-term Alfred surprised Angela by organising a ten day holiday in Italy. They travelled from Florence to Rome and then to Naples.

They went on a day trip to Pompeii where the guide took the tourists to a house, which still had a door whose knob was in the shape of an oversized penis.

"Ladies and Gentlemen, you now see the biggest penis in Italy."

"The second biggest," said Alfred, and everyone present laughed.

Angela was so embarrassed that she kept away from Alfred for the rest of the day's tour, especially as the other male tourists would come up to Alfred and whisper, "You lucky man." But thankfully the next morning, she saw the humorous side, and it was good to see her laughing again.

CHAPTER 74

LORD OF THE MANOR

1980

The Prime Minister's Office in Downing Street was circulating a profile of Vice President Mubarak, which described him as a future leader of Egypt, not intelligent, but having an affable exterior evidently concealing a degree of ruthlessness. It warned officials not to mention Mrs Mubarak's Welsh relatives unless the Mubaraks themselves brought up the subject, as it was thought they might wish to play the connection down.

Alfred was welcoming an old friend who too was not intelligent, had an affable character, enjoyed talking about his wife but would prefer not to speak about heirs.

"He says that he was your landlord—his name is Mr Kang," said the receptionist.

"My God. Mr Kang, how nice to see you. Come in and have a cup of tea with me. I remember you have half a cup with two spoonful of sugar," said Alfred.

"Good. You have done well. See your big office. I don't think you have time for me," said Mr Kang.

"Rubbish. You do not look a day older. Where have you been and how is Mrs Kang?"

"Well, a few years after you left, the Council bought our house under a compulsory purchase order as they had regeneration plans.

"We moved to Slough (a town about 20 miles west of Central London attractive to immigrants from Poland, India and Pakistan from the 1950s onwards) where there was a bed and breakfast place for sale.

"We still live in Slough, but we sold the bed and breakfast and I am no longer a bus conductor. Thanks to the grace of God, we own a small hotel now, ten bedrooms, and Mrs Kang is very busy."

"I must visit you. I would love to see her. What are you doing these days?"

"I am now a property speculator. I buy and sell in auctions and make small profits. I came to view a house in Brixton, and Mrs Kang said that I should come and see you, but not to take too much of your time."

"Time is not a problem. Mr Kang, you have made my year by coming to see me. By the way what happened to the other tenants?"

"When the local authority bought our house, the Alberts left and bought a house in East London with a Post Office mortgage.

"The accounts student, who had qualified by then, went back home. He sent us a postcard when he got there. The rascal was from Ghana and not Jamaica as he had told me.

"Mr and Mrs Malcolm were given a flat to rent by the local authority. You know Mr Malcolm has died. I got a letter from Mrs Malcolm saying he had died peacefully after lunch with her by his bedside." Alfred hoped his last meal was not mulligatawny soup.

"Have you heard from Miss Esme?" enquired Mr Kang.

"I did hear from her a few years ago. She is a nun working in a hospital in Central America. She is now known as Sister Martha. She is doing well," replied Alfred, but he could not help but feel sad whenever he thought of her.

"What a beautiful woman," said an admiring Mr Kang.

And so the conversation went, and after two half cups of tea Mr Kang asked Alfred for advice.

"I am somebody and nobody. I am richer than I look, but nobody knows. I want some standing in life, what do you suggest?"

"Excuse me, Mr Kang. I will be back," said Alfred as he left the room to stop himself from laughing.

When he returned, Alfred gave his advice.

"I have an idea. Why don't you buy a title? You will be a lord of a manor," said Alfred.

"You mean I can be Lord Kang?"

"No, but you can be called Suraj Kang, Lord of the Manor of, say, Brixton."

"How do I go about buying this?" asked a rather excited Mr Kang.

"You can buy a title at an auction."

Mr Kang went to an auction and bought a lord of the manor title, which he had printed on letter-headed paper, his business cards, his credit card and his chequebook.

When Angela asked how he got this idea, Alfred said that morning he had received several auction catalogues, and for the first time one was for the sale of such titles.

Mrs Kang never forgave Alfred for giving this stupid advice, especially as a result of an incident on holiday.

The Kangs had gone on a well-deserved holiday to Cornwall. She saw a nice dress on the sales rack, but when she handed over her Lord's credit card, the manageress had an opinion.

"Madam, your husband is a Lord. The sales rack is not the right place for you. Please come with me."

And, much to her annoyance but so as not to create a fuss, Mrs Kang bought a dress at full price.

A journalist from a national paper who happened to be at the auction was intrigued that a turbaned Indian had bought a title.

As a result there were on-going articles about Mr Kang with photographs of him looking dapper in a pin stripped suits, a Harris tweed jacket and grey trousers, and once in plus-fours with argyle socks, silk necktie and dress shirt. However at all times Mrs Kang refused to pose with him.

And thanks to Mr Kang, even Alfred was mentioned in an article in a national paper.

"All this has happened because my solicitor, Mr Alfred Stephens of Brixton, London and formerly of Darjeeling, India advised me to become a Lord," said the Lord of the Manor.

This sentence had an earth-shattering result for Alfred, as he would soon discover.

CHAPTER 75

Brixton riots

1981

1981 was the year when Prince Charles and Diana married, President Ronald Reagan and Pope John Paul II were shot and a number one hit was Stand and Deliver.

It was also the year when there was a riot in Brixton in which 149 police officers and 58 members of the public were injured, and 215 people were arrested.

The weather turned from cold to warm in mid-April, and on Saturday April 11, Alfred and Angela took the opportunity to drive to the countryside.

On their return, the telephone was ringing and Alfred answered.

"Have you seen the news?" said Maggie.

"No, we have been out."

"There is a riot in Brixton. All the news on TV is about it. Joe has been injured and I am at Casualty." She explained what had happened.

"I'm sorry. Let us know when you have any more news about Joe."

Joe Arthur was stationed at nearby West Norwood Fire Station. His day shift was about to end at 6 p.m. when the warning bell went and a message read: Car alight. Railton Road, Brixton. Riot in progress.

All the lights in West Norwood Fire Station came on, which was the second warning.

The fire engine was manned and Joe was the driver. When it reached Railton Road, the police waved it through their cordon.

A group of people let the fire engine pass. As it approached the vehicle on fire (a police car), there was another larger group who started throwing bricks and paving stones, one of which hit Joe on the chest, but he continued driving until he could park safely. He was rushed to the local hospital for treatment.

Joe's courage was acknowledged with the award of the Queen's Commendation for Brave Conduct.

The TV news showed shops looted, vehicles destroyed and other property (including private homes) seriously damaged. Brixton Road was empty of traffic. There were burning vehicles in the side roads and shops on fire; the Windsor Castle pub was blazing and burglar alarms were screaming.

"Alfred," Angela said, "I know you want to go and check the office, but it is too dangerous for you to go there now. Go in the morning."

"You're right."

The two of them could not sleep, and Angela wanted to know why the riots had started.

"You know, darling," said Alfred, "I have been telling you that our criminal work has been on the increase. There are more robberies in the area, druggies and squatters live in Brixton, there are illegal gambling and unlawful drinking and drug clubs, which the police are trying to close down.

"The police are heavy handed with their stop and search policy making black youths, most of whom are second generation, resentful. They believe that the police regard anyone who is black as criminals and act accordingly. You will be surprised at the locals' hatred of the police.

"Then there is unemployment especially amongst black youths. It is no good clearing the slums and giving people good homes and shops if there are no jobs.

"No, it does not surprise me that the riot has started—I am surprised it had not happened before."

Waking up on Palm Sunday, Alfred switched on the TV and the news was all about the Brixton riot and the authorities blaming outside agitators.

"That is not true," said Alfred. "The locals are economically deprived and resentful, and the Government is doing nothing about it."

On reaching Brixton, he found that the police had sealed off the area with a helicopter hovering above.

"Officer, my office is in Brixton Road—it is the solicitors," said Alfred. "Can I go and check if it is OK?"

"Speak to the Inspector over there."

Having been given permission, Alfred went past the police barricade, walked down Brixton Road and came to his office door, which had graffito reading: Kill the pigs.

Alfred was horrified to find that petrol bombs had been thrown and a large part of his office had been torched. He quickly left and went back to his car.

"How was it?" asked the Inspector.

"Most of my office has been gutted by fire," said Alfred.

When he got home, Alfred called his staff. Then he said to Angela,

"God knows what troubles are on their way for me."

However the trouble that did come in June of that year had nothing to do with the after effect of the burnt office.

CHAPTER 76

STAND AND DELIVER

1981

On the Monday following the riot, the streets were being cleared of burnt vehicles, goods and rubbish, and shops were being boarded up. Brixton opened again for business.

Alfred asked his support staff to help with the cleaning up, and told the fee earners to take on new business as fast as possible whilst he sorted out the problems.

That week the fee earners were busy representing new clients either seeking bail or appearing on criminal charges, taking instructions to sue the police, claiming compensation from them for unnecessary damage caused when gaining entry and searching premises (mainly for petrol bombs).

"I did not do it" "What is the evidence?" "Get me out" "I was hit by a policeman. I had done nothing wrong. See the scar here" "I am innocent" "The Police broke down my front door, the fireplace panelling was pulled away, and the two bedroom doors and kitchen door are damaged."

Settlements were achieved on many of these claims, although the police did note some were greatly exaggerated. A claim for loss of a television, fridge freezer and settee resulted in the claimant being charged with attempting to obtain money dishonestly.

But it was not just the police who had to deal with claims.

Like Margaret Thatcher who was working long hours to find the cause of the riot and the solution, so that in mid June that year she had been to New Scotland Yard at 7.30 p.m. on the Saturday and returned home at 3.20 a.m. on Sunday from Brixton police station, Alfred had been grafting all hours God gave him to sort out the office, get main services including telephones and telex working again and to reconstruct the files and documents. It was a relief that most of the clients understood but it brought out the greed of one.

Graham Saunders was a financial adviser struggling to earn a living with the help of an assistant. He had a one-room office a few hundred yards from Alfred's.

He had introduced himself to Alfred some time back, and had asked for help as he was not doing well, and his wife was threatening to divorce him.

He became the beneficiary of Alfred's kindness. Clients were recommended to him for mortgage loans and insurances.

"You have saved me from bankruptcy, my dear friend. I will never forget that," he would say and Alfred would feel pleased, and send him more work.

A month before the Brixton riot, Saunders had decided to speculate on the commercial property market.

On seeing an empty shop for sale he put in an offer, which was accepted. But he asked Alfred to delay the legal work as long as possible whilst he tried to raise the deposit and obtain a loan.

Alfred was inundated with telephone calls from the selling agent and the seller's solicitors trying to progress the sale but he could do nothing, as the finance was not in place.

As for Saunders, he was pretending and complaining to the agents about the delay on the part of his solicitor, and informing them that he was going to change to another but not admitting that he was the cause of the delay. Unknown to Alfred, Saunders' favourite expression to them was that his solicitor was useless.

The day before the Brixton riot, Saunders still had not raised the deposit or obtained a mortgage offer.

"My friend, I will let you know when we can exchange. Have a nice weekend."

A fortnight after the riot, Alfred received a letter from a solicitor representing Saunders, complaining that, according to the estate agent, his delay in the legal work had resulted in the seller withdrawing from the transaction; and because of his professional negligence, the claim was for compensation for the lost opportunity of making a profit from a sub-sale (£20,000) and reimbursement of his expenses to the tune of £950 (surveyor's and mortgage application fees) plus legal costs.

Alfred was gobsmacked at this claim, and replied immediately stating that their client had instructed him to delay the transaction, asked for written proof that he had the deposit and the loan arranged for the purchase, and accused him of attempting to obtain money from him dishonestly.

"Is it wise to make this accusation? It might make him more determined to press on," said Philip.

"In this case I know this is a try-on. The best form of defence is to attack."

The reply was that Saunders would accept £1,500 and legal costs in full and final settlement if the payment was made within seven working days, otherwise proceedings would be issued.

Alfred was so angry that he left the office and went home.

"Darling, you try to be kind and friendly with everyone, and someone will take advantage of you. You're kind of an easy mark. All I can say is settle the claim, let's get on with our lives and do not be bitter about it," said his wife.

The claim was settled without admitting liability for £750 (his legal fees), and Alfred was bitter for some time.

Two years later Saunders's assistant came to see Alfred.

"Mr Stephens, I have been sacked. Could you please represent me?"

The application for unfair dismissal succeeded, Saunders failed to pay the award, and Alfred, in the best interest of the client, was pleased to instruct bailiffs to go to Saunder's house and seize his goods.

"Mr Stephens, thank you for the money. I need to tell you something; it has been in my conscience. Saunders schemed to get money out of you as he thought you had enough on your plate with the riots and would cave in as you are soft. I am glad you did not. You know he is a racist and was jealous of you," said Saunders's former employee.

"It is a strange world," said Alfred when he got home, and thinking of Saunders: "Greed's worst point is its ingratitude."

Just as Alfred was getting over the Saunders episode, another problem, which also had nothing to do with the Brixton riots, raised its ugly head.

It was a June day, but not that warm. On the car radio, Tight Fit were singing The Lion Sleeps Tonight as Alfred was driving home after a hard day's work.

He was feeling tired and hungry. So it was good news that he remembered that Angela said she had cooked a roast.

When they were eating, Angela had something important to say.

"Darling, I have twice missed my period. So the other week I bought an EPT kit from the chemist. He recommended that I do two tests, preferably a week apart to be sure there is enough hormone in my urine. It looks like I am pregnant."

"Are you sure? How accurate are these tests?"

"I was told that they're as accurate as can be. I have made an appointment to see the GP tomorrow."

Alfred went to kiss his wife, and then straight to the drinks cabinet to take out a bottle of warm champagne; they had a glass each and the rest was wasted, as the couple were not drinkers.

"That's the last alcohol for me till the baby is born," said Angela and Alfred concurred.

"Darling, do you remember we said we would name a boy James after Major Mercy, and Lucy after your mother?"

"Of course, how could I forget?"

The couple went happily to bed, but they were slightly anxious as the GP still had to confirm the test.

Although they had agreed that no one should be told for the time being, they could not hide their excitement so, on their promises not to divulge the secret, the following day Angela told her mother and Alfred told Maggie.

The GP confirmed the pregnancy following which Alfred gave as stern a warning as he could to Angela that she should be careful not to be stressed, and not to lift or strain herself.

"Should you not give up work and take it easy?" asked an anxious Alfred.

"Darling, I have read the baby books before. These are all misconceptions about miscarriages. But I promise I will be careful, and I will give up work if it seems too taxing" said his dutiful wife.

Angela went through the normal symptoms of pregnancy, feeling of sickness (morning sickness), tingling and tender breasts, and moodiness. She noticed that her waistline was increasing.

She made arrangements to leave her teaching post at the end of the school year.

Angela had a temperature and backache, and took a day off work. There was also light bleeding but she thought this was not heavy enough to worry about.

However by the next morning, the vaginal bleeding increased, she was passing clots and she had severe lower tummy pain.

"The GP surgery is not open as yet. Perhaps we should go to A & E. Let me get ready," said Angela.

"I am going to call the ambulance," said Alfred, but Angela protested.

So Alfred took Angela to Kingston Hospital where she was seen by a doctor, who gave his opinion that Angela was miscarrying.

"Let nature take its course. As there are times when the pregnancy tissue does not pass out naturally and as this is your second miscarriage, an appointment will be given by the early pregnancy unit here to check that everything is OK," said the doctor.

When Angela attended hospital again, she consented to a minor procedure called ERPC, which would be carried out under general anaesthetic with the purpose removing pregnancy tissue from the womb.

"What is the cause of this miscarriage?" asked Alfred.

"Mr Stephens. I am afraid there is no ready answer. It could be caused, for example, by chromosomal abnormalities in the baby. A miscarriage can happen by pure chance, and it has nothing to do with your wife's health. We never find the cause of the loss with most miscarriages," replied the doctor.

That day Angela left the hospital very sad. She was heartbroken and Alfred remained by her side as she grieved; and she could only sleep with medication.

Alfred was relieved that Angela had already gone through the process of leaving her job, and he hoped that by being at home with no work pressure she would get over, however slowly, this tragedy.

CHAPTER 77

REUNION

1982

The day's post was brought to Alfred, and there was an unopened envelope marked: Private and Confidential. The letter was from a solicitor in Gray's Inn, which is about a quarter of a mile from Lincoln's Inn.

> "Dear Mr Stephens,
>
> I am writing on behalf of a client of mine on a personal matter. I would appreciate it if we could meet for lunch at the Law Society. Please ask your secretary to telephone me to make a mutually suitable appointment.
>
> Yours sincerely,
>
> Jonathan Ford"

Alfred was intrigued, and asked his secretary to make the appointment as soon as possible, as he wanted to strike while the iron was hot.

He went to the dining room of the Law Society three days later, and was taken by the waiter to a table for two, where Mr Ford a distinguished looking grey haired gentleman of average height and weight was waiting.

After the usual exchange of greetings and introductions, Mr Ford ordered Campari and soda for the two of them, and explained the reason for the meeting.

"As I said, thank you for coming. I have a client who lives in Portugal, who saw an article on a Lord Kang (an interesting man) where your name was mentioned and that you are from Darjeeling. My client was a tea planter there, and you will be interested to know that his name is Lewis Stephens."

"That is my father's name. He left Darjeeling in 1948 and never returned."

"And your mother's name is Mylie?" asked Mr Ford. "Yes."

'Would you like to meet your father when he is next in London?" asked Mr Ford.

Alfred thought about it and replied that he was not sure, but maybe there was no harm in meeting him.

"And what about your mother?"

"She died in 1974."

"I am sorry. I will let him know."

Alfred told Angela about the meeting, and she encouraged him to see his father.

"You never talk about your father, and when you have to mention him to people, it is to shade the truth. Here is the chance to sort out things, and then you can leave the past behind."

So it was in late July 1982 that Alfred went to the Royal Over-Seas League House in Green Park, London. Front desk staff escorted him to the Cocktail Bar where he saw a man nursing a gin and tonic and reading a newspaper to pass the time.

His father was 68 with wholesome good looks but seemed unconcerned about it. He was tall (six feet), light brown straight hair, large forehead, ice blue eyes, big ears and big nose with a high bridge and moderately thick lips.

On the other hand Alfred was five foot five, dark skinned, flat face with prominent cheekbones, small eyes, a broad nose with a low bridge but similar forehead and lips.

After an awkward silence, Alfred greeted him.

"It's nice to meet you. I never thought I would."

"Nor did I."

"Isn't the weather lovely? Summer has at last arrived. What is it like in Portugal?" said Alfred.

"I live in the Algarve, which is in the southern part of Portugal. The weather is hot but bearable. In the last few years I have come to London during this period to get away from the holiday package tourists. It also gives me the chance to see the doctor, dentist, Uncle Tom Cobley and all."

"Would you like another drink?" Alfred asked.

"What will you have?"

"A glass of lemonade will do, thanks."

So his father ordered for him, as well as another gin and tonic for himself.

When Alfred went home, Angela was curious.

"So how long were you together, and what did you talk about? How did he look? Did he recognise you?"

"Well, after our drinks, we had lunch, grilled Dover Sole with side orders, and then I had a trio of sorbets and he had a coffee. We were together for about two hours."

"And?"

"I would not have recognised him as my father, and he certainly would not have recognised me. When he looked at me, I got the feeling he felt guilty and embarrassed.

"I got the impression that he is a loner and a bit cold. He talked more than I did, about the Algarve and his life there, politics and how London has changed. But we did not talk about the distant past. It would have been difficult for both of us.

"When we parted, he said he hoped we would meet again, and we exchanged phone numbers."

At Christmas, Angela persuaded Alfred to telephone his father, who was on his own and seemed appreciative that the call had been made.

They met again the following July. They met again at Over-Seas House where Lewis stayed on his visits to London, and at restaurants nearby. The meetings were less awkward, and Alfred found his father had a cheerful, unreserved nature. They talked about the weather, fashion and films, countries visited, religions, what work Alfred did but never about what had happened in the Himalayas, other than Lewis commenting that he was sorry to learn that his mother had died.

The last evening together, Angela joined them. Lewis got on well with her and before you knew it, she suggested they spend Christmas together.

"I will have to see if I can reserve a room at Over-Seas House," said Lewis, to which Angela had a ready answer.

"Nonsense, you must stay with us. Don't you think so, Alfred?" and he agreed.

So it was that Lewis spent his first Christmas with Alfred and Angela, and from then onwards he would stay with them whenever he came over.

Did father and son speak about the past? They did not. But they did get to know each other and to become close, even if they did not have a proper parent/son relationship.

To deal with the past and the emotions for both men, Angela became the go-between. And it was to her that Lewis gradually spoke about his life after he left Sonada.

CHAPTER 78

THE PRODIGAL FATHER'S STORY

1983

Alfred went to work, and Angela spent time with his father when he came to stay with them.

One day when the two of them were sitting in the garden, Lewis told his story.

"I returned to the UK in the summer of 1948. I cannot remember the exact month.

"I went to stay with my parents, who were living in a small village in Sussex—Rushlake Green, where they had moved to after my father's retirement from the diplomatic corp.

"They were happy to see me, but I always felt that they were disappointed that I had not made something of myself, especially my mother.

"I spent the winter renewing old acquaintances, socializing with them; and as there was really nothing to do in the village, staying in London visiting the theatre and going to nightclubs, the usual things one does at that age.

"About five months after I had arrived, one evening my father went to call mother for dinner. She was sitting in front of her dressing table with hairbrush in her hand. She seemed to be about to brush her hair. She had died.

"It was all a terrible shock, mostly for my father who was suffering from a heart problem.

"I thought I would postpone my trip back, and re-book later.

"Later became several months and it was summertime of 1950. My father had taken the death very badly, and that August he died a few days after he had a heart attack.

"I was busy winding up my parents' estates, selling their home and just as I was thinking of re-booking my passage to India, I met a friend at the local pub. He was taking his girlfriend around Europe and he asked if I would like to come, as he needed a second driver. That said, his girlfriend's best friend was also coming.

"I thought, 'Why not?' and we spent that December driving around Europe and ended in Seville in Spain. There we met an English couple from the Algarve in Portugal, which was on the other side of border. They suggested we should go there, and they recommended a bed and breakfast place in a small town of Olhao.

"I found out that Olhao was the largest fishing port in the Algarve, full of character with Moorish-style houses an influence from the commercial links with Africa.

"We drove there; it did not take that long and we booked into the bed and breakfast that had been recommended.

"One morning I was sitting sipping a cup of coffee and gazing at the ocean.

"A voice said 'Mr Lewis, what you think of?' and when I turned around I saw our Portuguese landlord.

"I replied 'Mr Fernandes I was just thinking how nice it is here. I could easily live here,' to which he said, 'You can do.'

"We drove back to England to a very wet and unsettled February, and thought that there I was in the Algarve wearing shorts and keeping out of the sun. Am I boring you, Angela?"

"Don't be silly. It is fascinating. Please carry on. I am dying to know what happened next."

"What happened was that by March when the weather was no better, I decided to go back to the Algarve. I had more than enough money from my inheritance.

"I went by train to Lisbon, the capital and then onto the Algarve by train also, and my final journey to Olhao was by donkey cart. At that time the tourist industry had not discovered the region.

"I stayed in Mr Fernandes' bed and breakfast place for six months, and then moved to the provincial capital of Faro to a flat in a building, which was advertised as the highest building in the Algarve—four floors. I have remained there ever since. Well, that's enough for now. When is Alfred due from work?"

When Alfred did come back from work, Angela recapped his father's story.

"Angela, it's all very well. But did he mention Mummy and I?"

"Darling, give him time. It must be difficult for him."

Lewis had an important appointment to keep in London, besides seeing his medical practitioners. It had been years since he had attended, but he thought this year he would go to the annual dinner of the Indian Tea Planters Association, which was held at the Oriental Club off Oxford Street.

"Alfred, you go to bed. You look whacked. I will wait for your Dad," said Angela. And she did.

Just past one in the morning, a taxi pulled up and Lewis got out. Angela saw him and put the kettle on.

"Sorry, I am late. God, that was depressing. Some had died, others were in nursing homes and those that came had back problems, were waiting for a knee replacement, had a stroke or were heart patients. This is the last dinner I will go to. I felt depressed all the way back," said a slightly inebriated Lewis.

"So count your blessing that you don't look your age. Here, drink this. I have made you some strong coffee."

Whilst drinking the coffee, Lewis spoke again about the past.

"One day I was walking towards the dry cleaning shop when a Portuguese man, smartly dressed, came up to me and asked if I was the Englishman living in Faro. I told him I was. He told me in broken English that he was a lawyer and wanted to improve his English. He asked if I could teach him spoken English and he would pay me for my services. So I ordered a few books from Foyles and taught him three evenings a week.

"He then introduced me to others who wanted to learn, and the next thing was that I was teaching spoken English to waiters, cooks and kitchen staff at the newly opened hospitality school in Faro. That is what I have been doing all these years."

"What a story. And before we go to bed, Dad (as she now called him) tell me why did you not go back to India?" asked Angela.

"That will not take long. When I left India in 1949, or was it 1948 I had every intention of going back. But once I had spent sometime here I was less sure—why should I have to work so hard and have a lonely life in the tea estate for such measly salary? Then my parents died and I have told you how I got to Portugal."

"It's very late. Can I ask you a last question?" When he nodded, Angela asked one of the two questions Alfred wanted answered.

"Why did you marry Alfred's mother? I understand most of the sahibs did not. Dad, please do not answer if you do not want to."

"I can only answer in a roundabout way. The Second World War was on. I knew that I would be called for service. I asked the local priest, a Sicilian to come and see me. We had a long chat, and I told him of my worry—what would happen to Mylie, that's Alfred's mother, if anything happened to me? The priest suggested we get married so that if I were killed, she would be a British war widow and would be looked after by the State. That is why we married in 1942.

"You know, Angela she was a beautiful woman, just like you," said Alfred's father.

The old man looked very tired. Angela did not think it fair to ask him the second question ("Did you have a conscience abandoning your wife and child?")

"It will be breakfast time soon. Let's get off to bed. Good night, Dad."

CHAPTER 79

CRUISING THROUGH MID-LIFE

1983-1992

Since her father's death on New Year's Day 1980, Christmases and New Year Days had passed with no celebrations until Angela decided in 1983 that these festivities needed to be celebrated, and this would have been Daddy's wish.

Alfred was thankful, as he was tired of being a helper at Christmas lunches for the homeless at the parish hall instead of being a participant in a family gathering. What had Jesus got against him?

And as for New Year's Eve, did the year have to end with Mass, a glass of port and watching everyone else in the world having a good time on television? There were certainly no fireworks at the Stephens' home on New Year's Eve, although he could not say the same thing about his brothers in law.

Whenever Angela telephoned to wish them a Happy New Year just past midnight, the brothers' phones were never answered.

"We had an early night," both brothers would say on New Year's Day.

Looking back on his life, Alfred would say his most contented period was between the ages of 40 and 49.

Although the relationship was still awkward, he was reunited with his father; his practice was flourishing; Angela had come out of her gloom and she was now working as a part time teacher but only to occupy her time; they were enjoying regular breaks from work in their holiday homes and they were prosperous and healthy. Yes, the gods were smiling—for the time being.

CHAPTER 80

THE TAMIL PUSSYCAT

1984

From 1500 until the island gained its Independence in 1948, the Portuguese, followed by the Dutch and then the British controlled Sri Lanka or as it was then called Ceylon.

In the 19th century, the British brought Tamils from South India to work mainly in the tea plantations, and this group was known as Plantation or Indian Tamils. However there were Tamils already living on the island, who had migrated there as traders or invaders from South India and who lived mainly in the northern parts. They were the largest minority ethnic group at the time of Independence, and are now known as Sri Lankan Tamils.

But the main ethnic group that made up the majority of the total population was Sinhalese, and they had been living in the island for centuries.

When Sri Lanka gained its independence in 1948, there was no massive violence or social unrest, and there was no major conflict between ethnic groups as in India.

However in the General Election of 1956, the Sri Lankan Freedom Party led by S.W.R.D Bandaranaike campaigned as the defender of a besieged Sinhalese culture, with a policy to replace both English and Tamil with one national language, Sinhala.

A Buddhist extremist assassinated Bandaranaike in 1959, and his widow was elected as the world's first female prime minister in 1960.

Mrs Bandaranaike's policy, like her husband's, was that Sinhala should be the only official language of government, and this led to Tamil resistance and state-sponsored military action against them.

She lost the election in 1965 to the United National Party. But the new government's economic policies and its attempt to create Tamil as a second official language led to increased Sinhalese antagonism and the re-election of Mrs Bandaranaike in 1970.

She came to power this time as head of an alliance party. A new constitution, which included the support of Buddhism and discrimination against Tamils in areas such as university admissions, was passed in 1972 much to the dissatisfaction of the Tamil community.

The United National Party came back to power in 1977. However even this change in government did not stop the dissatisfaction of the Tamil community who had by now formed a new party, the Tamil United Liberation Front. This party demanded a Tamil homeland, and impatient younger Tamils formed separatist groups, one of whom, the Tamil Tigers, started on the road to violent rebellion.

In 1983 anti-Tamil riots escalated into a civil war between the Tamil Tigers and the Sri Lankan government. As a result there was a significant number of Tamils who left the island seeking asylum, amongst them lawyers who were unable to continue practising either due to the official language in the courts being changed to Sinhali or because they were in fear of their lives for having supported human rights.

Tamil clients pleaded with Alfred to help those lawyers who had come to London. Alfred remembered the Muslim bakers who had pleaded for help from his mother, who had supported them. Alfred acted likewise, and mentored many of these lawyers, who after working for him for a year or two went on to practise on their own accounts, except for one.

Philip Kesavan was born in the Tamil city of Jaffna. He worked as an advocate for two years in Colombo before coming to London due to the problems of language and prejudice, as well as the danger of returning to his hometown firmly in the control of the Tamil Tigers.

The first time he came for an interview, Alfred did not offer him employment, but a year later he was back grinning like the Cheshire Cat.

"What are you doing now?" asked Alfred.

"I am working in a travel agency, but I really want to be a solicitor. I was an advocate back home, so I can apply for the conversion. I will work hard for you."

Second time around Alfred offered him employment, and Philip never left him.

It soon became apparent that he was a person who wouldn't say boo to a goose, and therefore his nickname at work became the Tamil pussycat.

"We're the three Musketeers," was Philip's common cry to Alfred and Maggie.

"Give me a break," was Maggie's reply.

"I am the faithful Sancho to my Don Quixote," he would say to Alfred, who had a ready answer.

"Provided we're not tilting at windmills."

CHAPTER 81

Cut like a knife

1987

It all started with a cough.

"Angela, you must go and see your doctor. You are coughing all the time," said Alfred, worried about his wife.

"There is nothing to worry about. It will go away. I am trying another cough syrup."

This went on for several weeks and finally, due to Alfred's insistence, Angela made an appointment with her doctor. She was told that the cough should go away; and if it did not, then she would be referred to the hospital for tests.

Time did not resolve the coughing. So Angela attended the hospital on a routine appointment on her own, as she did not want Alfred to take time off. And when the results came, she attended the second appointment also on her own, as Alfred had to attend court.

"Darling, there is nothing to worry about. They gave me an appointment to go back in a month's time."

Before that appointment which Alfred insisted he must attend, three incidents took place that October.

Angela and Maggie had arranged a champagne reception at the Law Society on October 2 to celebrate Alfred's silver jubilee as a solicitor. The evening was a success. He was touched by the number of guests who attended and the speeches congratulating him, and more so when he saw the surprise guests whom Angela had traced, Mrs Sophia Mezetta, the Italian lady at the Law Society, who had given him a helping hand all those years ago, as well as "Lord" Kaur and his wife. Unfortunately Angela had not been able to trace the Fernandos.

"You deserve it, and from now onwards I want you to work less and enjoy the fruits of your hard labour," said Angela. "We do not need more money. I have not spent a penny of my salary since we married."

"Hurrah, we will now travel first class."

On October 16, there was the biggest storm disaster in Britain in recent times when 19 million trees were blown over and 13 people killed. A large oak tree in their garden fell thankfully away from the house, although it did destroy the fencing and the neighbour's garden shed.

Just three days later, on Monday, October 19 (to be known as Black Monday) the BBC reported that the world's stock market had collapsed after shares on Wall Street suffered a wave of panic selling. As far as our couple was concerned, their investments by the end of the month were down by 26.4%.

But there were even darker clouds on the horizon.

Alfred accompanied Angela to her next hospital appointment. The consultant asked her if her husband knew.

"Know what?" asked Alfred.

"Mr Stephens, I am sorry but I told your wife she has lung cancer."

'But my wife has never smoked and nor do I," said a shocked and worried Alfred.

"Because of the Government's advertisements, people know smoking causes lung cancer. That is not the whole case. Non smokers can also get lung cancer, and this is what has happened here."

The consultant then explained that a lobectomy operation was needed as soon as possible as he was shortly going on holiday.

As they left the consulting room, Angela had something to say.

"Darling, I did not tell you before as I did not want to spoil your celebration."

"Oh God, why is it that when everything seems fine, things have to go wrong?" thought Alfred, but said to his wife, "Darling, we will fight it. We will do all that is possible."

The journey back home was a sad one.

On the day of the operation, Alfred dropped Angela at the hospital and after making sure that she had settled down, he went to work. On the way, for the first time since the funeral service for his father-in-law, he dropped in at a Catholic church to ask Jesus for a favour.

That afternoon, the consultant telephoned to say that the entire lobe of her right lung that contained the cancer had been successfully removed, and her lungs could function with the lobes that remained. When this news was passed around the office everyone rejoiced, none more than the boss.

"Alfred, you look as if you had the operation. Relax and take Angela on a holiday when she has recovered," said their friend, Maggie.

So with Philip and Maggie managing the office, a month later Angela and Alfred flew via Los Angeles to Honolulu, and stayed at the Pink Palace in Waikiki Beach; life seemed good.

"Who would have thought I would be in Hawaii? Thank you, darling for everything," said a happy Angela.

"And thank you for making me happy. I love you," said her husband.

CHAPTER 82
PAN AM FLIGHT 103
1988

"Mr Pat Ryan is on the phone."

"Good morning, Pat. How are you?" asked Alfred.

"I'm OK. But I may need your help."

Patrick Ryan was born on August 27, 1937 and was of Anglo-Irish descent—his father, an Englishman, had been born in Fulham, West London and his mother in County Carlow, Ireland.

He was working as a customer service manager for Pan Am at London Heathrow Airport when he met an Indian girl named Farah at a friend's house party.

He was instantly attracted to Farah, and luck was on his side as she worked for another airline based at the airport. However it took four months of persistence on his part before she accepted his invitation to go out with him.

"He is not my type," Farah would say to her friends, so it came as somewhat of a surprise when they got engaged and married within the year of their first date.

Farah was a Parsi and therefore a descendant of Zoroastrians, who had fled to India when the Muslims invaded Iran more than 1,000 years ago. The Parsi community was diminishing because when women like Farah married non-Parsis, their children were not accepted as Parsis.

Pat was working in Operations when a plane was hijacked in Karachi, Pakistan. After this, his employers decided to increase security worldwide; they advertised for a new post of regional security manager for the whole of Northern Europe, and Pat was selected for this post.

The Ryan's had been married 15 years when on December 21, 1988 Pat took a day off from work to go Christmas shopping for their young son, Sean.

Just as they got home with their shopping, the telephone rang.

"Pat, I have been trying to get hold of you. There is a 704, which has crashed at Lockerbie. I think it is our aircraft. It is the only plane in that area," said an agitated colleague. The time was about 7.30 pm.

He switched the TV on. Michael Burke of BBC News was reporting that there had been an aircraft crash in Scotland. When the announcement came that it was a Pan Am plane, Pat left for work immediately.

'Don't forget that you have to drop Sean to school as I have a doctor's appointment," said Farah.

"Yes, darling" replied Pat, and smiled thinking that these two words must be the most commonly used words in their home.

The flight had started in a smaller plane from Frankfurt to London. Then Pan Am Flight 103 took off from Heathrow Airport carrying 243 passengers and a crew of sixteen.

Thirty-one minutes later, Control was issuing clearance for the plane to start the journey across the Atlantic to New York. Seven minutes later the plane exploded over the town of Lockerbie in Scotland. The time was 7.03 p.m.

The wreckage spread over fifty square miles. All 259 people on board and eleven residents out of about 4,000 were killed.

Pat was worried as to what would be required of him, and Farah had suggested he speak to their friend, Alfred.

Over several cups of tea, Pat explained his worry, and Alfred advised him.

"There are likely to be two investigations for which you need to be prepared. The first, the Fatal Accident Inquiry, will take place in Scotland (Dumfries), and the second will be looking into Pan Am's security procedure (New York).

"I know the inquiry under Scottish Law will be fact finding, like an inquest following a death in England, but I suspect the American one will be adversarial so you will need to be thoroughly prepared for it, and no doubt your employers will want to have an input. I think the American cross-examination will be quite harrowing for you."

So before he was called to give evidence, Pat spent time gathering the background information.

By the time of the Lockerbie incident, Pat had given training to the security employees in Northern Europe. He had realized that security at Pan Am needed to be comparable to that of El Al and Air India, who had experienced terrorism in the air.

He had warned the security employees about bombs in Toshiba Bombeat radio-cassette recorders used as altitude-timing devices, and about liquid nitrogen, which the Americans were unfamiliar with unlike the British who had experience of it due to IRA operations.

He did not know if it was the correct, but two senior colleagues had advised him that as long as baggage was x-rayed a plane was safe to fly even though the passenger was not on board.

Following the Dumfries inquiry, Pat telephoned Alfred to say that his evidence had been well received.

"Alfred, come quickly," said Angela.

"Look," and she pointed to the TV, and Alfred saw Pat, who was about to give evidence in New York.

"Never again. It was cut-throat with the American lawyers. They questioned me from all sides. Thank God I had gone there properly prepared. Thank you," said Pat later.

Yes, as Abraham Lincoln said: "Give me six hours to chop down a tree and I will spend the first four sharpening the axe."

CHAPTER 83

HOLDING ON

1988-1989

"It's hurting," said Angela. Alfred rushed for the painkillers.

He was getting more and more anxious about leaving Angela and going to work, but she was adamant that he did. In this battle of wits, Angela succeeded, as Alfred hated her being agitated.

Although the firm was functioning, there were clients who were being difficult and insisting on seeing Alfred. Before long, he found himself working full time and felt guilty about it.

When he was at home, he made sure that she took the painkillers regularly, helped her with arm (to avoid a frozen shoulder) and deep breathing (as there is less oxygen) exercises, pestered her to have afternoon siestas and kept a check on her weight. He continually worried that she would catch a cold, flu or a chest infection.

Angela started to feel better and was able to do light work, and was given permission by the consultant to drive short distances. Alfred wanted to take her on a holiday to a faraway place that they have never been to.

"No, darling. I would prefer to stay at home."

There were days when she suffered from depression, but for both their sakes Angela tried to be positive. But she told Maggie that she had a gut feeling that things would not get better.

"Are you experiencing any pain?" the consultant asked.

"I have a muscular pain in my right shoulder."

Following a scan, the consultant's facial expression said it all.

Angela was referred to another consultant, and after further tests she was seen with Alfred present.

"Mrs Stephens, I am so sorry. You have developed what we call metastatic cancer, in other words the cancer cells have spread to your shoulder. "

"What happens now?" asked Angela, as Alfred looked crestfallen.

"I suggest a treatment of radiation therapy, which will relieve the pain; and we may decide later if this should be combined with chemotherapy. My registrar will discuss your treatment with you beforehand and answer any questions. She can also give details of likely side effects. We should start the treatment immediately."

Alfred asked to be excused, and went to the toilet where he broke down.

"It never ends," he screamed at God.

When they got to the hospital car park, there was a parking fine because they had overstayed by 15 minutes.

The next few weeks went in a whirl. Alfred lost all interest in working, and was thankful that Maggie and Philip were in charge.

The couple comforted each other with Alfred wishing that he had the cancer, and Angela worrying about him.

Angela started a series of external radiotherapy treatment for ten days. Alfred accompanied her each time as the consultant had warned that she would be tired after the treatment and feel as if she was suffering from flu.

They would remind each other of the happy times.

"Do you remember when we were in Los Angeles, and you wanted to see the film Deep Throat. and you did not tell me what it was about. We had hardly sat down and there was a sex scene, so I walked out in disgust. You then exchanged tickets for the other theatre, and we saw Disney cartoons," said Angela.

"I know, and the theatre was empty except for the two of us, and we had to queue for Deep Throat," said Alfred.

"Yes, and almost everyone queuing were Japanese tourists."

And they giggled like little children do.

They also talked about future plans, enthusiastically by Alfred, and less so by Angela.

"Let's see, darling. Let's not rush into things," Angela would say, and a black cloud would come over Alfred's head.

Another day, another appointment with the consultant. It was time to talk about the treatment that would be of further benefit.

"The chemotherapy should mop up the cancer cells, and get your cancer under control," he said. "There is one other matter I would like to discuss with you. You do not have to, but would you like to participate in a study that we're running? We normally treat patients with six cycles of what we call MVP chemotherapy, but we're randomly asking patients if they would agree to three cycles so we can compare the two treatments.

Please think about it, and let us know if you will agree to the second option."

"I don't need time to think. If it will help your study, I agree," said Angela and she went on, "Doctor can I please ask two questions, first, will I lose my hair, and second, what is my estimated life span?"

"Darling, please don't worry," intervened Alfred. "If you lose your hair, I will get you the best wig money can buy, and do you really need to know the answer to the other question. Let it be."

"Yes, darling. I want to know."

The consultant said that there was always a danger of losing hair but it was not certain; and as to the other question, he, like the judges at the Old Bailey used to do, passed the death sentence.

"As a general rule the time span for your type of cancer is in the region of three years."

Alfred could not look at his wife, but looked out of the open window and saw that the sky was blue and there was a bird with long wings and long tail streamer circling gracefully. It must be a swallow, which winters in southern Africa and arrives for the spring.

CHAPTER 84

END OF A LIFE

1989-1992

Just as he would pursue a moneylender, defend an innocent person, fight for a child's custody or help someone move home, Alfred worked hard to trace wig manufacturers and visited specialist wig stores to find out which ones would come home to do the fitting, and to see the types of wigs, discovering that real hair wigs look and last longer than synthetic ones.

"Darling, we hope that you will not lose your hair during chemotherapy. But in case you do, shall I arrange for someone to come home to help you to decide the colour and style of a wig?"

"No, darling. I don't feel like it right now." Alfred discovered that the thought of losing one's hair is a very emotional experience.

In addition Angela was suffering from the side effects of chemotherapy treatment, which was being given at three weekly intervals. She suffered from nausea and vomiting resulting in the need to take anti-sickness tablets, and she lost her taste sensations.

Then she had fever and flu like symptoms, and Alfred had to rush her to the hospital where she underwent special antibiotic therapy.

Angela was also on morphine every four hours as the pain was excruciating.

"Remember, Mr Stephens if you miss giving her the morphine by more than quarter of an hour, you must bring her into hospital immediately so we can control the pain," said the senior registrar. This was the most important responsibility as far as Alfred was concerned, and one that worried him most.

He did not want his wife to suffer due to his fault, and that thought kept him awake at nights. He was able to keep awake because the office sent daily a courier with files to be worked on.

Angela knew the clock was ticking, but Alfred did not want to know.

"Darling, you look so tired," said Angela. "I had a word with the surgery and they have arranged for a Marie Curie nurse to call. This will allow you have a break. You are looking very worn out, and I cannot bear it."

This is how Alfred was able to take a day off each week, and he could go the office to deal with the administration work with Maggie and see difficult clients.

He was down with the flu, and after a few days Angela told him that she had arranged to go into a local hospice for respite care for three nights to give him a break.

The morning she was leaving, Angela asked Alfred to call for the parish priest. The priest rushed over and saw her, after which Alfred drove her to the hospice.

"Darling, do you really want to come here?" asked Alfred.

"Yes, I insist. You need to get better. Look at me—darling, always remember I love you very much," she said.

As Alfred was waking up the next morning, the hospice called to say that Angela had gone into a coma.

He sat beside her bed for sixteen hours holding her, but fate played a hand. When he went out of the room for a break and returned, the nurse came up to him and whispered.

"She is at rest."

Another staff approached Alfred and enquired if he would agree to donate Angela's corneas. He agreed.

Angela died on May 2, 1992 at the age of 47. It was three years, four months and four days since the conversation Angela had with the consultant as to her estimated life span.

Alfred did not cry until a week after the funeral, which was delayed by a fortnight due to a gravediggers' strike.

CHAPTER 85

THIS LOVE OF MINE

1992

"Do you want me to come and stay with you?" asked his father after the funeral.

"No, Dad. Don't worry. I am all right," replied Alfred.

But his father did worry, and would telephone Alfred every evening to make sure that he, at least, had a meal.

In his lonely house, Alfred realised that he and his wife had never talked about death, or his life after her death and there were so many other things that were never said. They never said goodbye.

He remembered her worrying that she had not asked his father a question he wanted answered—"Did you have a conscience abandoning your wife and child?"

"It's not important. What is important is that you get better," is what he had said to her.

Alfred felt foolish to think that even as death approaching he believed that she was returning home.

No one would ever find out if Angela had feared death: she never showed it. She appeared to be carrying on with life (so far as it was possible) as if there would be another tomorrow.

A fortnight after the funeral, Maggie went to see Alfred. When she saw him (disheveled, tired and sad), she felt acutely protective. But she had come for a reason.

"You have to get a grip of yourself. You need to come back to work. You do not want to hear it, but we're rudderless and our finance is not looking good. We're operating on an overdraft, and new clients are getting rarer by the day."

So whether he liked it or not, Alfred went back to work.

The first client he saw had been waiting for his return.

Mrs Stafford was an existing client and the wife of a secondhand car dealer in East London. She was petite, pretty and had bottle blonde hair at the request of her husband.

He had left her just before Christmas for a single parent. The new girlfriend was a cashier at the local betting shop that he frequented, but at one time she had been a bunny girl at the Playboy Club in Park Lane, London, which was the most profitable casino in the world when it closed down in 1981.

"He wants a divorce, but there is no way I will agree. I will not let him re-marry," said Mrs Stafford. "But I want you to sue him to get back the money I spent on his Christmas present."

"If you divorce him, then you can make money claims such as transfer of the matrimonial home and maintenance. But Mrs Stafford, it is difficult in law to get back money spent on a gift. Why do you want to be reimbursed? I don't understand," said Alfred.

Mrs Stafford then told her story. She was sure that she had been a good wife, looking after his needs and their home, not complaining when he was away on business, and always trying to look good so he would be proud of her.

"You would be the perfect woman if only you had larger boobs," was the only complaint of her husband.

So she had started saving, and when she had sufficient funds she went to see a plastic surgeon. She was booked for the operation, and told her husband she was going to stay with her sister so they could go Christmas shopping together.

"Darling, please go. If you want to stay a few days with her, by all means do so. Don't worry about me. I can manage. You deserve a break from me," said the duplicitous husband, who was already planning an overnight stay at his girlfriend's place.

"Do you know Mr Stephens, I thought how lucky I was to have him as my husband. How wrong I was. I suspect he was with his tart," said Mrs Stafford.

She had her operation, and came home with 36DD breasts, which she was going to display to her husband on Christmas Day.

However on returning home, she found a note from her husband stating that that he needed a bit of space and was therefore leaving her.

"I did not want 36DD breasts. I did it for him, and he betrayed me. I want him to reimburse me."

In the next few days, Alfred negotiated with the husband's solicitor. He offered a deal that if the husband reimbursed his wife for the breast implant, he would do his best to get her to grant his wish—a divorce, so that he could marry his bunny girl. The husband paid up, and when she received the cheque, Mrs Stafford came to see him.

"You are wonderful." Alfred did not feel wonderful.

CHAPTER 86

BRIEF ENCOUNTER

1993-2000

During this period Alfred lived on his own. He had a stab at cooking and failed, but he was never hungry due to ready to cook foods that he could buy and the hospitality of his friends.

And why was it that Alfred entertained his guests at restaurants that were usually empty and on the point of closure? Was it because he felt sorry for the owners?

What grief does is makes you addictive to work.

Years went by with Alfred drafting accumulation and maintenance trusts, discretionary trusts and bare trusts; putting life assurance policies into trusts; looking into special rules and tax advantages around trusts for vulnerable beneficiaries; keeping busy with such schemes to save inheritance tax on death. Clients wanted to be poor at moment of death and leave rich beneficiaries.

He was advising clients who did not believe their children would spend their inheritance wisely, and clients who did not want their widows to inherit all their estates to share with lovers—for why should others benefit from their efforts?

He was supporting disappointed beneficiaries; making claims on behalf of partners and children of deceased who had been left out of wills.

He was dealing with property investors and speculators who took it that the value of their investments would only ever go up, and who faced ruin with the property crash in the early 1990s following Black Monday in October 1987; acting for clients who wanted to sue their financial advisers and their banks, and then in the late 1990s representing another generation investing in property in anticipation of prices trebling in the next decade.

"I wanted to fear no one and stand up for the underdog, and here I am working for clients whose only worry is money," thought Alfred. But he realised he did what he had to do. After all how could he fail to take heed of Mrs Drummond's exhortation?

"Use your talent and make some money."

Alfred continued spending his time till the end of the 20th century assisting the better off clients.

"Did Alfred enjoy this stage of his life?" Not really.

"Was it a waste of time?" No, for it gave Alfred the financial security that most humans seek.

But this did not stop him from speaking to Maggie.

"I need to work on some cases where at least where I can feel I have helped someone in trouble," said Alfred to his practice manager.

"But do they want your help? Just concentrate and make money for yourself. There will be no one there to help you when you get to old age and are poor," Maggie replied.

Alfred had just come home and changing his clothes when the doorbell rang. It was Lee Drake, the son of a former neighbour.

"I saw you coming in. Sorry to trouble you. My mother has just died, and here is her Will. Please could you do the needful?"

"Are you sure this is her last Will as I remember writing a Will for her and this is not the one?" said Alfred.

About 5 years previously Lee Drake had knocked at his door, and asked if he could bring his mother to see Alfred, as she would not have been able to travel to the office.

Mrs Drake was a quiet old woman who lived across the road. Alfred had never spoken to her.

"Mum, shall I tell Mr Stephens what has happened?"

The mother nodded, and Lee told the story.

"As you may know, my mother is a widow. My younger brother Sam and I are the only children.

"My mother showed me a letter from her bank demanding repayment of a loan of £45,000 secured on her house. I knew nothing about it. It appears Sam took Mum to the bank, and borrowed this money to start a business, and promised Mum that he would pay the monthly repayments.

"Anyway after making two payments, he and his girlfriend left on a two-year round the world trip. Mum got a postcard about three months ago from Brazil.

"The bank want the arrears settled and confirmation that future payments will be made on time. I have paid the last five months, but I really cannot afford to continue paying."

Mrs Drake said nothing.

Alfred discussed the matter with the bank, who reluctantly agreed not to seek repayment for a year provided Mrs Drake placed her house on the market for sale. So she had to move to a one bedroom flat nearby.

Alfred advised her to make a Will and she nodded when he advised that her estate could be divided between her two sons, but would it not be fair if, first, her oldest son received an additional £45,000?

Neither her oldest son nor Alfred knew that two months after making this Will, she had gone to another solicitor to make a new Will giving the money in her bank account (£9,216) to Lee, and the flat to Sam as he would need somewhere to live when he returned from his travels.

Alfred was one of about half a dozen who attended her funeral at the local crematorium where the priest, who did not know the deceased, said what a wonderful mother she had been to her two sons.

"Have I come to the right funeral?" thought Alfred.

As for Lee, he was inconsolable—was it because he had lost his mother or that he had realized, if he had not done so already, that whatever he had done for his mother, her favourite son was the prodigal?

2000 was supposed to be the year there would be computer failures due to Y2K bugs, making them believe they were a century back causing havoc. But this did not happen. What did happen is that Alfred received an unexpected letter.

"Dearest Alfred,

I am so excited that I have been offered a chance to visit Lourdes with a small party of the sick from here, and more so when I was informed that on the return journey I will be staying with the Sisters of Mercy in Twickenham for three nights.

I am looking forward to meeting you again, and being introduced to your wife.

I will let you know the dates as soon as the program is finalised. The aim is to be at Lourdes on July 16 when the last apparition to Bernadette occurred.

Yours in Christ,

Martha"

Alfred replied immediately.

"My dear Esme (forgive me, I find it difficult to address you as Sister Martha),

I am so pleased that you are passing through England and we will have the chance to meet. I am still living in Kingston so it is just a hop and a skip to get to you in Twickenham. I know where the Sisters live.

I am sorry to say that you will not be able to meet Angela as she passed away some years back.

Please let me know the dates and I will clear my diary.

Affectionately,

____ "

The pilgrims from Belize arrived in Lourdes in time for the services taking place on July 16, and two days later they arrived in England, the sick staying at a hotel near London Heathrow Airport, and Sister Martha at the convent in Twickenham.

Alfred went to the convent and waited for her to come from her room. He was expecting to see her in her nun habit; somewhat to his surprise she was in jeans and a white shirt.

They both felt shy when greeting each other.

Esme looked no different other than she had a few grey streaks in her hair, a few wrinkles and wore no makeup. Her face glowed with a peace and calm that radiated to all around.

As for Alfred, he was still slim, had thinning hair and wore tortoiseshell spectacles, as he was now short sighted. He was dressed in a sharp navy blue suit, pure cotton white twill shirt, pale blue Hermes tie and Church's Consul black shoes.

"Alfred, you look very nice," said Esme.

"I'm not sure if I should say so, but you are not bad either," he replied.

They laughed as they did in the years gone by.

"You must be tired, and I'm sure you have not eaten properly. Let's go to the Alexander Pope," said Alfred, and he took Esme to the pub almost opposite the convent and at one-time part of the garden belonging to the great poet's house.

As they were sitting down, Esme laughed again.

"Alfred, do you know this is the first time we have been to a pub together."

Once they settled down, they ordered salads, a glass of cider for Esme and half a pint of Young's Bitter for Alfred; they talked, Esme about her calling and Alfred about his marriage and deaths of his mother and wife.

"I'm so sorry," said Esme when he finished, and asked to see a photo of Angela, which Alfred showed her.

Seeing Alfred looking upset, Esme comforted him.

"I spend a lot of my time comforting families when their loved ones have died. I tell them that an Irish writer (C. S. Lewis) wrote that grief and pain are the price you have to pay for love."

Esme had to take the rest of her party on tours of London, so she could only met Alfred once more.

At her request, Alfred drove her to Brixton.

"Oh Alfred. I cannot believe it. You have bought a black Mercedes. I remember you told me that when you were a child you would see the Maharajah of Cooch Behar being driven in one, and you said one day you would have your own."

"You remembered. Yes, I did dream of having one. But I still have not achieved another goal."

"What is that?"

"Making cream horns like I ate at Lobo's Restaurant."

"You know I used to try to make one's for you, but never succeeded. Looking back I think I was using the wrong type of flour. Someone did tell me I should have used Canadian flour."

When they got to Brixton, Esme found it was now a colourful urban area (due to the gentrification in the 1990s) and had a mix of residents, from people that had lived in the area for generations to new residents attracted by the trendy image and the Brixton Tube station, which meant easy access to Central London. It was also, as Alfred told her, the place to go for clubbers, artists and druggies.

Esme was saddened to see that Speenham Road no longer existed, the second hand shop in Acre Lane had closed down and the fleapit cinema had been converted to a multiplex.

"So, Esme will you be staying in Belsize for the near future? Do you miss Jamaica?" asked Alfred.

"Funny you should say that. I think this trip is like a thank you gesture. Mother Superior has been telling me that there is a probability that I will be moved back to our convent in Kingston next year. I would like that. I have not seen the family since most of them came to see me take my final vows, and that was almost 23 years ago. Thankfully my siblings are all alive. And I am aunty to 6 kids.

"You know Alfred, whenever I hear a Jim Reeves song on the radio my mind goes back to our time in Brixton, those were happy days."

"I too. Remember we used to dance in your room to 'Welcome to my World,' and the Albert girls would join in?"

On the way back to the Twickenham convent, they drove via Kingston and went past the house that Alfred had selected for Esme to view and which he had bought later, and the house he now lived in.

By the time he dropped her at the convent, they were both silent.

When they were parting, Alfred remembered what Bowju had told him when he was leaving Sonada.

"Esme, I was just thinking what Bowju told me when I left for England—you do what you have to do; and as we all have to do, you must follow your destiny."

"Yes, dearest Alfred, it is all in God's hands."

"Am I allowed to kiss a nun?"

"Of course, on both cheeks."

This brief encounter was the last time they saw each other.

CHAPTER 87

9/11

2001

The Millennium year, which many had wrongly celebrated the previous year, started on a low note for Alfred.

Meeting Esme again after 28 years did not bring joy to his life. On the contrary whenever he thought of her, it brought great sadness and loss.

The early part of the year went by as it had recently done.

However on June 1, the Crown Prince of Nepal killed most of the Royal Family including his parents, King Birendra and Queen Ashwarya. Alfred was shocked to learn of these deaths as he had been at school with the King and his youngest brother, and he had known their two sisters who were also murdered.

Then on September 11, 2001, 19 men hijacked four commercial airlines. The end result was that 2,977 people were killed in New York, Washington, DC and outside Shanksville, Pennsylvania.

Two interesting facts on the day of America's worst terrorist attack which the public did not know about were—the top search-topic on Google was for: Nostradamus; and Alfred was being interviewed at the local police station on an allegation of theft when American Airlines Flight 11 and United Airlines Flight

175 crashed in the north and south towers of the World Trade Center site in Lower Manhattan, New York killing 2,753 people of whom approximately 75% were men. It can be said that neither Nostradamus nor Alfred had foreseen the event in London.

"As you keep on wanting to help a person in trouble, you may like to take this on?" Maggie had said.

An old criminal client, long term unemployed, had brought his daughter, also unemployed, to see Alfred following the death of her boyfriend who had been accidentally killed by a police car when he was running away from a possible attempted burglary.

There was the question of several thousand pounds deposited by the deceased in a bank account, which was not being released by the bank until grant of probate was produced. This court order would state who would administer the deceased's estate.

The girl thought that, as she was his common law wife, she was entitled to the money, but as this designation had no legal validity and there was no Will giving the estate to her, the rules of intestacy applied. The rules stated that the beneficiaries would be in the following order—the deceased's spouse and if he had none, his children, and then his parents.

"He was never married, but we have a two year old son," said the young woman, who looked pleased at this revelation.

"Is he registered as the father in the birth certificate?"

"Yes, here it is," and she handed over the certificate.

"In that case, we can get the grant of probate in your son's favour. But as he is a minor, two trustees have to be appointed to administer the money till he reaches 18," advised Alfred.

The father interjected, and said he and his daughter could be these trustees.

Unfortunately Alfred's habit of being unreasonably responsible came to the forefront, and taking into account the father's criminal record (which he was well familiar with) and his assessment of the daughter's attitude at the meeting he decided to protect the child.

"Your daughter can of course be one of the trustees, but the other should be a professional as you will need one for tax and legal advices," said Alfred, and suggested that they go away and decide who it should be.

"Can you give us any ideas?" asked the daughter.

"Yes, your doctor."

A few days later they came back and said that the doctor said she would not have the time and, as Alfred anticipated, her opinion was that the co-trustee should be the solicitor. This is how Alfred became the second trustee, which he would regret later.

It was correct that the deceased had £5,017 in his bank account, which had recently been opened. Alfred remembered seeing advertisements about incentives for opening an account with the deceased's bank, so when he next spoke to a bank official he raised a query as to whether or not the deceased had taken up all his incentives.

Well, blow me down the incentive was one year's free accidental death insurance, so the child inherited £55,017.

"Now you know why I brought you to see Mr Stephens—he is the best around," said the father, and his daughter planted a kiss. Alfred felt quite proud of himself.

The two trustees obtained grant of probate, the money was collected from the Bank, the reduced legal fees were paid and the net asset of £53,000 was available for the boy.

"Before we invest the money and by the way the income will come to you for your son's maintenance, we could pay any expenses you may soon have for your son," said a helpful Alfred to his co-trustee.

"My son does not have a bed," then "He desperately needs some clothes and shoes." There was a litany of what her son needed, and it was agreed that she could be given £3,000 towards his maintenance for the coming year.

Two months went by, and then another appointment was made. This time her father accompanied her, and both of them were suntanned in an autumn day.

"We have just come back from Gambia. It was lovely," said the father, and he went on to brag that he had feigned a heart attack at the airport and they had come back by business class, and that his daughter had fallen in love again which was good as she was too young to be grieving.

"How did you meet him?"

"He is a waiter at the hotel where we stayed. That is why we have come. You told me that I could draw money out for my son. I am getting married, and intend to live in Gambia and will be taking my son with me. I would like to buy a house there, it is much cheaper and my son will have a better quality of life. I want the remainder of the money."

Alfred took a deep breath, and explained that the child's money could not be used to buy a foreign property.

"In that case can I have £5,000 so I can bring my fiancée to England so he can help with my son?"

"I am sorry this is impossible. The money belongs to your son and he can have it when he gets to 18. In the meantime the trustees can only release bits and pieces for his maintenance and advancement. Full stop," said Alfred. They left in a huff.

Hell has no fury like a woman scorned, as Alfred was to find out.

"There is a man from the Law Society (the governing body for solicitors) on the phone. He says it is urgent," said his receptionist.

"Mr Stephens, I am sorry to trouble you, but we have a young lady here in a very distressed state claiming that her solicitor has stolen her son's money. I am sure that is not the case. What explanation can I give her?"

There are a few occasions when Alfred was angry. This was one of them. He explained what had happened, and the Law Society official understood.

"Some people will try anything," he said, and complimented Alfred.

It was the turn of the police. On September 10 they telephoned.

"Sir, there is a lady and her father with me wanting the police to investigate the loss of her son's inheritance, which I believe was last with you. Can you please help with my investigation?"

An appointment was made for the following day at 1 p.m.

This is how Alfred was at the local police station on September 11, and giving a voluntary statement when there was a knock on the door.

A constable informed the investigating officer that a plane had crashed into a tower in New York.

He then returned and said a second plane had flown into another tower. The meeting was postponed, and everyone rushed to watch the TV in the waiting area.

The re-convened meeting petered out and after Alfred signed his statement, he was leaving the station.

"Before you go, Sir, I would like to thank you for your co-operation. You know this will not go anywhere. If I was you, I would give up the trustee lot," said the investigating officer.

Alfred followed this advice, contacted the Official Solicitor (an independent statutory holder who provide last resort trustee service for person who are vulnerable due to age) and resigned in his favour knowing that the child's money would be very strictly controlled bearing in mind the history.

This incident was the straw that broke the camel's back.

As John Ruskin had said: "The highest reward for a man's toil is not what he gets for it but what he becomes by it." Alfred had become disillusioned.

CHAPTER 88
BEFORE I MISS THE TIDE
2002

Alfred remembered long ago that there was love in the air. Now he felt lonely and bereft, and it did not help that he was not doing what he had set out to do, giving a helping hand to those who were faltering.

He realised that he was using compulsive work to escape from dealing with his disappointments and sadness. This work and the world were not giving him satisfaction, and therefore were they worth investing in?

Alfred had spent his adulthood giving advice to others, but he did not want to advise himself. As the saying goes, a lawyer who acts for himself has a fool for a client. So he went to see his father to talk about his future plans and ask for advice.

"Do what you want to do. Don't waste time just talking about it," said his father.

"Maybe, it's a mid-life crisis?" said Philip when Alfred had a meeting with Maggie and him.

"Are you sure this is what you want?" asked Maggie.

"I'm sure. I would have preferred to let you two carry on in case I later change my mind, but you know that it is a hard to keep on generating income," said Alfred.

"There's no way that the practice can run successfully without you. I'm going to retire with you, and go back to Sri Lanka," Philip said.

"Except for eighteen months on maternity leave, I have been working all my adult life. I too will stop working," Maggie said.

So they took steps to sell the practice with staff transferring to the new owners, and to prepare for the future.

Reluctantly Alfred agreed to a farewell party on October 2, 2002, being the 34th anniversary of his qualification.

Those closest to him noticed that Alfred was on edge throughout the evening, periodically looking at his watch and not saying much other than to acknowledge the guests' good wishes.

Then after dinner had finished, Alfred asked everyone to be silent as he had a few words to say.

> "Thank you all for coming to celebrate my retirement; some of you have come from faraway places. Thank you Maggie for organising this do. Thank you and Philip and the rest of our staff, past and present, for your support all these years, particularly during the time Angela was ill.

> "Time has passed so quickly. When I arrived at Liverpool Docks in February 1962, I only had one friend in England, Gerry—over there. Now I have all of you, and my father is here also. Thank you all for everything.

> "Looking around and seeing you, many memories flash by—mostly happy ones, but I do miss those I have loved and who are not here.

"Since Angela passed away ten years ago, I have been asking myself 'What should I do with the rest of my life?'

"Well, I have sold my home and everything else, and I have decided to leave England.

"The dancing will start soon. Please enjoy the rest of the evening. As for me, I have a taxi waiting.

"I must leave now before I miss the tide."

And to everyone's astonishment, our 59-year-old Anglo-Indian, having lived in England for 40 years, left taking with him the last gold bracelet of his mother, the paper red roses given to him by Bowju and the tin suitcase he had brought from Sonada.

Alfred had decided to turn the corner and live a different life—just like his father; but this time, no one was being abandoned.

To be continued.